More Praise for *Windrusher and the Cave of Tho-hoth*

"Superbly written, *Windrusher and the Cave of Tho-hoth* is thrilling, touching and unforgettable. With vividly drawn characters and a unique and distinctive voice, DiGenti grabs you from the first page with this exciting, fast-paced adventure and detective story. The touching denouement brought tears to my eyes. The enchantment of *Windrusher* belongs on the silver screen."

—Marilyn Parrish, author of *Song of Surrender* and *The Presence*

"*Windrusher and the Cave of Tho-hoth* is cat fantasy in the honored tradition of Tad Williams' *Tailchaser's Song* and Gabriel King's *The Wild Road* series. It's fast-paced action with strong mystical echoes and a thoroughly likable and resourceful feline hero."

—T. J. Banks, Author of *Souleiado*

"In his entertaining sequel to *Windrusher*, Victor DiGenti takes us into the secret inner world of cats, which is every bit as intriguing as the lively adventures of his feline hero."

—Gerald J. Schiffhorst, Ph.D., author of *Writing with Cats*

"The mystical world of felines is further revealed in this exciting sequel. Windrusher & the Cave of Tho-hoth is an incredible journey of a cat with a higher calling."

—Elaura Niles, author of *Some Writers Deserve to Starve:
27 Brutal Truths About the Publishing Industry*

Reviewers Loved *Windrusher*

"I literally couldn't put it down—it is so beautifully written. What a wonderful read, I can't wait for Windrusher's next adventure."

—Betty White, actress and animal rights advocate

"Touching, mystical, completely engrossing. Put this on your bookshelf next to *Call of the Wild* and *Black Beauty*. Windrusher's great adventure belongs with the animal classics."

—Linda Stewart, author of the *Sam the Cat Mystery* series

"Prepare yourself to be swept up in the breathtaking adventures of Windrusher, a.k.a. Tony. Do yourself a favor and pick up this book. It's a guaranteed good read that will make you look at y~ ~al articles

—Nancy

"Beautifully written, the characterizations, whether human or animal, are so well done that I could visualize each and every character."
—William Kerr, author of *Death's Bright Angel*

"Cat people will love this riveting fantasy."
—Alex Matthews, author of the *Cassidy McCabe* mystery series

"More than just an adventure and more than a fantasy, *Windrusher* works on several levels. Victor DiGenti has realistically captured the plight of homeless cats. His story goes right to the heart of the matter. And right to the heart of the reader."
—Darlene Arden, author of *The Angell Memorial Animal Hospital Book of Wellness*

"A delightful tale…for lovers of adventure and cat lovers; poignant with moments of great humor. Tony/Windrusher is an endearing hero for this new series."
—Blether, the book review site

"*Windrusher* takes readers on a wild ride through the fascinating and mystical world of cats."
—*The Gainesville Sun*

"Victor DiGenti's new book *Windrusher* opens an imaginary world for juveniles to adults unlike any other I've ever seen. From one animal enthusiast to another, read this book."
—Amy L. Clark, *The St. Augustine Record*

WINDRUSHER
and the Cave of Tho-hoth

Also by Victor DiGenti

Windrusher

Victor DiGenti

WINDRUSHER

and the Cave of Tho-hoth

Published by Ocean Publishing
Flagler Beach, Florida

Copyright © 2004 Victor DiGenti

ISBN: 0-9717641-7-4

Library of Congress Control Number: 2004112455

Printed in the United States of America

Published by Ocean Publishing
Flagler Beach, Florida

Ocean Publishing

For
Chloe, Rocco, Gage, and Sami.
You taught us well.

ACKNOWLEDGEMENTS

IN RESPONSE to those readers who wondered what more could happen to an amazing cat with the power to communicate with the gods, I offer you this book. Windrusher has taken on a life of its own, and I found myself carried along on his adventures surprised at the twists and turns this feline made. Thanks to Evanne for her constant encouragement and support that helped me move past those days when I doubted Windrusher would ever emerge from his cave. To Greg and Brian, who filled my head with music, talked tough when I needed it, straightened my crooked prose, and gave it order. I'm grateful to Frank for his confidence in Windrusher, and, finally, thanks to Andrew, a master illustrator and friend, for giving a face to Windrusher.

Swiftly walk over the western wave,
Spirit of Night!
Out of the misty eastern cave,
Where, all the long and lone daylight,
Thou wovest dreams of joy and fear.
Which makes thee terrible and dear,—
Swift be thy flight!

To Night — Percy Bysshe Shelley

PROLOGUE

"WARNING! Step through these doors at your own risk. The results could be CATastrophic."

The man in the yellow and lime green Madras jacket smiled at the sign and pushed through the double doors, carefully holding the pet carrier in front of him. Once he was inside, the noise hit him flush in the face; hundreds of voices competed with a public address announcer calling out a series of numbers in a voice tinged with impatience.

A compact and solid five foot ten inches, he walked with a slight swagger, and had an open, expectant expression on his face that seemed to welcome the chaos swirling around him. Pausing on the landing inside the auditorium, he lifted the carrier to eye level and crooned to the sleek blue point Siamese inside.

"Here we are, baby. Does it smell like championship time to you? These other fur balls won't know what hit them when you enter the ring."

He surveyed the multiple layers of walkways circling the center of the auditorium like some gargantuan wedding cake. Each level was crammed, side by side, with large pop-up shelters, looking like acrylic Quonset huts. A mob of humanity crowded the aisles, stalking particular breeds, and engaging the proud owners in conversation about everything from behavior to birth parents. They peered intently through the mesh and vinyl doors of the shelters, scrutinizing the felines and mentally comparing them to their own favorites.

Each of the shelters sat on a six-foot table and great care had been taken to give the space a distinctive look to match the elite breeds dwelling within the cages. Frilly curtains were draped over some exteriors, and the tables were covered with fancy cloths and skirts, damasks and silks. Some tables held accessories for their dwellers—toys, brushes, and combs—while trays of snacks rested on others, as if they were expecting guests for tea. Inside a few of the shelters were miniature couches, tables, and chairs, furniture that the felines ignored, but gave the space a cozy lived-in look.

Cats of all sizes, colors, and coats lounged in their holding cages, some sleeping soundly, as only cats can amidst the din and rumble of conversations, and others suspiciously eyeing the crush of people slowly working their way along the narrow walkways.

It was easy to spot the owners. They were nervously grooming their show animals, carefully combing longhaired Himalayans and Maine Coons. Across the aisle, an elderly woman cleaned the eyes of a submissive Ragdoll, while her neighbor wiped the sleek coat of a rambunctious Oriental Shorthair with a chamois cloth until it glistened like a ceramic figurine.

"Ring six is looking for Persians one-ten, one-eleven, one-twelve, and one-fourteen. Please bring your Persians to ring six."

The public address announcer's voice slashed through the clamor and dozens of people moved deliberately toward the side rooms to see the judging. In Ring 2, the judge lifted a silky Chocolate Lynx Point Birman named Sinhs-Sational Jitter Bug Dandy, standing the stocky cat on his hind legs, staring attentively into the round blue eyes, and turning him over as though examining a cashmere sweater. Then he teased him with a dangling toy on a long stick flicking it high above the cat and watched him leap to capture the prize. The spectators applauded enthusiastically at this athletic display as if an Olympic record had just been broken.

"Ring six is still waiting for Entry one-twelve. This is your second call, number one-twelve, where are you?"

The man in the Madras jacket smiled broadly at the Siamese he carried. His teeth gleamed like those in the television toothpaste commercials. "There seems to be some delay with Entry one-twelve, doesn't there, Snickers?" he said to the cat. "Let's see if we can help."

Nearby, a woman pulled a contentious Persian from a silk-lined cage. She was in her mid-fifties and wore a stylish navy blue pantsuit, her neck, wrists, and fingers festooned with gold jewelry. She plopped the cat indecorously on the table, grabbed a sterling silver comb, and attacked a knot of hair.

"Honestly, you pick the worst times to throw one of your fits, Katmandu. You know I love you to death, baby, but we're late as it is and this isn't helping. One more Grand Championship and you'll break all records, so let's shape up."

She combed desperately at the tangle on the cat's left side, causing the Persian to turn her pansy face and laser her blue-green eyes at the woman. Katmandu was a handsome cat, wearing a resplendent coat of cream shaded with delicate silver markings and a mantle of black flowing from her back down her sides. She lifted her brick-red nose leather slightly in apparent acknowledgement of the woman's remarks, turned back, and closed her eyes.

"I can see that you've poured all your love and attention into this beauty," the man said, suddenly appearing next to the woman. "It's no wonder she's a champion. But then, I see you have no shortage of beauty and love to give, do you?"

The voice dripped with liquid velvet. It was the sound a Chocolate Grand Marnier Truffle might make if it could speak. The woman's eyes cut toward the man, startled by the stranger with the silken voice. There stood a balding man with the most blinding smile she had seen this side of a movie screen. For the first time in twenty years, she felt a blush creep across her face.

The man leaned in and peered at the engraved plate on the cage and read the name aloud: "'Best of Breed GC, NW, RW Katmandu Moonstar of Valhalla.' And you are a beautiful Grand Champion, aren't you, girl?" he said to the cat.

He turned his round face toward the woman and fixed her with green eyes that she would swear actually twinkled as he spoke, emphasizing his words with slight nods and a bright smile. "She is a worthy champion. You should be proud of what the two of you have achieved."

The woman felt herself blush again. There was a seductive aura to the man, as though his sole desire was her well-being, and she unconsciously found herself nodding in a mirror image of his own head movements. She wondered how he could speak while maintaining such a broad smile. That must have taken practice.

"She is the love of my life, but sometimes she can be rather petulant. Like now. Isn't that right, honey?" The woman shook her head in mock aggravation, but by the tilt of her head, the set of her shoulders, and the smile that had replaced the pinched mouth; it was obvious that this friendly stranger had lifted the mantle of tension from her just as a magnet lifts iron shavings.

"She wants you to know that she's worth the effort, and you can't take her for granted," he said. "It's amazing how cats can read our innermost feelings, isn't it? And instinctively they know that we would do anything for their happiness." As he spoke, his head bobbed earnestly and his free hand floated over the champion cat, as though he was conducting an orchestra. His incandescent smile punctuated the brief conversation.

She flipped back her bangs, and took another long look at the man. There was something about the round face and fleshy jowls that made her want to reach out, grab his cheeks, and playfully squeeze them. Those rubbery mounds looked as though they could be twisted and pulled into a hundred different shapes, like balls of clay in the hands of a potter. She resisted the temptation and for the first time noticed that he was carrying a cat of his own, a lovely Blue Point Siamese of obvious good breeding.

"I don't remember seeing you at any of the shows, Mister..." She paused as if she may have forgotten the introduction.

He smiled again and extended a hand. "Where are my manners? I'm John Morrow, my friends call me Jake."

"Esther Corcoran, Mr. Morrow. Very pleased to meet you. So, are you new to this game of ours?"

"Of course, I've always been a cat lover, but I've just begun to dangle my toes into the competitive waters. It's fascinating the way—"

"This is the final call for Entry one-twelve for ring six. Final call

for number one-twelve." The announcer's voice broke into Morrow's statement.

"My God, that's us," Esther said with more than a trace of panic. "We only have a minute to get to ring six or we'll be disqualified. Come on, baby." She picked up the handsome Persian and tenderly settled it over her right forearm, careful not to disturb the mantle of flowing hair.

She took a step toward the ring, and John Morrow, Jake to his friends, turned quickly to move out of the woman's way. His arm banged against Katmandu's table as he turned and he clumsily dropped the carrier he was holding. It landed at his feet with a loud crash, and a frightful yowl rose from the floor.

"Snickers, are you all right?" he cried, bending over and pulling the cat out of the carrier. He clutched Snickers to his chest tenderly and kissed the cat's head over and over.

Esther stopped in mid-step, horrified to see the Siamese plunge to the floor. She watched Morrow sweetly kiss the poor cat and reached out her hand to scratch Snickers under the chin, letting her fingers trail lightly over Morrow's jacket. He put a hand on her arm in return.

"I really must go," she said breathlessly. "Why don't you come with me to ring six and see Katmandu make—"

She didn't finish her sentence, which surely was going to be to see Katmandu make history. Her voice stopped in mid-thought, as did hundreds of others, dropping an eerie blanket of silence over the huge auditorium. At that precise moment when Esther Corcoran and Katmandu were about to dash to ring six where the champion Persian would make history, the hall went dark.

The darkness that descended like a heavy shroud over the International Cat Fanciers Show was so complete, so dense and unyielding, that she could no longer see John Morrow and his shining teeth. Perhaps if she had the eyes of a cat, she might have seen his yellow pants pass in front of the table when he brushed against her arm.

Unfortunately, there were no windows in the auditorium to help wash away the blackness, no sky lights to relieve the tension and fear with refreshing beams of sunlight. And what seemed most strange, and would receive an abundant amount of conversation by the New York

City investigators later that day, the auditorium's emergency generator lights were also dark.

The stunned silence was abruptly broken by shouts of alarm, and the sounds of more than one person toppling off the walkways. Then, just as suddenly as it went dark, the hall was again bathed in light.

Esther saw no reason to panic. Her mind had been racing while she waited for the lights to come on and she actually said a prayer of thanks to whatever technical goblins had picked that moment to scramble the lighting system. Surely, this electronic glitch had upset the judging timetable and there was no way they could disqualify her.

The first thing she noticed when the lights came on was that John Morrow was nowhere in sight. Then she looked down at the pliant feline dangling from her arm and saw that it wasn't GC NW Katmandu Moonstar of Valhalla, but a lovely Blue Point Siamese named Snickers.

That's when she screamed.

1

SUNLIGHT BLASTED THROUGH the bay window, engulfing the eight-foot-tall ficus tree standing guard over a deco-style reclining chair. The morning light swept past the tree, casting leafy patterns on the floor, and spread over the sleeping form of Windrusher sprawled across the seat of the recliner.

The large gray and orange cat was in that nether period between sleep and wakefulness, hanging tenaciously to the last threads of unconsciousness while the sounds and smells of the morning beckoned him to open his eyes. Outside, two jays were loudly quarreling over the feast of sunflower seeds in the bird feeder while a squirrel stood watch below the feeding tray hoping to rescue any seeds that dropped to the ground.

Windrusher filtered the sounds through his drowsy brain, felt the warmth of the sun on his back, and finally, with a ferocious yawn, opened his eyes and greeted another beautiful West Florida day. He peered over the side of the chair, then dropped to the floor and sat motionless for a moment. Finally, he stretched himself out to his full length, his stomach scraping against the carpet.

There were moments when he had to remind himself where he was, which of the families of two-legged beings, known to cats as Hyskos, that he was living with. His journey had introduced him to many kind Hyskos who took him in and cared for him like one of their own. There was the old woman who called him Crackers, the young sisters who rescued him from the room of cages, and, of course, the Hyskos home where he met Silk Blossom. Each stop he made in his long, harrowing journey was now assimilated into his ever-shifting field of memories so that it was easy to become momentarily confused upon awakening. Those moments were becoming less frequent, however, and he knew that this was the only family he wanted, the one that called him Tony, the one he would live with the rest of his life.

He padded into the kitchen; following his nose toward the mouthful of nuggets he had left earlier that morning when the older high-legged male had fed him. It had still been dark when he heard the muted sounds of the Hyskos attempting to slip quietly from the house. He had planted himself between the man and the door leading to the garage. Noisily, he announced his presence.

"I just can't get past you, can I, Tony? Well, be quiet, you'll wake Amy and she needs her sleep," said Gerry Tremble in a stage whisper, reaching down to give the cat an affectionate scratch on the head.

"Come on, I'll give you a little food, but I have to get to the hotel."

That was more than two hours ago, and after eating, Windrusher had returned to the recliner for another nap. Now, with the warm rays of Rahhna polishing the surfaces of the room, he began to wonder if everyone had left the house while he was napping. He sat in the hallway, his solid body fully awake now, and scratched at his right ear.

Many night globes had passed since he had returned to his Hyskos family. He tried not to think of those troubling times in search of… In search of what? Fulfilling Irissa-u's holy mission? Finding his family of high-legged beings? Yes, he was home, but he'd rather forget the pain and loss he suffered during his travels. He was proud that Irissa-u had chosen him to be one of her seven followers, but did he have to relive it each time he visited the Inner Ear?

The Inner Ear was the gift of the great god Tho-hoth, according to the legends passed along by his mother and all the mothers before her for the past four thousand years. These nursing tales shared the incredible history of cats and the divine guidance their gods had provided to draw the feral creatures from the jungles and into the stone villages of the high-legged beings. He had never taken them very seriously, not until he was visited by the goddess Irissa-u who urged him to fulfill the grueling quest to locate his family.

He was content in his role as a house cat, enjoying the rewards

Irissa-u had promised him in those incredible dreams. He was doted upon by the high-legged female, his food bowl filled at regular intervals, and he could curl up in a patch of sunlight and nap whenever he wished.

Was there anything more a cat could want? He didn't think so. Yet, despite his conscious desire to put the past behind him, there were times when thoughts of Lil' One and Silk Blossom crept into his mind and he relived the journey.

The feelings usually passed quickly, and he had to admit that as one day slid into another, these excursions into the past were not as common as they once were. This was the life he really wanted, not one ruled by mysterious dreams and cryptic messages from ancient gods. He was now an ordinary cat, living an ordinary life, and that was fine with him.

It was past time for the older female Hyskos to join him in this ordinary life of his, he thought, and padded toward the master bedroom to find her.

Amy Tremble eyed the clock on her bed stand, rolled away, and pulled the sheet over her shoulder. She was aware of the stillness around her, the soft sighs of the breeze tapping its wake-up call on the windows. She should have been up hours ago, kissing the kids goodbye as she left for her early morning shift at the hospital. Amy was always the first out of bed, rolling through the quiet house with the energy of a waterspout, fixing breakfast, making lunches, and rousing the other members of the household.

Yet, here she was still in bed at 9:30 in the morning. An insidious transformation had changed the familiar patterns in her life, and instead of facing the day with hope and expectancy, she awakened afraid, anxious, and disoriented.

After twenty years in the medical field, she knew the symptoms of depression as well as any psychologist. At first, she tried to convince herself that it was a mid-life hormonal imbalance that had her feeling a little blue. "Must be going through menopause," she told her concerned husband. "I'll get a check-up and take a few pills." Of course, she did neither because her case of the blues had started when ten-year-old

Tabitha Worrell had died on the operating table.

Tabitha, with her glorious red hair and freckled face, had pulled through two earlier life-saving surgeries after a hit-and-run accident left her broken and bleeding next to her bus stop. After five days in intensive care, the girl had opened her eyes and began what the doctors called a miraculous recovery. Amy had taken a personal interest in the girl, perhaps because Tabitha was so close in age to her own daughter, Kimmy, and visited her several times a day.

She was there shortly after Tabitha emerged from the coma. Over the next three days, Amy looked forward to her brief visits with the injured girl, bringing flowers to brighten the room. And she was on the surgical floor that night when Tabitha was rushed in with multiple-organ failure. Despite all their efforts, ninety minutes later, the ten-year-old who had been proclaimed a living miracle, was pronounced dead.

Amy had witnessed death in all its ghastly forms during her career as a surgical nurse, but this one left her bruised and wounded, as though she had been the one on the operating table. Her quiet confidence was replaced with self-doubt, and she felt herself sinking into a morass of hopelessness. The feelings of gloom intensified when she learned that her sister, Jeannie, in her eighth month of pregnancy, had been diagnosed with preeclampsia.

Preeclampsia, she knew, was one of the most serious diseases of late pregnancy, and if it advanced to its next stage, eclampsia, it could be fatal for both Jeannie and her baby. She had flown to Connecticut to be with Jeannie as soon as she heard. Her sister's doctors had already put her on a low-salt diet and prescribed medications to lower her soaring blood pressure. When she arrived, Amy was struck by Jeannie's puffy face and hands, but she stroked her swollen cheeks and tried to comfort her sister, who had been instructed to lie on her left side to relieve the pressure on her uterus. She stayed with her for three days before returning to Crystal River to care for her own family.

That was when she decided she needed to take a sabbatical from work and get her life together. But it didn't happen, and she slipped into an even deeper funk. She felt like she was disassembling, grasping for a foothold in reality, yet finding nothing of substance, like a mountain climber sinking his axe into a wall of soap bubbles.

More and more, she thought back to her days as a nursing student, those high-energy days filled with idealism and high hopes, and wondered now if she should have followed her father's advice and majored in business. A CPA never had to watch a helpless child die on the operating table. She berated herself for her weakness and knew she had become a burden to her family, especially her husband.

This couldn't have happened at a worse time for Gerry Tremble. In three weeks, his hotel, the King's Bay Resort, would host its first professional golf tournament, and the hotel was booked solid. On top of that, he was overseeing the last stages of an expansion of the hotel's ballroom, and there was no margin for error or time for distractions. No, Tremble wasn't prepared for the emotional maelstrom Amy brought into their home.

He tried hard to understand what his wife of twenty years was going through, and delicately suggested medication or therapy, but she ignored him, saying she only needed more rest. When Amy said she would be taking time off from her job, he readily agreed.

It frightened him to see this woman of strength and intelligence morph into an irritable, angst-ridden stranger. He explained to twelve-year-old Kimmy and her older brother G.T. that their mother was under a lot of pressure at work and concerned about Aunt Jeannie's condition.

"People react in different ways to these kinds of situations," he told them. "Your mother has worked so hard taking care of other people for so many years, and now we have to give her all our love and support."

Amy finally decided to help herself and went to her doctor who prescribed Zoloft. That was less than a week ago and the antidepressant was just starting to equalize her mood swings. Still, she felt adrift in the big house and hated herself for causing problems for Gerry and the kids. She sat up in bed, shaking her head to clear it of the stereophonic conversation that was caroming through her brain, and pulling her from one invisible counselor to the other.

What a sorry piece of baggage you've let yourself become, Amelia Rustin Tremble. Look at you lying there so filled with self-pity that you don't have the energy to move. Where does it say that you deserve any better treatment than anyone else?

"Shut up, you old scold," Amy said aloud.

Ignoring her, the shrewish voice continued, gouging at her raw emotions. *Did you think the world was a fairy palace where the good and innocent people, like Tabitha Worrell, are protected from pain and death? It doesn't work that way, girl. Get your sorry ass out of bed.*

The voice in her head left her feeling like a child being scolded by her mother.

No, the world's not a fairy palace, but reality sucks, doesn't it? This was another, more gentle voice. *You deserve to take some time for yourself, ponder what twenty years of hospital work has really achieved if you can't save a ten-year-old girl. Face it, Amy, what difference does it make if you stay in bed for a few more minutes? For the rest of the day? You have to take care of number one first.*

She took a deep breath, and imagined her brain clenching like the setting of her jaw, and shut out the tiresome discourse. Looking down, she noticed for the first time that Tony was lying by her knees. She had no idea how long the sleeping cat had been there, and as she watched him, a quiver ran over the cat's muscular shoulders and a soft mewing rose from his throat. She laid her hand gently against the dreaming feline, feeling the rise and fall of his chest.

Somehow, touching this innocent creature lifted her spirits and, for the moment, at least, the voices ceased, and the suffocating visions of failure and frustration faded away.

2

WINDRUSHER FELT THE BLISTERING SAND against his feet, saw waves of heat rising from distant dunes like a flock of translucent doves, and realized he must be dreaming again of Irissa-u, trekking toward the stone villages. Above him, Rahhna, the day globe, ignited the atmosphere, and turned the earth into a fiery kiln.

He turned and scanned the horizon for any sign of life, searching for the Holy Mother and hoping to find the reassurance that he was once again part of her inner circle. One of the seven followers of the Holy Mother.

He was alone. A desert of sand and stones stretched around him in a vast panorama of desolation. The only hint of relief in sight was a bleached cliff of crumbling limestone rising in front of him. At the base of the cliff, among the tossed and broken boulders, he saw shadows and a promise of salvation.

He hesitated before limping toward the life-saving shade, waiting for a sign from Irissa-u that she was awaiting him. There was no sign. He sucked in another mouthful of torrid air. It seared his chest and lungs and left him gasping as though he had inhaled ribbons of glass.

He wanted to drop to the desert floor and wait for this nightmare to pass, but knew he had to keep moving. If he stayed here, beneath the punishing sun, he would surely die. With that thought firmly in his mind, he willed his feet to scramble those last few yards over the feverish sand and find shelter in the shadows of the cliff.

Minutes later, he collapsed in the shade of an overhanging lip of rock, the searing blades of Rahhna hidden for the moment. He lay in a heap, his legs splayed, his head against the hot sand. Let me rest and regain my strength, he thought, and then I can continue on this incredible trek if that's what the Holy Mother requires of me.

Exhaustion permeated every fiber of his being, and deep inside he knew there was no way he could continue, even if Irissa-u herself implored him to keep moving. He closed his eyes, retreating from the brutal heat. A low rumbling noise awakened him, and he jerked his head reflexively, his ears fluttering in confusion.

Even as fatigued as he was, there was no way he could have missed seeing the dark opening in the cliff face that stared out at him. The irregular fissure looked like it had been carved into the rock, curving like a fifteenth-century scimitar from a ragged point at the top to an opening several meters wide next to his head.

Perhaps the heat had muddled his senses, leaving him blind to the obvious. Perhaps. That might explain how he could crawl to the edge of the cave without actually seeing it, but there was no way he could have avoided feeling the impossibly cool breeze that fluttered over him from deep inside the cave's opening.

"Why don't you join me in here, Pferusha-ulis?"

The voice was deep and compelling with a slight vibrato as though the words were notes strummed from a string instrument. And it had used his familiar cat name, Pferusha-ulis, Windrusher, as though he knew him. The voice came from somewhere within the cool recesses of the cave, and as he stared into the darkness, stupefied by his exhaustion and the shock of hearing his name, he tried to muster the strength to find the source of that voice. He edged forward, his rear legs scraping against the sand, and then collapsed unable to move further.

"Do I need to come out there and pull you in?"

The condescending tone angered him and he shot back with a passion that surprised him. "By the head of Tho-hoth, doesn't it seem like I could use your help? If you had the sense of a floppy-eared snouter you would step from inside your burrow and lend me a paw before I pass on and join my ancestors."

The speech drained what little energy he had left, and he lay back hoping the cave wouldn't disappear before he regained his strength and crawled inside. He swallowed, feeling the grit of sand on his tongue, and rested his head against a rock. Wind waited for the mysterious voice to retort to his angry jibe, watching the mouth of the cave for any sign of movement.

A faint light broke through the murky shadows like the first rays of Rahhna in the morning. As he watched, the light grew brighter and he could see the sides of the cave gleaming in reflected brilliance. Transfixed, he marveled that the light's intensity seemed to rival the day globe shining overhead. He closed his eyes briefly to shut out the glare and when he opened them there stood the source of the light.

The cat was half a head taller than any feline Windrusher had ever seen. Except for a vibrant splash of white across its chest and paws, the cat had a flowing coat of black hair that stood out from its body and surrounded the massive head like a lion's mane. Great white whiskers and tufts of hair grew recklessly from its pink nose and dagger-pointed ears. Its pale green eyes had an oriental cant and they shone with an internal luminosity that seemed to regard him with a curious sadness.

There was no way to judge the age of this cat, but he wouldn't have been surprised if it was as ancient as the limestone cliff itself, and it had been waiting an eternity for him to arrive.

The old cat lowered its regal head and for the first time he noticed the glimmering red stone dangling from a leather collar around its shaggy neck. The stone glowed with a fire of its own and seemed to pulse to an internal rhythm. Wind's eyes widened at the sight and his heart raced. The Stone! Could it be? But before he could speak, the old one licked him along the side of his face, from his jaw line up to his ear, and then moved back into the shadows of the cave.

A surge of energy ripped into him at the touch of the cat's tongue. The exhaustion that paralyzed and threatened him with an agonizing death had disappeared. Windrusher jumped to his feet and scrambled forward into the darkness. He followed the traces of light into the subterranean depths until he was smothered by a blackness so encompassing that it shut out all traces of light. Where was the burning face of Rahhna now when he needed it to find his way? He stopped, his eyes wide, his ears searching for a clue, fighting the panic that was pressing in on him.

He remembered his younger days when traveling in a Hyskos vehicle or being closed in the carrying cage would trigger powerful emotions of fear and rage. Fighting those feelings of claustrophobia, he took a step forward trusting that he was going in the right direction. He had to continue on, had to find the glowing cat wearing the Stone of Life. There was no choice now that he knew this was no ordinary dream, but a summons from the great god Tho-hoth.

After wandering the earth to introduce cats into the kingdoms and villages of high-legged beings, Irissa-u proudly proclaimed that the cat would multiply and be revered in the Hyskos households. Irissa-u was right, yet she was wrong.

Cats had migrated from the jungles to live in and among the Hyskos, reproducing at a prodigious rate. Almost everywhere the high-legged beings traveled they took cats with them. In some kingdoms, cats were even celebrated as gods, venerated along with other deities worshipped by the Hyskos.

These were the tales that Windrusher and generations of cats had heard from their mothers. The cat world knew that even though Irissa-u succeeded in spreading cats across the globe, there was a darker side that had threatened the future of cats.

While the cat was revered in some of the Hyskos kingdoms, in others cats were mistreated and met horrible deaths. Still, the cat population grew rapidly. Too rapidly. In some places it was out of control and cats turned on each other, fighting for food and mates. Those that lived in homes with high-legged beings became fat and selfish, caring nothing about the homeless cats forced to fight for their survival.

Windrusher recalled the stories of how the gods were so concerned that everything Irissa-u had accomplished would unravel unless they did something. It was then that Tho-hoth, the god of wisdom, came to earth and witnessed for himself the chaos and brutality. Cats were battling the twin scourges of famine and pestilence while fighting viciously among themselves for survival. Tho-hoth realized that cats, despite their historic and noble antecedents, were no better than other jungle animals. Saddened by what he saw, it is said the great god vowed to find a solution and retreated to a cave in the desert to meditate.

Legend had it that when Tho-hoth emerged from the cave he brought with him the precious gift that would forever link cats to each other and render them a singular and remarkable species among all creatures: The Akhen-et-u.

The Inner Ear, as it was known to those fortunate enough to be able to tap into this communication tool, allowed cats to share knowledge and grow together while they slept. It evolved over the centuries into more than a medium of communications, but a repository of knowledge, a window into the feline soul, and a shared experience that bonded cats together no matter where they were on the planet.

Sadly, there were some cats, known as Wetlos, unable to make the connection. These cats were typically a bit slower than their connected counterparts, but it didn't seem to bother them since they were in the dark as to what they were missing, and most Hyskos considered them to be cute and charming, if a bit eccentric.

The darkness pressed against Windrusher like a tangible force and he gulped down musty air and wondered if he would ever awaken from this dream. Relying on his sense of smell and the touch of his whiskers to guide him along the narrowing path, he edged forward. Moments before the harsh desert sun had threatened to incinerate him, now a sharp chill furrowed through the fibers of his muscles.

The glow emanating from Tho-hoth split the blackness once again, and Wind now saw that he was in a high chamber with highly reflective curved walls. Tho-hoth sat upright regarding him with somber eyes. An involuntary shiver erupted on Wind's neck and coursed across his back.

"Pferusha-ulis, perilous times are coming. Be on your guard. You will once again find yourself far from the home you love; the fate of others will depend on you. Are you prepared?"

Windrusher's eyes grew wide and black specks swam in the periphery of his vision. Had he lost his senses or did he just hear Tho-hoth warn him that…? What was he telling him? None of it made any sense and he suspected the heat of Rahhna's rays had damaged his brain. He opened his mouth to reply, but his throat tightened and nothing emerged.

"You have proven yourself to be a cat of incredible resources, and you must do so again or the shifting sands of fate will swallow you." Tho-hoth's pale green eyes seemed to bore into his soul. "But it's not just you who will be in danger. The life of your Hyskos rests on your back. Prepare yourself, Windrusher. Prepare yourself."

3

RIDING THE SLIPPERY CUSP of the wave that carried him from the deepest stage of unconsciousness, Windrusher popped through the last vestiges of sleep and opened his eyes. He blinked at the bands of sunlight pouring through the window, stared at the room around him, and tried to focus his thoughts.

Recognition of the female's bedroom finally tore through the gauzy curtain that encased his brain, and he remembered snuggling against her legs while she slept. One moment he was dozing by her side, enjoying the comforts of the soft bed, the next he was struggling to survive in the scorching desert heat.

Such an abrupt and surreal transition might have plunged another feline into madness. Looking back on his desert experience, however, Windrusher accepted it as another of those inexplicable demonstrations of the will of the Holy Ones overcoming reality. He knew he had been singled out by Irissa-u to fulfill a mission on her behalf. Why not a visit from the great god of wisdom? For whatever reason, he had received a forewarning that his life was about to change.

He told himself that perhaps it was only a dream. Yet, he couldn't deny that something had swept him from this bedroom to the Cave of Tho-hoth. Just as he now lay entangled in the female's sheet, with her scent still strong in his nose, he knew that he had been in that cave. He had heard the great god issue a warning—a warning that still rang in his head.

"Perilous times are coming. Prepare yourself."

Windrusher scurried through the Trembles' house searching for clues that his family was planning to move and leave him behind once again. There were no telltale packing boxes, no flurry of activity; nothing that he saw raised any warning signs that they were about to abandon him. Everything was peaceful. He padded silently into the kitchen, lapped at his water bowl, and spotted the older female Hyskos sitting alone at the counter, quietly drinking coffee.

The big orange and gray cat sat at the woman's feet and scratched roughly at his left flank in confusion. His mind was awhirl, tormented by the dream and its meaning. He closed his eyes and saw the ghostly vision of the magnificent old cat standing over him, the pulsating Stone of Life dangling from his neck.

Wracked with doubts, he moved to the back door, feeling the need to do something. He stood there for a moment, his tail a pilose whip swishing back and forth across the floor. He meowed loudly in exasperation, heard the scraping of a chair behind him and the sound of approaching footsteps.

"Guess you want to enjoy some of that Florida sun, huh, Tony? You let me know when you've had enough of the outdoor life," Amy said.

Wispy gray clouds straddled the horizon, framing a brilliant azure sky that hung over the Championship Course of the King's Bay Golf Club. The Trembles' house sat in the crook of what many golfers considered to be the most treacherous dogleg on the course. It was flanked on one side by a sparkling serpentine water hazard in which several young alligators were known to sun themselves in the afternoon. One of the most imposing of the thirty-five sand bunkers on the course jutted from the middle of the 8th fairway.

The Bermuda grass turf vibrated with a brilliant viridescence, a result of the nearly maniacal attention needed to stave off the unrelenting advances of insects and weeds. Mix together tons of pesticides, tinker with pH balances, spew the liquid iron, and the result is a perfectly natural Florida golf course.

On the other side of the split rail fence separating the Championship

Course from the Trembles' backyard, Windrusher ambled past the massive clump of giant philodendron that ruled one corner of the yard. Stalks as thick as a man's wrist snaked up from its dark and tangled body ending in expansive green leaves resembling the hands of a giant. They fluttered in the warm breeze, dipping toward him, each broad finger reaching out, grasping at him, as though attempting to pull him into the maw of the plant.

He had spent many afternoons in the welcoming shade of the philodendron, but today he felt a vague discomfort, and a wave of uneasiness surged along his back. He quickly stepped past the plant, toward the flower bed with the concrete birdbath casting a puddle of shadow over a patch of soft dirt. He settled in between two glossy, multi-colored crotons, determined to sleep away any nagging questions about Tho-hoth's puzzling prediction.

He pulled doggedly at a nail on his left paw until he lost interest, then began a slow, methodical grooming. In the willow tree to his right, he saw a flash of red as a cardinal alighted on a drooping branch. The bird eyed the cat suspiciously as though weighing its chances of swooping down on the birdbath for a quick drink and escaping unharmed. Wind ignored the bird and his eyes slid across the fairway where a cart with a single golfer was parked between the bunker and the fence.

The golfer seemed to be talking to himself, and Windrusher heard snippets of nonsensical syllables float across the yard on a warm breeze. Cats might not understand the exact meaning of the Hyskos words, but they could intuit the emotional signposts contained in a high-legged being's voice, their body language, and the expressions on their faces. He watched for a moment as the Hyskos, wearing gaudy pink knickers and an orange tam-o'-shanter style cap with a white pompon, pulled a shiny wedge from his bag and peered into the sandy crater. The golfer shook his head vigorously, the pompon jerking from side to side, muttered something to himself, and stepped into the bunker.

Windrusher settled his head on his paws. The hot breath of Rahhna and the Florida humidity combined to drain his energy and he could no longer resist the comforting and insistent tug of sleep. It had only been a short time since he had awakened from his deep sleep and the disturbing dream, but since when did a cat need to worry about getting too much sleep? As the golfer approached his ball, Wind's eyes fluttered and closed.

He had taken only a few steps along the winding path leading him to deeper layers of sleep when he heard the soft *twack* and felt a spray of water across his face. He jerked his head up, fully awake, and saw water dripping down the sides of the birdbath. His first thought was that the red bird had decided to take a quick bath while he napped. He stretched his long body toward the top of the birdbath to investigate.

A golf ball sat in the middle of the shallow pool, the water rippling from the impact. He lowered himself to the ground, just as the high-legged being with the garish clothing was lifting a leg over the top of the split rail fence. He carried his wedge in one gloved hand and held onto the railing with the other, balancing his compact frame for a moment, and swaying precariously.

Wind watched in bemusement as the clumsy Hyskos nearly toppled from the low fence, thrusting the sand wedge into the lawn to regain his balance. He saw the man stumble forward, his round face flush with the effort, and moist with sweat. As he searched for his ball he was never quiet, a constant stream of words tumbling from his mouth.

"I'll never know why I continue to punish myself with this game. Game? Huh! This isn't a game, it's the cruelest form of torture designed to reduce us all to gibbering idiots." The words flowed like he was talking with another golfer. And although he expressed the frustration that most golfers frequently encounter, there was a warm open smile on his round face that seemed to indicate that despite his exasperation with his game, he was still enjoying himself.

The golfer hitched up his pink knickers, placed one hand above his eyes as a shade from the brilliant sun, and stepped toward the flower bed. "I know that darn ball is somewhere near that birdbath," he said to himself. "How could I have shanked it so badly?" He shook his head and his rubbery jowls sprang to life, quivering and shaking like two water balloons about to be launched at some unsuspecting pedestrian.

Windrusher stood as the strange Hyskos approached the flower bed. He was obviously searching for the little white ball. He liked the sound of the man's deep voice, it was low and soothing, and there was a brightness to his eyes that suggested he wasn't taking this too seriously.

Since his return, Windrusher had been the center of attention. So many Hyskos had come to see the cat that had survived the long journey that he was accustomed to their strange behaviors and displays of affection. He understood that he was an ordinary cat who had done an extraordinary thing, and eventually became accustomed to the attention. This one, with his foolish clothes and constant chatter, seemed different than the others. At least that promised to make this encounter more tolerable.

"Can you believe it? Look where that ball landed. I couldn't make that shot again if I took a hundreds strokes. Heck, a thousand." The golfer stood over the flower garden, snatched the tam-o'-shanter from his head and rubbed the sweat from his balding pate with the cap before replacing it. He blinked at the hot Florida sun and wondered how people could live in this hellish climate. He couldn't wait to get back to the West Coast.

With a slight shake of the head he let his eyes settle again on his amazing hole-in-one in the birdbath as if seeing it for the first time. He shook his head so that his rubbery jowls trembled slightly, but he stopped abruptly when he saw the cat step out from the garden.

"Ah, look at you, my beauty," he said, fixing the cat with a high-intensity smile. "Standing guard over my ball, were you? I do appreciate it. Heaven knows someone has to watch over me."

The golfer squatted down on his heels and cautiously extended a hand toward the cat. He had laid his wedge on the lawn and he used his other hand to steady himself. "You are a magnificent feline specimen, let me tell you. And I'm a good judge of all things furry and proud."

The cat stared at the golfer with bright green eyes that seemed to reflect an uncanny intelligence, and dipped its head slightly. The golfer's smile broadened, exposing his whitewashed wall of teeth, and he gently ran two fingers across the cat's scalp.

"Listen to you purr, you've got your machine running in high gear." The golfer was rubbing the cat's left ear between his fingers now, and with his other hand he scratched under the cat's jaw. The purring grew even louder and the cat rolled his head back and closed his eyes.

"Why is a pretty cat like you out here all alone? That's what I want to know. If you belonged to me, I wouldn't let you out of my sight. Not a majestic feline like you, one that looks like he's capable of heroic acts." He smiled once more, crab-walking forward so that his knees were almost touching the cat's side.

The golfer felt a twinge in his right calf and for a moment feared a painful cramp was about to seize his leg. That's all he needed was to cramp up and scare the critter away. He must be getting old, or not eating enough bananas, but for some reason he was getting more cramps than ever. It was as if he had awakened some sleeping beast that feasted on the sinews and muscles of his leg.

He put that troublesome image out of his mind and continued massaging the cat, feeling the ropey neck muscles shift under the pressure of his fingers. "You deserve to be pampered after all you've been through, Tony. Yes, you do. Deserve it and should demand it. I'll bet these people don't even appreciate what they have; take you for granted."

Although this Hyskos was much like the others who touched and petted him, wondering, perhaps, if some of the magic of his adventures would be transferred to them, there was something different about him. Something lying below the surface of this overly friendly high-legged being. It nagged at him momentarily, but he put it aside. This was a Hyskos, after all, and he couldn't expect to fully understand them.

Perhaps it was the morning sun, or the dream, but he found himself drawn to him. His gentle voice melted his defenses like hot water poured over a sheet of ice, washing over him in soothing waves. Windrusher let his head roll back as the man massaged his neck, closed one eye, then the next.

The golfer felt the cat's muscles loosen and smiled broadly. He gently edged his left hand beneath the cat, still kneading its neck with his other hand, and lifted the cat to his chest. The cat squirmed slightly, opened its eyes and stared at him suspiciously, but relaxed as he cradled him confidently in the crook of his arm and began talking once again.

"Oh, you are an armful, big boy. But don't you worry about a thing. Old Jake has you and won't let you fall. No, he won't." He gave the cat a small squeeze and kneaded the folds of skin at its neck in the balls of his fingers. When the cat closed its eyes again, he rose to his feet, briefly awakening the spiteful beast that was resting inside his calf muscle, and felt its teeth nip at him in a gesture of defiance. He stood there for a moment until the pain eased, the creature retreating into its lair.

Turning his full attention to the cat again, he leaned down and whispered in the cat's ear: "Ah, you are a trusting soul, my tabby friend. Just when you thought your journeys were over you're on the move again. But have no fear, you have proven that you have the heart of a warrior, and this journey will be much safer and faster than your last one."

The golfer took a step toward the low split rail fence, one hand holding tightly onto the scruff of the cat's neck, the other now not simply supporting the feline's ample body but compressing it tightly against his chest. He took another step, then another.

Now he was running with the cat clutched against him in an iron vice, one leg swinging smoothly over the top rail of the fence, the golf cart with the empty sports bag waiting just a few feet away.

4

AMY TREMBLE WAS SEARCHINg for her old self. She knew that she needed to find that missing person if she was ever going to return to some semblance of her old routine.

"A journey of a thousand miles begins with a single step," she murmured to herself, and smiled when an image of her father popped into her head. She remembered her science fair project, and how he tried so hard to get her past the frustrations of a twelve-year-old with no inkling of how to complete the task.

She had two months to prove that plants respond to music. What kind of plants should she grow? How many? What kind of music to play? What ever made her select such a stupid topic anyway? It's not like playing music to plants was going to change the world, or help her become a better speller or catch the attention of that cute Aaron kid who sat three desks away.

But Dad told her to take it one step at a time, and together, they worked out a plan and developed a hypothesis. As she thought back on the project, she remembered building the crude hothouse, selecting seedlings from the local nursery—what were they, zinnias, tomato plants?—and selecting a variety of music. Thanks to her father, she received an A on the project, and even gained an appreciation for Mozart.

Yes, Dad was right; she had to take that first step. Had to start. She started with the pile of dishes in the sink. Then she went up to the bedrooms, stripped the sheets off of all the beds and began a wash.

The activity felt good, each chore moving her on to the next one. While the sheets were in the dryer, she picked up dirty laundry from both Kimmy and GT's bedrooms, and ran the vacuum cleaner across the floors wishing the kids were here to see her acting like the mother they remembered. Kimmy and G.T. were enjoying their summer vacation, Kimmy was at tennis camp and G.T. had spent the night at a friend's.

The morning blew by and it was early afternoon when she realized she hadn't seen Tony since she let him out in the backyard. He must be hungry by now, but surely he would have scratched on the door and made his presence known. He wasn't shy about that.

She opened the back door expecting to see him standing on the stoop, his tail swishing impatiently. But Tony wasn't there. "Tony," she called out, knowing that she was going to get the silent treatment for leaving him outside for so long.

When the cat didn't appear, she walked into the backyard, squinting while her eyes adjusted to the sunlight. God, it felt good to be outside. The aroma of freshly mowed grass tickled her nose, and she heard the sound of distant laughter. A warm breeze caressed the side of her face.

"Tony, where are you? Aren't you ready to come inside and eat?"

Still nothing. He was probably asleep under a bush somewhere. She was amazed that he had stayed awake long enough to find his way from Connecticut to Florida. That, she would never understand. She walked to the back of the yard and looked over the low fence, not really expecting to see him on the golf course. He hardly ever strayed from the yard.

Next, she wandered over to the monstrous split-leaf philodendron, one of his favorite napping places, and bent over to see if he was sleeping under one of the huge leaves. She walked completely around the massive plant, lifting the leaves, calling his name. Amy stood by the philodendron and let her eyes roam across the large backyard, her fingers unconsciously scratching the back of her right hand. Maybe he was in the front yard, she thought, and took a step in that direction before stopping, her head swiveling toward the small island of plants surrounding the birdbath.

A reflection caught her eye, the sun glinting off what looked like a shiny pipe or metal rod. Squinting as she walked forward, she now recognized the object as a golf club, but it pulled her up short. Staring at the club, she attempted to make a connection, see the pieces come together. It certainly didn't belong to Gerry. No way would Gerry be so careless as to leave one of his prized titanium and tungsten clubs lying on the lawn exposed to elements.

Bending over to inspect the club, she confirmed that it wasn't one of Gerry's. Of course, they lived on a golf course and there had to be dozens of rational explanations for why that club was there. She pictured a furious and frustrated golfer flinging it into the air and walking away.

There was probably a simple reason why that club was in her backyard, but something made her uneasy, rapped lightly at the back of her mind like a bird at a window pecking at its own reflection. Shaking her head, she caught sight of the slight depression in the sand and froze. She had seen too many of these not to recognize it immediately. She pictured Tony sleeping in the flower bed, shifting from time to time to get more comfortable, leaving behind this telltale impression. But that wasn't what bothered her; it was the imprint of a shoe with spike marks pressed into the dirt next to the depression.

They had waited a day for Tony to return. Kimmy and GT searched the neighborhood, going from house to house, taping flyers with Tony's picture on it to street signs, and slipping them in mailboxes. Amy called the Humane Society and Animal Control to see if Tony had been picked up or dropped off. She backtracked with the kids, walking up and down each street in a four-block area, calling his name, talking with neighbors.

No one had seen Tony. It was as if he had melted into the dirt, leaving behind the impression of where he slept and the mysterious golf club. The next day, she insisted they call the sheriff's office.

The sheriff's deputy walked around the yard, stared at the golf club, the footprint, and the impression in the sand without saying anything other than an occasional *hmm*. He was young and listened politely, his head cocked slightly to one side like he may have been a little hard of hearing, occasionally jotting a few words in a small notebook. The shiny nameplate on his breast pocket indicated that his name was Weed, and it suited the tall, gangly young man with the deep voice.

Officer Weed finished his survey of the yard and they went back into the house where he quickly wrote up a report. "I'll take the club with me, if you'd like, but I don't think it'll lead to anything." He seemed to lose his concentration for a moment, letting his eyes slip to his wristwatch, and then back to them.

"Personally, I think Tony will show up before long, Mrs. Tremble," he said, signing and dating the report. "Didn't you say he had found his way to Florida from Connecticut?" He gave them a quizzical glance as though he may have confused Tony with another cat that had traveled over a thousand miles on its own.

Amy, who had been holding herself back, was ready to erupt. She could see that the officer, for all his politeness, had no interest in Tony, didn't believe he had been abducted, and wanted to move on to a real case as soon as possible. She opened her mouth to tell him what she thought of his investigative technique, but Gerry jumped in before she could speak.

"Officer, believe me, this isn't like Tony at all. Since he's been here, he doesn't even wander out of the backyard."

The deputy nodded and opened the front door. "I'm sure you're right, Mr. Tremble, but my guess is that he's not too far away and will turn up soon. My mother had a cat that would disappear for days, but he always returned, fat and happy, if you know what I mean." He tore off a copy of the report and handed it to Gerry with a perfunctory nod.

"I'll be sure to call if anything turns up. And you do the same."

Amy and Gerry stood in the doorway and watched the young officer get in his car, close the door, and pick up the radio mic before pulling away from the curb. They saw him nod vigorously a few times. He seemed to be laughing as he turned the corner.

5

HIS NAME WAS RUNYAN MCWATERS. Not John Morrow or Jake. At this moment, driving from Crystal River to the Orlando Airport in his rented Buick, he was doing what he did best. Talking. McWaters rejoiced in the sound of his own voice in a way a sculptor might admire one of his singular creations, or a jazz pianist would listen to a recording of his latest effort and realize that something amazing had happened on that track.

McWaters didn't need any feedback to spin out his phrases, although having an appreciative audience certainly was welcome. He was aware that words were his special gift, that he had powers of persuasion that baffled even him. He was still awed by what came out of his mouth and how people reacted to him. Growing up, his mother would tell him he was going to be a lawyer. Either that or his mouth was going to get him in lots of trouble.

He talked to the cat in the soft carrier on the seat beside him from State Road 44 to the Florida Turnpike. Two hours and fourteen minutes later he drove into National Car Rental, returned the Buick, and hopped aboard the airport van with his overnight bag in one hand and the carrier in the other.

"You are one lucky cat, my boy. Taking your first plane ride, and finding a new home with a rich sugar daddy." He spoke to the cat at his side as he entered the Level 3 departure terminal of Orlando International and threaded his way through the crowds of July 4th holiday travelers. "I don't know about you, my furry friend, but I'll be happy to leave this swamp behind and get back to San Diego."

A young man in an expensive suit and a styled haircut sporting blond highlights and enough mousse to raise the Titanic shouldered his way through the mob of people. He clutched a leather brief case and spoke loudly into a telephone headset oblivious to the people around him. The man brushed against McWaters, knocking him off balance, and continued on his way without saying a word. In one fluid motion, McWaters dropped the overnight bag and whipped out his hand grabbing the man's bicep and spinning him around.

"I'm sorry sir, but did you forget something?"

Startled into temporary silence, the man looked down to be sure he still had his briefcase, shook his head and started to move forward. McWaters tightened his grip, digging his fingers deep into the muscle, constricting nerve against bone, until he cried out in pain.

"Ah, but I'm afraid you did forget something. And aren't you lucky that I'm here to remind you that you forgot your manners?"

The young man jerked his arm violently. "Let go, you crazy son of ahh—"

McWaters' fingers dug deeper and the man's face contorted in pain and rage, his arm raised away from his body like it no longer was a part of him. "Okay, okay," he gasped. "Whatever you want."

"No, it's what you want, isn't it? Maybe you weren't paying attention when your mother was passing down life's little lessons—like actions and reactions." He increased the pressure on the man's arm, pulling him forward until their faces were inches apart, and gave him one of his most brilliant smiles. "Let me hear you say *excuse me*, please."

"Excuse me. Excuse me. Now, let me go—please."

He released the arm, giving the man a slight push to send him on his way. "Very good. Your mother would be so proud," he said to the man's retreating back. He bent over and picked up his bag, smiled and nodded at the dozen people who had stopped to gape, and continued on his way to the Delta counter.

Assured that his flight was on time, he checked the gate departure against his boarding pass. Gate 68 was on Level 4 and required a short train ride on the airport AGT system. First, however, there was the matter of passing through the security checkpoint.

Fifteen minutes later, he presented his ID and was shuttled to another guard at a table behind the X-ray machine conveyor belt. She handed him a plastic tray. "Empty your pockets, and place any jewelry in the tray," she said politely, but firmly. He dropped his overnight bag on the conveyor belt without prompting but held onto the cat carrier raising it toward the guard.

"Put the cat on the table, please, and empty your pockets," she said, her voice a bit sterner this time.

He did as he was told.

"Sir, you'll have to remove the cat from the bag."

He hesitated, glanced at the concourse ahead of him, the line of people behind him, and then back at the guard who was frowning at him now. He unzipped the bag without another word. Wrapping one hand tightly under Tony's front legs, he lifted the cat out of the bag.

The guard examined the inside of the soft carrier briefly and placed it on the moving conveyor belt. "Please carry the cat through the metal detector with you, sir."

He murmured something unintelligible to the cat, holding it near his face with both hands. Turning toward the box-like metal detector, he smiled at the other guard standing beside it. "Are you sure that it's safe for me to take my cat through that thing? I'd hate for anything to upset him, or scramble his genes." Still holding the cat next to his face, he smiled broadly at the stern-faced guard to let him know he was only joking.

McWaters had immersed himself into the role of loving cat owner. He truly felt affection for Tony at that moment, and wanted the world to instantly recognize him as a protective father figure caring for his beloved feline companion. The guard's face relaxed and he nodded encouragingly at him as if to say nothing would happen to your cat.

With the smile still on his face and the cat held up like a trophy, he stepped toward the metal detector unprepared for the violent hiss that erupted in his ear and the fiery pain that coursed down his cheek. He yelped in surprise, slapping a palm against his stinging face and looking at his hand as though seeing it for the first time. There, on his palm, was a tracing of three thin red lines. He was so shocked that it took him a moment to realize what had happened, and that he was no longer holding the cat.

Windrusher treaded his way through the hordes of long-legged beings that pressed in on him from all sides. He had finally escaped from the Hyskos with the soothing voice, escaped from the bag he had been crammed into since he was snatched from his own backyard.

Still in shock and disbelief that such a thing could happen, he had silently endured the long ride with only an occasional whimper, and wondered if he would ever be allowed out of his soft prison. After a lengthy ride in the noisy vehicle, with the man babbling on nearly the entire way, he was carried through this noisy, frightening hall. Finally, he was pulled from the bag by the foolish Hyskos who held him up for everyone to see, as though the two of them were family.

Family? Could it be? He was momentarily confused. Did he now belong to this round-faced being? Was it possible his family had given him away, that they didn't want him anymore? No, that wasn't possible.

Windrusher was certain that he did not belong to this Hyskos, could never belong to him. But if he was going to return to his own loving family he would have to take some action. Wildly, he raked his unsheathed claws across the man's face causing him to clutch the wound and drop him to the floor.

He was free and running as fast as he could through the crowded corridor. He retraced the path they had taken, looking for an exit, but everywhere he turned there were legs; tall legs, legs covered in pants and dresses, legs trailing bags on wheels behind them. The legs jumped back as he bumped against them and he heard expressions of surprise as he cut one way and the next, weaving through the throng, hearing snatches of unintelligible conversation as he ran.

He darted past lines of people, his nails clicking on the tile floor. The din seemed to converge into a single rumble that roared through and over him in a bewildering cacophony. Ahead he heard an even louder noise, repeating itself over and over as it approached. He jumped aside as a small vehicle, much like the ones he saw on the grassy fields next to his home, slowly rumbled by with its cargo of high-legged beings.

The vehicle had cleared a path through the crowd, and he was able to get his bearings. He thought he recognized the moving staircase they had taken, and beyond that he knew was the exit to this place. If he could only make it down to that next level and outside, he might be able to find his way back to his family.

Cautiously, he surveyed the lines of Hyskos on the moving stairs, one going down and the other up toward him. Down. He needed to be on the one moving down. Positioning himself behind a potted palm between the two stairwells, he observed how the high-legged beings stepped onto the plate and rode it down to the next floor. The plates seemed to grow out of one another, rising out of the floor and folding back onto themselves. He saw that he would have to leap on it as it extended outwards, without being stepped on, without being swallowed by the folding metal plates.

It all seemed so bewildering. He had come so far, yet he was gripped with indecision, unsure of whether to keep running or hop onto the moving stairwell. Instead of running or hopping, he dropped to the floor, flattening himself, pressing his head against the ceramic pot.

He squeezed his green eyes shut to block out the frenzied confusion surrounding him, hoping that when he opened them he would find himself back in his sun-drenched yard. Instead, an image of Tho-hoth reeled through his mind, and he saw the ancient god of wisdom, great tufts of fur surrounding his head like a fiery mane, penetrating eyes cutting through him.

You have proven yourself to be a cat of incredible resources, and you must do so again.

He heard the words deep within him as he had in the Cave of Tho-hoth when the holy one had spoken those very words. Tho-hoth had warned him that he would once again face danger and perilous times, that he would be taken far from home, and that he must act to save himself and others.

He inhaled deeply, drawing in a mélange of odors from the constant flow of bodies passing by him. He stood and stepped onto the moving stairwell, feeling the surge of the plate carry him down. Ahead of him and behind him were the tall-legged beings. He shuffled toward the side as one of the Hyskos almost stepped on him moving past him even as the stairs took them lower.

Voices jumped out at him from above and below, but he remained calm, fighting the inner furies that called on him to flee. Step by step, he approached the floor, where one after another the high-legged beings stepped from the moving platform. It was his turn now, and he jumped forward, sliding on the slick tiles before regaining his footing and turning toward the bright windows and doors.

His stomach suddenly lurched as though falling from a great height. Except he wasn't falling, he realized, but had been jerked upwards. Something, someone, had gripped him tightly and he had been lifted violently off the floor.

"That was quite a scare you gave us, Tony. You could have got lost or got hurt, or, heaven forbid, been stolen by some maniac, and I'd never see you again." McWaters shoved the cat into the bag, zipping it quickly closed. "But you're safe now, my little friend."

6

MᴄWᴀᴛᴇʀs ʜᴇʟᴅ ᴛʜᴇ ᴄᴀʀʀɪᴇʀ protectively against his chest in the slowly moving line of passengers inching their way up the aisle. He waited patiently as they stowed their luggage, and finally reached his seat. At least he had an aisle seat, although he knew that each seat in coach class was equally rotten. The next cross-country job, he would insist on first class. Von Rothmann could certainly afford to spring for a few hundred more, he thought.

He had hoped the seat next to him would be vacant and he could slide Tony in front of the empty seat rather than his own, giving him a little more leg room. He saw the woman in the middle seat and tried to hide his disappointment with a polite nod. At least he would have someone to talk with to help pass the hours until they landed in San Diego.

He placed the carrier on the seat while he found a spot for his bag in the overhead compartment. Lifting the cat carrier, he sat down, balanced Tony on his lap, and turned to speak to the woman next to him. It was impossible for him to spend five hours sitting inches away from a stranger without offering a little friendly conversation. Sleep would come later, but there were social conventions that must be adhered to, introductions, polite explorations, hearty expansion on whatever subject arose. And the cat in his lap was a good place to start since she was staring intently at the carrier.

"Is that a cat?" she asked before he could speak, her voice tinged with disbelief and horror.

"Why it is indeed, a fine and wondrous creature of the genus *Felis*, subgenus *Felis catus*, which incorporates most of the domestic cats in—"

"I'm terribly allergic to cats, and I'm not about to sit next to that thing for the entire flight." The woman stood up and attempted to force her way past McWaters. Of course, she couldn't. There was no room for her to pass unless he got up from his seat and let her out. Ever the gentleman, he did just that and she brushed by him without another word.

He sat back down, held the carrier up to eye level, a hint of a smile on his lips, and whispered, "Sometimes it's the little things that make life worth living, don't you think?"

He only had time to slide the carrier under the woman's seat and buckle the seat belt before a flight attendant approached followed closely by a tall, exceedingly thin woman wearing faded jeans and a far-away look on her tanned and lined face. The attendant scanned the paper in her hand before leaning in close to McWaters, as though they were co-conspirators.

"Mr. McWaters?"

"Yes."

"The passenger in the seat next to you has requested to be moved to our cat-free section, if you know what I mean." She smiled kindly at him before nodding to the woman who had taken a position directly behind her. "Ms. Swinson here was kind enough to swap places, and assures me she is fond of cats and not the least bit allergic. Isn't that right, Ms. Swinson?"

"Yes, of course, I don't have any problems with cats, have five of my own. I'd have more if—"

"Right," the attendant cut her off. "So, if you would move your traveling companion to the seat in front of you and allow Ms. Swinson to have a seat, we'll be able to take off."

He did as he was told, unbuckling, moving the cat over, then stepping into the aisle while Ms. Swinson slid into the middle seat trailing an overpowering stench of cigarette smoke. Hopefully, she was the strong, silent type, but he didn't think so.

"I'm Tracy Swinson, and did I tell you I have five cats. Most of them are rescues from the Humane Society; but I found one in a garbage can. Can you imagine that? I'd fill up the house with cats, but my boyfriend,

Terry, his name is Terry Strong. TS and TS, isn't that a hoot? Terry thinks that five is enough in our small house. It only has two bedrooms, but it's comfy, and we're lucky the rent is so low, because we're in a great neighborhood. So close to work, I'm not stuck in that god-awful traffic every day like poor Terry. Don't you just hate it?"

McWaters' head was reeling, and he realized he was holding his breath. He let it out slowly through pursed lips, inhaled deeply and stuck out his hand. "I don't think we were properly introduced. I'm Runyan McWaters. My friends call me Mac, and I'm so happy to meet another cat lover. I know exactly what you mean about that horrid traffic, let me tell you about what happened to me last month..." If there was one thing McWaters adored, it was a challenge.

"I understand, Officer Weed, but you will keep trying, won't you? Yes. Yes. Goodbye."

The conversation had been brief and decidedly one-sided, but Kimmy Tremble understood the news was not good as her mother put down the telephone. "What did he say?"

"The same thing he's said the last two times I've called—*You have to be patient, Mrs. Tremble. I'm sure your cat will be back soon.* It's the same old song and dance we've been getting from them. I get the feeling he doesn't believe Tony was taken. If he does, it isn't worth his time to go looking for a cat."

"Of course, he was taken. We know Tony wouldn't just leave." Kimmy's eyes were red and she could feel her self-control dribbling away, more tears welling up, preparing to join the others she had shed over the past three days. Someone knew where her cat was, had deliberately entered their yard and stolen him. She felt the need to lash out; yell and throw a tantrum. But there was no one available to direct her anger toward, and now that she was twelve years old, she knew that tantrums wouldn't bring Tony home again. Besides, her mother was just as worried as she was.

"What are we going to do, Mom? The police don't believe he was stolen. We have to do something." The tears were coursing down her face now and she swiped at them with the back of her hand. Her mother placed an arm around her and gently wiped her cheek.

"We're not going to give up, Kimmy. You can believe that. We'll do something—offer a reward, go on television—I don't know what, but we're going to bring Tony back where he belongs. Here, with his family."

The soft rumble of the airplane engines vibrated through the cabin. Most of the passengers were unaware of it as they read, slept, or watched the movie on one of the small screens that peppered the ceiling. They were sitting in padded seats, cushioned from the vibrations, but Windrusher was on the floor and felt the constant strumming deep within his belly. It wasn't an uncomfortable feeling, but it served to remind him that he was on the move again. He recognized the mechanical sounds and feel of a Hyskos vehicle; although this one was different than the other large vehicles he had stolen rides in during his journey to the land of warm waters.

He was on another journey, but this time it wasn't his choice. He hadn't slept since being snatched from his family's backyard and slid quickly into the comforting grasp of Hwrt-Heru, the goddess of sleep, felt her loving embrace and released his tenuous grip on consciousness. He dropped into the spiraling vortex and heard the rising chorus of voices reaching out for him, imploring him to link his mind with theirs. Only by sharing himself, by releasing control, would he become one and tap the wisdom found within their universal soul.

The compelling attraction of the Akhen-et-u lured him on and he rode through increasingly louder waves, letting the sounds wash over him, willing his inner consciousness to focus on the direction of the flow. Windrusher floated toward the peaceful center and when a break appeared, as he knew it would, rushed in and introduced himself to the multitude of sleeping cats using his Mother's name, Son of Nefer-iss-tu, and his call name, Pferusha-ulis, Windrusher.

He was aware of the rise in the noise level at the mention of his name, but ignored it and told the listeners his story of being snatched by a strange Hyskos, brought aboard yet another vehicle taking him far from home. He shared with them each detail he could remember, including the powerful thrust of the vehicle as it began its journey and the sinking feeling in his stomach. As he hurried through his story he realized there wasn't much to tell. It had all had happened so quickly.

Even as he told his story to the listening multitude that now had grown uncommonly still, he knew how hopeless his situation must sound. It wasn't like the last time he turned to Akhen-et-u for assistance. Because cats were everywhere, they were able to provide clues to conditions and locations, suggestions for dealing with the challenges he had faced while trying to find his family. But he didn't have any idea where he was, where he was going, or when he would get there. How could he expect these cats to help him?

While the voices bubbled and chirped, parsing every bit of his story, Wind remembered his dream visit with Tho-hoth and cut through the din to share these important details with the Inner Ear. "There was no doubt that it was Tho-hoth himself, speaking to me from his cave in the desert. And he told me that there was great danger in my future, not only to myself but to my own Hyskos family."

The effort involved in telling his story had left him exhausted and he fell quiet, waiting for what he knew would be an outpouring of opinions and comments. Much of it would be useless, of course, but it was up to him to winnow out the meaningless, the inconsequential, and find the scrap of wisdom among the mass of jabber. The feelings of hopelessness that had enveloped him just moments before were slowly washed away as he listened to the voices. His past experiences, even if they were unique, had proven that the Inner Ear was a vital lifeline and if he listened carefully he would find that bit of knowledge that might save his life.

One queenly voice identified herself as Laris-ens-la, Rainwalker, and she provided him with information that explained the transport vehicle he had described. "From what you say, Windrusher, it seems you are now on the Hyskos vehicle that flies like the feathered chirpers. Surely, you've seen them buzzing overhead, sometimes trailing long white tails? My Hyskos has taken me with her on these carriers many times. Of course, we have two homes, which, I'm sure, most of you don't since—"

"Windrusher," a familiar voice filled with the weight of authority cut the queen off. "It's been a long time since you visited with us."

"Short Shank, it seems we only speak during my troubled times. I have a bad feeling, old one, that I may have had one adventure too many. Perhaps the end of my journey will be coming soon."

"You were chosen because of your special gifts, Pferusha-ulis. Remember what Tho-hoth told you and be ready to face the danger, whatever it might be. Along with the gift of wisdom, Tho-hoth has blessed you with a vision of your future. Accept these gifts for what they are since very few cats are fortunate enough to know what fate awaits them."

7

VIEWED FROM A PASSING CAR on I-5, the house perched atop the bluff was all glass and reflections. The roofline swept up at one end, like the prow of an ocean liner, giving the house the angular shape of a four-sided polygon.

It would be nearly impossible to see anything behind the massive thirty-foot high windows, especially now that the setting sun had painted the glass with florid strokes. Karl von Rothmann paced behind the huge expanse of windows, specially tinted to block out harmful ultraviolet rays, and barely noticed the stream of traffic below him or the blue waters in the distance.

Von Rothmann wasn't immune to the beauty of the view—it was the reason he had purchased the entire bluff and built his dream home here. Architectural students might notice the resemblance to Frank Lloyd Wright's Ablin house in Bakersfield, although there was no attempt to organically blend this structure into the landscape.

Von Rothmann craved privacy, among other things, and he didn't want to share his view with anyone, even though he thought he could have purchased an entire city block in downtown San Diego for the same price. But California real estate was the best investment anyone could make, and one day he'd sell to a developer who would build a dozen or more homes on this same bluff.

For the third time in the past five minutes he glanced down at his wrist and checked his watch, as though he was afraid some thief had made off with his custom-made chronograph. It was impressive to behold, a chunky gold creation that seemed to be hammered from a five-pound nugget and polished to a high sheen. Either the craftsman or the buyer must have decided the bulky gold watch, with its carved twenty-four-carat case and bracelet, was not gaudy enough and added a sprinkling of diamonds for good measure.

A matching gold and diamond ring sat upon a stubby middle finger, and it was this finger that he ran over the face of the watch before letting his eyes drift toward the line of traffic below. He told himself that everything had gone as planned, but still the doubt remained. Shouldn't he be here by now? Did he have an accident? Maybe he'd been stopped by police and taken off for questioning.

No. He was letting his imagination take him in illogical directions.

He knew there was nothing to worry about. McWaters had called as soon as they landed in San Diego. He glanced down at the streaming traffic and knew McWaters was somewhere in the mass of commuters inching their way north. He looked at his reflection in the window and canted his head one way and then the other. Lifting his hand, he carefully patted a head of hair the color of a dirty brick and swept back from his forehead in a stiff pompadour.

His head was shaped like a large, squat pumpkin that had sat exposed to the elements for too long and was beginning to fall in on itself. His puffy, flushed face was a ruinous terrain of brown spots and lesions caused by a succession of carcinomas that left a cancerous trail along his arms and hands as well.

He took a deep breath, brought his hand up to his chest and felt the delicate silver cross hidden beneath his Tommy Bahama silk shirt. His mouth twisted into a tight smirk that cleaved a grim line across his odd-shaped face as he fingered the tiny cross. Abruptly, he turned his back to the wall of glass, crossed the vast open area with its tableau of art deco style chairs and tables, and walked toward the hall at the southern end of the residence.

A visitor to von Rothmann's mansion might have thought the hallway led to bedrooms, an office, or even a library, but once he turned the corner he encountered another wall of glass. There was no view of mountains or ocean through this window. Instead, it revealed an interior courtyard, encased in waist high glass blocks on two sides, with tempered glass rising to the fourteen-foot cathedral ceiling.

A large tree grew inside under a skylight, and in each corner stood a multi-layered, carpeted structure with platforms and covered hideaways. Scattered around the room were a variety of playthings, catnip-filled mice, plastic balls, and feathery contraptions. A television set sat on a stand in another corner, its screen alive with dazzling tropical fish swimming in endless circles.

It was a bright and cheerful room. A white waist-high counter with rows of storage drawers covered one wall, and above it, flowing onto the other wall, was a colorful mural of jungle foliage, flying parrots, and crested cockatoos against an indigo sky. It might have been a child's playroom except for the pet toys strewn across the floor, the large bottle of water that flowed into a gray dish, and the four sets of matching Waterford Crystal bowls lined up on the floor.

He noted that the three occupants were asleep, which wasn't surprising. Two of them were on a rattan couch, the other on one of the carpeted platforms. He squinted at the four bowls across the room. Three of the bowls, standing exactly sixteen inches apart, each on their own squares of beige carpet, were filled with brown pellets. The other was empty.

His head moved from the first bowl to the large marmalade-colored tabby sleeping atop the carpeted stand. He spoke aloud, knowing he couldn't be heard through the thick glass walls. "Murray, you're still the top cat," he said, his voice thin and reedy with a hint of a European accent. Next he turned to a small kitten sleeping on a pale blue pillow covered with fluffy white clouds. "My little Darwin. Still lost in the clouds, aren't you?"

At the other end of the couch, completely covering another fleece pillow, was a stately Persian with a magnificent cream coat. The Persian, like each of the other cats, wore a bulky collar. The cat opened one blue-green eye and stared directly at him as though some signal had passed between them.

"Nothing gets past you, my magnificent Grand Champion. Yes, we're about to receive another important guest, and I expect you to welcome him properly." He smiled his mirthless grin and let his eyes slide back to the empty crystal bowl.

"I'm telling you, be careful with this one, boss. Look what he did to me at the airport." McWaters pointed to the ragged scratch running down his left cheek. "There I was chasing him down the concourse, zigging this way, zagging that. We must have made for a funny picture. But here he is, next day delivery. Just like FedEx."

Von Rothmann's ravaged face softened as he held the cat carrier up to eye level. They were standing in front of the feline bed and breakfast, as he referred to it, and the smile that creased his face this time was real enough, all teeth and gums. "Tony, Tony, Tony. You don't know how long I've waited for you." He paused and inhaled noisily. "To have you here where you belong with your other celebrated brothers and sisters of the fur." He cast a sideways glance at McWaters who took the cue and laughed loudly at the little joke.

"No, I don't think we're going to have any trouble with you, are we? Runyan, open the door, and let's introduce Tony to his new roommates."

McWaters pushed the door open, the bottom edge of it scraping on the sisal mat inside the door. Von Rothmann placed the carrier on the counter, zipped it open and plucked the cat out. He hugged him to his chest, supporting the cat under one arm while he gently stroked his head with the other. His face took on a beatific cast, as if he had entered the cathedral of Chartres, and his faded blue eyes glowed with a liquid brightness. Bending his head to Tony's ear, he whispered, "Now, she'll know what it feels like to lose someone you love."

He straightened and turned toward McWaters, "He is a fine specimen, isn't he?"

McWaters nodded.

"You've come a long way, Tony, but now you can rest. You'll never want for anything."

Von Rothmann twirled slowly, both arms around the cat. "See your beautiful new home. You'll soon forget about that other place and those other people who left you behind." He reached into a pocket of his linen trousers and pulled out a handful of cat treats. Walking toward the

Persian who was still lying on the couch, he placed several of the fragrant treats on her pillow.

"Tony, I want you to meet Katmandu. Katmandu, Tony." He made a small mock bow with the cat in his arms. "She was the last boarder to join us before you arrived. You must show her some respect because she's a National Grand Champion." Katmandu's eyelids closed and opened again in response to von Rothmann's voice.

"She may seem a bit cold and reserved to you at first, but when you get to know her, you'll find out she's very cold and reserved," McWaters said.

Both men laughed.

The small gray and white kitten was lurking at the base of one of the cat stands, playing with a catnip mouse. As von Rothmann approached, it released the mouse and lifted its head expectantly showing large curious, dark blue eyes.

"We're standing before a scientific miracle, Tony" von Rothmann said. "This unassuming young feline is named Darwin. I know you didn't have time to read the paper over the past few months, or watch CNN, but Darwin was all over the news." He squatted in front of the cat who cut her eyes right and left as though preparing to run for safety.

"Darwin is the very first cloned cat," McWaters added. "Amazing isn't it? Little Darwin here was quite the achievement. Everyone in the scientific world was agog over her until they went on to their next splashy experiment, that endangered marsupial—what was it, boss, some kind of kangaroo?"

"The Lumholtz Tree-Kangaroo," von Rothmann answered testily, tossing several treats to the small kitten.

"Right. Then, poor Darwin was just another old experiment passing her time in a cage in some lab at Texas A & M University, where, I must say, they have very cooperative lab assistants."

Von Rothmann straightened slowly, carefully holding the big gray and orange cat to his chest. "You'll have a chance to get better acquainted with Darwin shortly, but there's one more roommate you must meet."

He stepped toward the carpeted cat stand where the large marmalade cat was lying watching the tantalizing tropical fish on the television screen. "Murray here is a true media celebrity." He reached up and scratched the tabby behind one ear. "Isn't that right, big boy? Murray was the star of many a cat food commercial, and even had a part on that horrendous sitcom…"

"*Larry's Life*," McWaters completed the sentence. "I guess you could say that Murray still performs for the cameras," he said, flicking his eyes toward a high corner where a small industrial camera was mounted. "He has a much smaller audience now, but you don't seem to mind, do you, Murray?"

Von Rothmann was eyeing McWaters with open hostility. He turned his back and crossed the room to the built-in counter with its storage cubicles and drawers. "Runyan, if you can stop talking long enough, would you find Tony's collar. Then fill his food bowl. And I think their litter boxes need cleaning."

McWaters pulled one of the drawers open and withdrew a thick leather and metal collar, identical to the ones on the other cats. Quickly, he placed it around Tony's neck and silently did the other chores.

"Now, we'll leave you alone with your new friends, Tony, so you can get better acquainted," von Rothmann said, bending over to place the cat on the floor. "I hope you get along, but you have the rest of your lives to work out any differences."

The glass door closed behind the two men and the cat they called Tony turned and watched them walk away.

8

WINDRUSHER AND THE OTHER CATS eyed one another in silence. The small kitten wrinkled her tiny pink nose as though a malodorous air had swept through the room. She took one hesitant step toward Windrusher, then two quicker ones before losing her balance and falling against him. Her large luminous eyes gleamed, and she emitted a high-pitched meow.

He lowered his head and licked the kitten several times until she rubbed against him so hard she tripped and fell over one of his paws. He watched her jump to her feet, and waited until she regained her footing to formally introduce himself. "I'm the Son of Nefer-iss-tu. My call name is Pferusha-ulis, Windrusher. What do they call you, little one," he said, giving the kitten a gentle head butt.

The tiny cat was staring at him as though she expected Windrusher to sprout wings and fly around the room. As the silence grew more awkward, his thoughts flew back to his first meeting with Lil' One, and wondered if this cat was too young or too much the Wetlos to be able to communicate.

"Don't expect much from that one."

Swiveling his head to the top of the carpeted stand, Windrusher was relieved to find that at least one of the cats would speak to him. The ginger red tabby was at least as big as he was, with massive jowls and distinctive dark stripes around his legs and tail. The marmalade gazed down at him with intense copper and black eyes then hopped from one platform to the next until he was standing beside them.

"She means well, but she doesn't have much to say, and spends most of the time playing when she's not falling down or going in circles. We call her Blank Eyes because she acts like a poor Wetlos and we're not sure there's anything in her head."

"Even a Wetlos may surprise you once they find themselves," Windrusher said, recalling the remarkable transformation Lil' One made from tentative kitten to rambunctious and assertive cat during their journey.

"I hope that's true for this kitten, because she seems to have strayed far from the Path. Perhaps you can instruct her while you're here, Windrusher. I'm called Chaser, and that silent sack of fur with the pushed-in face is Rahhna's Light. She will tell you that she shines brighter than any other cat, but only if she decides to share her royal thoughts with you."

Windrusher's head was filled with many questions. He had been stolen from his yard, imprisoned by a strange Hyskos, and now found himself here with these other cats. Have they always lived here in this Hyskos home, he wondered, or were they stolen, too? And most importantly, was there a way out of this house?

He studied the three cats, the friendly and talkative marmalade, the stumbling kitten with the huge eyes, and finally the Persian with her luxuriously long creamy hair and turned down mouth. She was draped across the pillow as though posing for a photograph, and she glared at him in silence. Wind grew uncomfortable under her stare, and realized there was something about her that reminded him of….

Of Scowl Down, of course. Poor Scowl Down. An image of the cantankerous old female leaped into his mind. He would never forget his old friend, but now he concentrated on the big-boned ginger cat. "Thank you for your welcome, Chaser," he finally said. "You will have to tell me what you know about this place, how you got here, and how you are treated." Edging closer to the cat, he lowered his voice and said, "There's something about Rahhna's Light that makes me feel like a whiskerless kitten. I'd better pay my respects since she's obviously a cat of fine breeding."

He approached the Persian and stopped at the foot of the rattan couch directly below her. She stared at him with large aqua eyes, and ran her tongue delicately over her mouth.

"Perhaps you were sleeping when I introduced myself," he said politely. "I am called Windrusher, and Chaser tells me you are called Rahhna's Light. A name certainly befitting such a fine cat. Do you know why I have been brought here?"

The longhair remained silent. He stood waiting for her response feeling the glare of her unblinking eyes pressing on him like a heavy weight. "Were you also brought here against your will," he tried again, "or is this your home?"

"Do I look like a cat that would live in a room with such ordinary cats as you and those Wetlos friends of yours?" she suddenly snapped. "Of course, this is not my home. My Hyskos had a large and beautiful home and I was free to wander through its many rooms. Not confined like a snouter in a cage." The Persian was on her feet now, standing on the pillow, the words fired at Windrusher in a high-pitched growl, one after the other as though she had been saving them up for just this moment.

"She had fine beds for me to sleep on, and she groomed my coat until it shined like my namesake, Rahhna. I am an important cat, can't you see that? Or are you as blind as that kitten is dumb? I've been with only the very best cats, and I can tell you that none of you is worthy to clean my whiskers."

Rahhna's Light inhaled loudly, turned away from Windrusher, and dropped to her belly on the cushion. He remained motionless, still struck by the vehemence of her words. He could see now that she was nothing like his old friend. Scowl Down was defending her home when he and Lil' One invaded her territory that stormy night. Perhaps Rahhna's Light believed she was defending her territory, or maybe, as he suspected, she was always this contentious.

Windrusher's drooping tail mirrored his feelings as he turned away from the angry Persian. It was going to take time and patience to break through the wall of resentment this cat had built around her, but he didn't know if he wanted to try. Certainly not now. What he wanted now were some answers and the only one who was not railing at him or falling over his feet was Chaser.

The big marmalade had been watching the interchange with Rahhna's Light from the base of the tree growing in the center of the room. "I should have warned you about her. That Setlos must have been a snouter in her last life. She hasn't said a kind word to me or Blank Eyes, but she saved her worst poison for you. I don't know how you made such an enemy so quickly."

"Irissa-u gave me special gifts."

"I can see that. It's best to leave her alone in her misery."

Windrusher's head was still reeling from the longhair's tantrum. Frustrated, he stretched himself to his full length against the tree trunk, dug his claws into the smooth bark and raked downwards with all his strength. Twice more he clawed the trunk, leaving behind deep furrows and dissipating the pent-up anger and hurt the Persian had heaped on him.

Now he was ready to resume his conversation with Chaser. First he asked him how he came to be here, and the big marmalade told a remarkable story.

"Like you, I consider myself blessed by Irissa-u. Born behind some Hyskos buildings, I lived with a small colony; eating scraps from garbage or whatever the high-legged beings might leave for us. It was a hard and dangerous life for a cat. Predators stalked us, sickness felled us, and there was always hunger. But I was young, and I had my mother nearby to nurture me. At least until that day when the Hyskos came with their nets and vehicle and took us away.

"We were placed in cages in a room filled with other cats. The crying and misery was almost too much for my young mind to endure, especially after my mother and sister were taken away from my cage. I never saw them again."

Chaser paused; his eyes clouded and seemed to turn inwards as though seeing himself in that cage once again watching his mother taken from his side and carried away. Listening to Chaser's story, Windrusher recalled his own imprisonment in the Hyskos cage and how close he had come to a similar fate. He knew exactly what the young cat must have endured.

"My mother was a friendly cat who had lived in a Hyskos home until they moved away and left her behind to care for herself," Chaser continued. "Still, she wasn't bitter, and she taught me not to fear the high-legged beings. The other kittens in our colony were frightened and would run from them when they brought food, but I understood that they were there to feed us and I would let them touch me and scratch my head."

Chaser had been a trusting, friendly kitten when the two men from animal control appeared in response to complaints from a store manager. While they set traps for most of the cats, Chaser walked boldly up to one of the men expecting to be fed. Instead, the surprised trapper picked him up and placed him into a cage in the truck.

From there, he was transferred to another cage inside the animal control facility with his mother and another sibling. After five days, an employee made an early morning visit and removed Murray's mother and sister, who had been crying the entire time she had been caged.

"I was totally alone, wondering what had happened to my mother and sister, worrying that I would be taken away next. But I tried to make friends with the Hyskos that visited me, and soon a female Hyskos came and brought me to her home.

"She was kind but needed constant attention. She called me Murray, and would get down on the floor and play with me. Each time, she clicked a little noise thing then gave me a tasty cruncher. It was a foolish little game, but I found satisfaction in pleasing my Hyskos and training her to give me more crunchers."

Her name was Iona Wager and she was a respected animal trainer specializing in cats. Her credits had appeared in dozens of television programs and motion pictures and she was always searching for intelligent young cats to add to her stable of felines. Marmalade cats were in high demand ever since Morris the Cat had made such a big hit on the 9Lives commercials, and when she received a call from one of the animal control workers about a friendly, fearless young cat, she went to see for herself.

That turned out to be the luckiest day of Murray's young life. Iona worked several times a day with her young rescue, although never for more than a few minutes at a time, and always making it seem like a game. Starting with sitting on command, an easy trick, Iona used a pet clicker and treats to reinforce the behavior she wanted the cat to perform. When the cat sat, she clicked the clicker, gave him a treat and praised him. From there they moved to sit-ups or beg-ups, getting the energetic kitten to lift its paws up in response to the clicker and treats.

It took patience and time, but Murray was intelligent, and soon he was introduced to a television studio with its overhead lights, cameras, and workers. Murray and Iona had worked on developing a trademark Murray look that was soon the centerpiece for a series of Kitty Cuisine commercials. Murray had mastered what amounted to a double take, a shake of the head and a stare into the camera with hooded lids that conveyed a *what the hell?* skepticism. Viewers came to anticipate the look each time Murray was presented with a competitor's brand of cat food, and his success led to a part in *Larry's Life*, a slapstick comedy that brought instant recognition to the marmalade cat, and a People's Choice Award for the star.

"After living outside and knowing hunger and fear, this new life was like a blessing from Irissa-u. I never completely forgot that other part of my life, but more and more it seemed like almost a dream, or a story that my mother told me as a kitten."

"You were most fortunate," Windrusher said, thinking about the many cats he encountered in his journey that struggled to survive. "But how did you come to be here. Surely, your female Hyskos didn't give you away?"

Chaser didn't answer; instead he padded over to the water fountain and lapped at the liquid in the bowl. Windrusher waited for Chaser to resume his story, noticing that Blank Eyes had quietly slipped in beside him. He didn't know how long she had been lying there apparently listening to Chaser's life story. He licked her lightly on the head, and the kitten meowed loudly and flattened herself, one leg extended in front of the other.

Chaser turned back to his listeners, licking drops of water from around his mouth. They both looked at him expectantly. "I remember that we would travel together to far-away places," he said.

Larry's Life proved to be so popular in its first season that the network ordered another twenty-two programs. In mid-August, two weeks before the premiere of the second season, Murray and Iona Wager were sent off on a much-ballyhooed, ten-city publicity tour. At the Chicago tour stop, Murray and Iona were to appear on three TV talk shows and at two pet stores where Murray fans lined up to meet their favorite cat actor and get his autograph, a postcard with his picture and paw print.

Iona made sure that Murray looked his best and was well-rested before each appearance. This meant taking a long nap in the hotel room while she worked out the details of the next stop. She knew that outsiders probably thought that being interviewed on television and meeting the fans was the glamorous part of show business, but Iona found it tedious and uncomfortable. She was ready to go home and get back to her cats. They still had three more stops to make, and she was exhausted from the schedule of appearances and constant travel.

She looked fondly at Murray, asleep on his own double bed, and decided he had the right idea. They still had three hours before the 5:30 p.m. appearance at Pet World, and she thought a power nap would do them both good.

Iona was about to call and ask for a wake-up call when the phone rang. She plucked it from the cradle quickly so it wouldn't bother Murray, expecting it to be the studio publicist telling her of another addition or change to the schedule.

"Ms. Wager?" a mellifluous voice asked.

"Yes."

"Ms. Wager, this is the front desk. We have a package down here from Los Angeles marked urgent delivery."

"Thank you, can you have it sent up to my room, please?"

"I would, but the delivery man is in a hurry and says he requires your signature before he can leave. I was wondering if there was any way you might come down here and sign for it, then I'll be happy to have someone carry it up to your room for you."

Iona hesitated, eyed the sleeping cat, and then said, "Okay, I'll be right down."

She checked to be sure that the security pass key for her room was in her purse and slipped out the door. She was only on the fourth floor and decided that she needed some exercise and didn't wait for the elevator. Iona hadn't noticed the man at the other end of the hall, fumbling through the pocket of his madras sport coat as though he was looking for the pass key to his room. He held a shiny new bag in his other hand, one with a mesh top. But Iona didn't see that either.

After the door to the stairwell closed behind her, she couldn't see the man walk briskly toward 414, her room, and insert a pass key. Nor did she see him exit the room carrying Murray in his new carrier and walk around to the east exit on the far side of the fourth floor where he disappeared down the stairwell.

A desperate search of the hotel and a visit by the Chicago Police Department proved fruitless. Since there were no signs of a forced entry or anything else stolen from the room, the police at first seemed to think that she had accidentally left the door open when she went downstairs to retrieve the package. Of course, when she finally made them understand that there was no package, that the front desk had not even placed a call to her room that afternoon, then they admitted there was a possibility Murray had been stolen. She would probably receive a call or letter from someone claiming to have the cat and wanting a reward, a bored detective surmised.

"Sure it's extortion," the detective with bloodshot eyes and a baggy olive green suit said. "But Murray's a famous cat, and some small-change chump thinks this is a sure-fire way to make a quick, clean bundle." He had a way of shifting his eyes past her, then staring over her shoulder like he was talking with someone else in the room.

"How much is a cat like that worth?"

"I don't know. How do you put a price tag on Murray? His only intrinsic value is as a performer, and if he's not there to perform, then he has no value, does he?" She stared into the detectives bloodshot eyes, determined to get him to look at her.

"Yeah, but you'd pay to get him back, wouldn't you?" he mumbled to the invisible person behind her.

"Well…sure. Murray means a lot to me, and I mean more than just as a paycheck."

"Uh huh," he stuck a hand into a coat pocket so misshapen that it looked like he might have carried a Sears' Catalog in it, and pulled out a card. Let me know if you hear anything, though I guess you'll be returning to L.A. Right?"

"I'll hang around for a few days to see if anything turns up, but then I'll have to get back to work." She cast a desperate glance around the room, her eyes brimming with tears, as though hoping she had overlooked some hiding place and Murray would appear. "I don't know what we'll do," she said quietly.

Actually, Iona Wager knew very well what she and the studio would do. Few people outside of those involved with television and feature film production know that key animal actors have two, three, or even four doubles. Murray had three, and Iona used them for different tricks during the shooting of *Larry's Life*. They were virtually identical, but each of them had their specialty: Rhoda did the "duck and cover" perfectly, lowering her head and placing her two front paws across her face, one eye peeking out between the paws; while Pumpkin expertly chased his tail and sat up on his hind legs.

Each of them had their time under the lights, but it was Smuckers who she had been working with on the "look." She almost had it down, and Iona knew that Smuckers could slip into the role with just a little more training. That was one of the cruel facts of this business—animals, like people, were dispensable, and the show must go on.

"And he brought me here." Chaser's eyes were trained on the two cats sitting silently before him, absorbing the impact of his story, but he wasn't truly seeing them. Images of his past life flickered by and he saw them in a series of vivid scenes. There was the large space with the household furnishings where his female Hyskos took him each day. Despite the blazing overhead lights, the room was always cold, and all around him high-legged beings were in constant motion, shifting objects, talking to one another.

He stared directly at Windrusher and Blank Eyes, but what he saw was a life that had been stolen from him. "Then he took me out of the box and I was in this strange room." His eyes shifted away briefly and he flicked his tail from one side to the other in irritation. "I was alone, but soon I was joined by Blank Eyes and then Rahhna's Light made her grand entrance."

"And now I'm here," Windrusher added.

"And now you're here. But we're not alone. We're never alone," he said with a slight quiver in his voice.

"What do you mean?" he asked, turning his head to follow Chaser's fearful eyes that were leveled at a spot directly behind him. The Hyskos peered through the window, his arms folded across his chest, a broad smile etched on his rubbery face.

Chaser feared that this Hyskos and his odd-smelling companion would never let them out of this room. The life he knew was certainly over, but it was better than living outside and begging for scraps of food. Still, he had a feeling that they should fear this high-legged being with the shiny teeth.

9

DAYS HAD PASSED; filled with hope and despair, high expectations and complete frustration. Amy had worked hard to console Kimmy, to keep the family's spirits up as they searched for Tony. Kimmy had taken to wearing the large photo button a teacher had given her after Tony was first reunited with his family. The teacher had used the *People Magazine* photograph of a smiling Kimmy holding Tony in her arms, and she had worn it for weeks before putting it away. Now, it was pinned on her shirt again, and she wore it as they went door to door, looking for anyone who might have seen something, handing out fliers with Tony's picture and their phone number.

It was an unsolved mystery, but Amy had promised Kimmy that they were going to bring Tony home, and she had every intention of keeping that promise. Yesterday was the fifth day of Tony's disappearance, and sitting alone with her check list of agencies and phone numbers, she found herself staring at the couch where Tony would take his naps each afternoon. Tony was gone, and as much as she tried to remain positive, to remember the miracle of Tony's travels from Connecticut to Florida, she realized her promise was an empty gesture.

There didn't seem to be anywhere to turn or anybody that really cared about Tony. After all, shake any bush near the clubhouse or behind most restaurants and shopping centers and you'd find more cats than anyone could count. All of these negative thoughts piled together in her mind like a freeway wreck.

But that was yesterday.

She couldn't believe that on this Saturday afternoon, just the day after she was on the verge of giving up, they were all sitting in the living room, and a man they had just met was offering them hope.

"The first thing we have to do is track down the golfer who left that club behind," Quint Mitchell said. "Did the police follow-up on that, do you know?"

Gerry answered him: "No, they didn't do much of anything, although they took the club and dusted it for fingerprints. But there was nothing."

"I assume they checked with the Pro Shop to see which golfers were scheduled for starts that morning."

Amy and her husband looked at each other with quizzical expressions. "Uh, I don't think so," Amy said with more than a hint of exasperation. "Now, why didn't we think of that?"

Quint gave them a broad smile that subtly altered his tanned and handsome face, and suddenly he looked ten years younger. That face, along with the mischievous glint in his eye and the small scar on his chin, brought an image of a young Harrison Ford to Amy's mind. Not as young as the *Star Wars'* Han Solo, but maybe Ford in the first *Indiana Jones* film.

"Hey, isn't that why you folks called me? I'm the trained private investigator, so I wouldn't expect you to think of everything, especially with the pressure you're under."

Amy may have had her doubts when she called Quint Mitchell, but she was rapidly becoming a believer.

Yesterday, as she sat fighting the despair that threatened to send her back to her bed in search of comfort and solace, she had received a telephone call from a resident on the other side of King's Bay Landing. "Mrs. Tremble, we're new to Crystal River, moved here from Jacksonville a few months ago. But I had heard about Tony, and I'm so sorry to hear that he's missing."

"Thank you," she replied. "Do you have any news?"

"I'm sorry, I don't, but I wanted to tell you about a man who did some work for us last year. His name is Quint Mitchell, and he's a private investigator who lives in Jacksonville Beach. He's quite good at his job, but what makes him special is that he has this knack for finding things."

"Finding things?"

"He finds missing persons and runaways, like most private investigators, but he specializes in finding lost or stolen heirlooms, paintings, and other valuables."

"Uh huh." Now she understood why this woman had called her.

"He's an amateur archaeologist on the side, so I guess this kind of investigative work is in his blood. I highly recommend him, and this is the kind of case he'd love if he's available."

He was available and made the 155-mile trip across the state to Crystal River in just over three hours. While Quint didn't have any cats—his chocolate Lab, Digger, was more than enough for him to handle right now—he was intrigued by the case of the missing cat.

He had asked a lot of questions, reviewed the backyard scene, and left with a photo of Tony tucked in his briefcase. His first stop was the obvious one, the King's Bay Landing Golf Club. He introduced himself to the club manager, Todd Peters, and told him he was working for Gerry and Amy Tremble to help locate their missing cat. The manager, who also doubled as an assistant pro, jerked his head toward the bulletin board behind him where one of the fliers with Tony's photograph was tacked.

"We know about Tony, he kind of put us on the map here in Crystal River," Peters said. "It's a shame he's gone. Are your saying he was stolen...cat-napped?"

He nodded to the sincere young man with the telltale golfer's tan on his neck and arms. "It's a good possibility. Apparently, this wasn't a cat that wandered off. Consider what he went through to get back home."

"Hmm," Peters offered, scratching the back of his head with the pen he was holding. "How can I help?"

"First, tell me if the police have been by to interview you or check your books."

"Why would they want to check our books?"

"It seems that the Trembles found a golf club on the lawn next to where Tony had been sleeping. So it's possible—"

"You think a golfer might have snatched Tony," he said excitedly.

"Anything's possible at this stage. But I was wondering if you could show me last Friday's starting times. You probably know most of the regulars here and can vouch for them. It would be a great help to the Trembles if we went through the names together and narrowed the field, if that's possible."

Peters popped up from behind his desk and ran to the counter where he retrieved a large notebook. "Last Friday morning, right?" he said flipping back a few pages. "Yeah, I was on duty that morning."

"Good."

"Here it is. We started at 7:30 Friday. Any idea when Tony was taken?"

"As far as we can tell it was sometime between 9:30 that morning to noon or maybe even 1:00 P.M. The Trembles live on the 8th fairway so it would have taken a golfer, what, an hour or so to work his way up to the 8th? That's if he played through. I guess he could have followed the cart paths right to the 8th green."

"Yeah, I guess," Peters was running a finger down the list of starting times. "This shouldn't take long; there are only a couple of dozen groups here. A lot of these guys are regular Friday morning foursomes, a couple of doubles, and some threesomes. There are some names I don't recognize, but we have phone numbers for everyone."

"That's a big help."

"Of course, we get a lot of guests from the resort. We have a deal where they get a certain percentage of the starting times."

"I thought the King's Bay Resort had a championship course of its own," Mitchell said.

"Oh, they do. It's a first rate course. But you know golfers, they can't get enough. A lot of guys will come here on a golfing weekend and play both courses, sometimes twice. Plus, they're hosting a PGA Tour event next week and they've cut way back on the number of rounds over the past few weeks."

"Makes sense."

"Huh!" Peters was staring down at one of the names. "Here's

something a little strange; a single. We don't get too many of them. Usually we hook them up with another group, but this guy—I remember now—he was in a real hurry and said he might not …" His voice trailed off as though he was trying to remember the exact conversation.

"What?"

"He said he might only have time to play nine holes."

Quint was peering over the manager's shoulder at the name above Peters' finger. "Jack Morrow," he said aloud as he wrote down the name and phone number beside it. "And was this guy one of your regulars?"

Peters was shaking his head. "No, don't know the name. But if he's the guy I'm thinking about, he was real friendly. Liked to talk. Big smile, gaudy clothes."

"Gaudy clothes?"

"Yeah, this guy stuck out like a peacock in a pigeon coop. Had on knickers and one of those Scottish caps, what do you call them…a Tam? I thought he must have been a real Payne Stewart fan. God, I miss old Payne."

Quint was writing it all down in the steno pad he always carried with him.

Peters scratched his head again and looked up with a puzzled expression. "A guy that was going to do a crime would try to blend in, wouldn't he? Be as forgettable as possible."

"Not if he didn't think he'd ever get caught."

Quint thanked the eager young pro and was already in the parking lot when he heard his name called.

"Mr. Mitchell."

He turned and saw Peters at the door of the clubhouse waving at him. Peters hurried down the stairs and jogged across the parking lot. "I just thought of something. Might not be anything but could be connected. You never know."

"What's that?" Quint asked.

"It came to me after you walked out of my office—the guy in a hurry."

"The guy in a hurry?"

"Uh huh. It was about quarter to twelve last Friday when some guy squealed out of the parking lot and almost hit Rudy Carrola. Didn't even stop, spun out of here like someone was chasing him."

"And you're sure it was last Friday?"

"Positive. I checked the starting times to be sure and saw Mr. Carrola had a 12:15 start."

Quint had his notebook out and was scribbling rapidly. "That's good work, Todd. It could be our man. If I can get Mr. Carrola's phone number, I'd sure like to talk with him and see if he remembers anything about the car."

A broad smile spread across Peters' face as he opened a hand to reveal a yellow sticky note. "I've got it right here, Mr. Mitchell. Oh, did I tell you that Mr. Carrola is a retired New York City policeman?"

"Excellent," Quint said knowing the old cop would probably have a description of the car and possibly the driver.

"One other thing," Peters said, still holding on to the yellow note.

"Yeah?"

The young manager paused dramatically and his smile grew even broader. Holding the note out towards Mitchell he said: "Would it help if we had a license plate number?"

The picture most people have of private investigators has been colored by years of sensational fiction. They loved Thomas Sullivan Magnum with his Detroit Tigers ball cap racing around Honolulu in Robin's Ferrari. And in the hard-bitten crime novels, the hero often provides solace of an intimate nature for a beautiful client who has just been told her husband was a cheating sack of roach droppings. When he's not in bed with his clients, he's punching it out with the bad guys.

Quint enjoyed the stories as well as anyone, but like every P.I. he knew, he spent the majority of his time cruising the Internet, not on stakeouts or in hand-to-hand combat. Computers are the essential tool for every investigator who earns his way by providing clients with the information they could probably find themselves if they knew which databases to search.

Despite what had become a cliché on television shows, obtaining motor vehicle information through a source in the police department or the DMV office was difficult to do because of the penalties established when the Driver's Privacy Protection Act was passed in 2000. Scriptwriters usually fall back on the confidential source rather than the more accurate, if more boring, use of search engines and the growing number of data providers.

He returned to the Trembles' house and, after explaining what he had learned, used the family computer to access AutoTrackXP, one of the best tools in any P.I.'s arsenal. Within minutes of logging on, he had learned that the car was a Buick Regal and was registered not to an individual, but to National Car Rental.

"I was afraid of that," Quint said to Amy and Gerry who were looking over his shoulder. "But we're still a lot closer than we were an hour ago." He swiveled the chair around and stood up to face the Trembles. "This is going to take some calling and some legwork to track down the car, but I think we've got a solid lead. I'll put Charla on it." Charla Jolly was his office manager, and, he often thought, the very backbone of his business. Her computer savvy topped his, and she had absorbed so much of the investigative side of the business that he felt comfortable leaving her alone to deal with any customers that might walk in while he was out of town.

"Do you think you'll be able to find him," Amy asked.

"It's not going to be easy. He's got a week's head start on us, and we have no idea where he rented that car, but it shouldn't be too difficult to find. Once we locate the rental office they'll have driver's license information on…" he paused, picked his notepad up off the desk and flipped a page… "Jack Morrow—if that's his name."

Amy squeezed her husband's hand tightly. "Thank you so much, Mr. Mitchell. Is there anything we can do to help?"

"You can call me Quint."

"Quint," she repeated.

"And I have a lot of telephone and computer work to do. I don't want to bother you people anymore—"

"Oh, you're no bother." Amy cut in. "You can do all of that right here, if you want."

"Thank you, you're very kind, but I've intruded enough on you, and I like to operate in private, if you know what I mean. Can't give away too many of my secrets. What I'd like is a nice motel room that has a computer terminal for my laptop. Can you recommend one? And remember it will show up on your bill later so make sure it's affordable."

The Trembles grinned at one another, and then Gerry Tremble said, "I think we can help you with that."

The room overlooked a sparkling lagoon that acted as a feeding stop for dozens of Snowy Egrets and Blue Herons. Quint stared entranced by the great birds gliding across the water and landing in the shallows to wait for an unsuspecting fish or frog. Life is good for you guys, he thought. Free food, free transportation, stay at the best spots.

It wasn't too bad for him, either, now that he thought about it. It had only taken a call from Gerry Tremble, and he was ensconced in a corner room, a junior suite they called it. Not too shabby. I'll have to tell mom and dad about this place.

He had already spoken with Rudy Carrola, and, just as he expected, the old New York cop had given him a description of the car and the driver. "Round, fleshy face. Well-lived in, I'd call it," Carrola told him. "If I was on the beat at home, I'd say he was an Irish guy. In fact, he could have been on the job himself, he had that kind of look to him. Except for the hat, of course."

"He was wearing a hat?"

"Don't know if ya'd call it a hat, exactly. One of those beret type things, 'cept it was big and puffy and a gawd-awful orange plaid and had this little white tassel on top."

"A tam-o'-shanter. It's a Scottish golf cap named after the hero of a Robert Burns poem."

"If you say so, but I don't know anybody that'd wear such a thing. 'Cept Andy Ferguson, maybe. I remember when Andy wore those skirts, the kilts, to the Captain's Ball one year. Never heard the end of that."

After his conversation with the retired cop, he called the phone number that Jack Morrow had given to the club attendant when he made his reservations. He wasn't surprised to find it was a gas station in Oakland, a small town outside of Orlando. It all fell in place when he convinced the National Car Rental customer service representative to look up the tag number and tell him where it had been rented. He was ready with several good cover stories, but after a little chit chat with the woman, he decided the truth was his best story—at least the first time around.

He first checked in with the Trembles before making the long drive. He was sure they would want him to pursue his lead, but it was their money, and they deserved to know where he was headed. He hadn't even had time to unpack his overnight case, so he carried it and his laptop to his Toyota Camry, checked the map, and headed west on State Road 44. He figured it would take him about two-and-a-half hours to get to Orlando International Airport.

10

It took all of his charm before the supervisor pulled the record for the man in the Buick Regal. The National Car Rental supervisor, an attractive redhead with a sprinkling of freckles across her cheeks and perky little nose, listened politely to his tale.

"Mom's getting up there, seventy-five next September, and doesn't see very well. She and a friend were coming out of a store at the mall and she slips stepping off the curb, and takes a pretty good fall."

"Oh, I'm so sorry. Is she alright?"

"She's fine, a little sore. She's lucky she didn't break anything, but you should see the bruises. Anyway, down she goes and this elderly gentleman stops his car, jumps out and helps her. Mom can't stop talking about him, how sweet he was, how concerned for her welfare. How cute. He even offered to take her to the hospital, but once she was on her feet she knew she was okay."

The redheaded supervisor shook her head sympathetically, probably relieved to hear that there was no liability on their part. "I'm so glad she's doing well, but how can we help you?"

"It's like this," he said, reaching over and touching the supervisor on the wrist. "Mom wants to thank the driver, but she didn't get his name or anything. Fortunately, her friend has this incredible memory for numbers…I hear they've banned her from the gambling casinos because she's a card counter…but she saw the license plate as the car drove away. And I have a friend in law enforcement who looked it up and told me it was one of your cars. So, here I am." He shrugged, gave her his most boyish grin, and passed the plate number across her desk.

The redhead raised an eyebrow and sat silently staring at the slip of paper. He could imagine the questions circulating in the supervisor's head, doing her mental review of company policies, and knew he better not give her too much time to think about it. He plunged ahead.

"Mom wants to send him a loaf of her famous banana nut bread." Leaning closer, and giving the supervisor a conspiratorial smile, he continued, "To tell you the truth, I think she has a bit of a crush on him. She's been widowed for twelve years, and who knows what can happen? Right?"

Five minutes later, he left the rental agency with a copy of Runyan McWaters' driver's license.

Orlando International Airport was awash with humanity; all of it seemingly on a caffeine high, pushing through the crowded halls at a drum major's pace, pulling luggage, carrying children, talking in a dozen different languages. Quint went directly to the first uniformed guard he saw and asked for directions to the security office.

Virtually all airport security responsibilities now reside with the Transportation Security Administration (TSA) since the passage of the Aviation and Transportation Security Act of November, 2001. He knew these workers had more serious issues than a missing cat, but if anyone saw anything that day, it was one of the security guards.

Sitting in the austere office, waiting for the TSA Security Director, he again felt the thrill of discovery, unearthing a link to the past as he had done at archaeological sites throughout the country. He had first participated in digs as a college student where his interest in archaeology confounded his mother and father.

He surely was a disappointment to his overachieving parents; a mother who was one of the first female partners of a Wall Street brokerage firm and found time to paint strikingly good watercolors. His father effortlessly climbed the jurisprudence ladder from trial lawyer to managing partner, to Circuit Court Judge to State Supreme Court Judge. Now retired, both of them lived full and active lives without ever a worry about whether the Social Security cost of living adjustment would be 1.5 or 1.9 percent. His father, who always had a flair for the dramatic, surprised everyone by churning out a legal thriller that hit number six on the *New York Times* Bestseller List.

They had come to terms with his independent streak long ago, and if he was still a disappointment in their eyes, they hid it well. He certainly gave them every opportunity to shower him with criticism, dropping out of Syracuse in his junior year and joining the Navy. He served through the first Gulf War and served his last year at Mayport Naval Station. He liked the slow pace of Jacksonville Beach and decided to remain there while getting his degree at the University of North Florida.

He had been raised in upper New York around Rochester, and had seen enough snow and ice to last him a lifetime. So he traded winter sports for the more mellow life of a surfer, and with the nation's oldest town, St. Augustine, a few miles to the south, he returned to his archaeological interests.

Quint drifted into the investigative field through the back door. His service with the Military Police while on active duty led him to take a number of criminal justice courses at UNF. Upon graduation he joined a small investigative firm run by a former FBI field agent. In his first year with the firm, he was given the case of a stolen painting that was taken from an oceanfront home in Ponte Vedra Beach. He surprised everyone by tracking the painting to a buyer in Belgium. He realized this was just another form of archaeological fieldwork and several years later opened his own investigative firm.

The fact that money was never a concern certainly helped. His parents had established substantial trust funds for their two children and he had used part of his to purchase a two-story, four-unit building several blocks off the water in Jacksonville Beach. He lived above his own office, and leased out the other two units.

Security Director Winston Holloway entered the room with a female uniformed guard who stood next to him as though her only assignment was to protect the director from a sneak attack. He shook hands with both of them and offered his ID card to the former secret service agent.

"This is a strange request you've made, Mr. Mitchell, but I've learned not to be too surprised by anything these days. I was in Washington last weekend, so I had to check the records. Do you know how many people pass through this airport every single day, Mr. Mitchell?"

"I'm afraid I don't, but by the looks of the terminal it has to be huge."

"That's a good word, huge. Oh, we're not Atlanta or Chicago, but we see almost 75,000 people every day, that's nearly twenty-seven million people a year. I couldn't tell you how many animals are transported, but finding any trace of a cat coming through here on a given day would be pretty remote. But I asked around and they told me about the runaway cat."

"Runaway cat?"

"Right, a runaway cat. Ms. Lopez, tell Mr. Mitchell what happened at the Level 4 security checkpoint last Friday."

Quint sat mesmerized while Ms. Lopez related the story of how the cat had scratched its owner and run loose through the terminal for fifteen minutes until the man finally corralled it near the front entrance. He had familiarized himself with the story of Tony's journey across country. How he had survived a tornado and miraculously ended up with Kimmy Tremble just miles from his home.

From what the guard was saying, the cat almost beat the odds again. It sounded like he was only a few steps from the exit and freedom. Of course, once outside, he would have had to navigate his way through the hellish roads and traffic surrounding the airport and find his way back to Crystal River. A tall order, but he wouldn't bet against this feline.

He pulled out the photo of Tony and showed it to the guard. "Does this look like the cat?"

"Yes sir, sure does. I couldn't be positive, but it was a cat with green eyes. Gray with orange stripes. If that's not the same cat, it's his brother."

"Thanks, you've been a big help. I don't suppose you know what flight the guy was taking?"

"No sir. I did check his ticket, but I don't recall."

"Most of the gates beyond that point are for Delta flights," Holloway said. "It's not like this guy is a terrorist or anything, but we frown on criminals using our airport to transport stolen goods, even if it's only a cat. I'll be happy to cooperate with you. Of course, it would help if we had a name."

The weakness came upon him with such speed that he thought his legs would give way. He felt a tremor in his extremities and a throbbing in his temples that was growing stronger with each pulse of blood through his arteries. Von Rothmann reached into his pocket and pulled out a glucose tablet. He popped it into his mouth and waited for the shakes and sweats to subside, for his blurred vision to clear. He didn't have to look at his expensive chronograph to know that it must be nearing 4:00 P.M.

The excitement of last night was making him careless. Finally capturing his prize and knowing that he alone possessed this special creature was such an unexpected thrill that he had forgotten to check his blood sugar level. He would have to be cautious since one insulin reaction could lead to another. He sat in a high-wing chair in his bedroom with his head back and eyes closed.

Everything had gone perfectly, just as they had planned. He had to admit that McWaters, despite his annoying habits and runaway mouth, had proven to be reliable and resourceful. Keeping him around after the sale of his company was a smart move since he would never have been able to pull off the string of thefts as nimbly as McWaters had. But then, it takes a corrupt former cop to know how to bend the law, doesn't it?

He rose from the chair and walked the few steps to his king-size bed. A nap was what he needed; regain his strength so he could enjoy the incredible bliss he felt having Tony in his house. It was like owning a treasure, a Michelangelo or Van Gogh that had been lost to the art world. There may be photographs of the artwork in books or prints hanging on walls, but he owned the real thing, and only he alone could enjoy it, could bask in its splendor.

Tony and the other felines were his private collection. He may add others over time, but one thing was certain, he would never give them up. He would rather see them dead. His hand again went to the small cross under his shirt, and he smiled grimly, knowing his actions were justified and long overdue.

He didn't mind being alone; in fact, he craved the rich experiences that could only be found within his own intellect. Von Rothmann didn't need other people except to help him attain his goals. His mother had taught him that. Taught him well after his father walked out and returned to Germany, leaving them alone in a foreign country. But he learned that he didn't need other people, and he learned what happened when he reached out for the comfort and love of another person.

His breathing became regular and he felt himself slipping into the welcome arms of sleep. He let himself drift away still thinking of that time so long ago when he allowed himself a rare display of emotional weakness, searching for a relationship that only brought him rejection and more pain.

Yes, that was years ago, but he had learned his lessons well, and he never forgot. No, he never forgot.

10

WINDRUSHER DIDN'T HAVE any of von Rothmann's medical symptoms, but his grueling experiences had left him exhausted and craving the healing power of sleep. He curled up under the skylight letting the heat of Rahhna wash over him. Lowering his head on his front paws, he tucked his tail alongside his body, the tip of it brushing against his whiskers. He closed his eyes and, using that incredible gift all healthy felines enjoy, was almost instantly asleep.

Caught in the stream of unconsciousness, his mind passed through the shallows of light sleep and into more rapid channels taking him deeper into the loving arms of Hwrt-Heru. He was immediately buffeted by the eddies and whorls arising from the depths of Akhen-et-u, beckoning him to bond his mind with the millions of other cats, but he avoided the nearly irresistible tug of the Inner Ear and embraced the sweetness of sleep.

A shiver coursed through his muscles as his sleeping mind divided itself, like a cell undergoing mitosis, leaving his physical body unconscious to the world around him, still asleep under the skylight. Through whatever heavenly calculus the gods used to alter his life, part of him was transported to another time, another place.

The cold permeated his fur, and he strained to see through the oppressive blackness. He was pushing through a narrow passage, rough walls scraping at him from all sides. The roof of the passageway pressed down on him, and jagged outcroppings scoured the top of his head. His legs were tight against his body, scratching at the flinty dirt, clawing his body forward.

Where was he? The walls had narrowed, of that he was certain. Soon he would be wedged tight, unable to push his way forward or retreat, and this black burrow would become his underground tomb.

He fought the panic that threatened to immobilize him. Keep moving, he commanded his cramped and trembling limbs. Keep moving or risk never moving again. His head and shoulders abruptly broke free of the rough walls of the tunnel. He caught the trace of a musty odor, the scent of earth and fire, a holy temple of wisdom and meditation locked away for eons.

Windrusher knew at once where he was: He was back with the god of wisdom, back in the Cave of Tho-hoth. A flickering red light approached, and the cave was bathed in the soft warm glow of a setting day globe. Once again, he stood before the great god staring with awe into those hypnotic pale green eyes.

In some part of his mind, he understood that he was asleep in a spacious and bright room with three other cats who had been stolen from their families and homes as he had. Yet, if he was lying beneath a tree inside that room, how could he be here in this holy cave?

But here he was. And there was Tho-hoth, his eyes glowing with the wisdom of the ages. "Tho-hoth," he said, lowering his head before the legendary cat. "Your warnings have come true; I am far from home once again. But my new home seems to be safe and we are fed and cared for by the two Hyskos males. Am I still in peril?"

Tho-hoth sat quietly. The Stone of Life hanging from his neck pulsated like a beating heart, throwing off muted rays the color of fresh blood. He bent his head forward, "Windrusher, listen carefully to my words. There is no safe haven in that home. It is a den of cruelty and injustice. If you do not find a way out, you and the others will die there. And it will be soon."

Windrusher heard the words but for a moment he was unable to understand their meaning. He stared with wide eyes as the old cat faded away and the light in the cave went with him. The words swam through his mind and he let each one resonate in his brain: *There is no safe haven in that home. It is a den of cruelty and injustice.*

How could this be? Chaser, Blank Eyes, and Rahhna's Light had been there far longer than he had, and they were treated well. They were fed and had a warm and comfortable room with pillows and toys. Wouldn't Chaser have told him if the two Hyskos had harmed him in any way?

If you do not find a way out, you and the others will die there. And it will be soon.

Tho-hoth's last prediction had proven to be accurate, so he had to take this warning seriously. Still, he wasn't convinced that he or the other cats were really in danger. If the high-legged male wanted to harm him, why would he steal him and carry him to this place far from his own home? He could have hurt him at any time, especially after he had scratched his face.

No, it didn't make any sense, but when did the actions of the Hyskos make sense? He might not understand, but he now had a new mission. When he awoke, he had to lead the other cats out of that den. And do it quickly.

Quint's copy of Runyan McWaters' driver's license listed a Southern California address. He wasn't sure that the document given to the Orlando car rental agency was legitimate, but the security director found a match on the Delta flight to San Diego. He debated about whether to call the California police, but in the end knew he needed more evidence. He wanted to check out the court house records and see what he could dig up on McWaters and his residence. He might be able to find some records on Internet databases, but California was where the trail was leading him, and that's where he should be—with the Trembles' permission.

"We've been very lucky so far, Mrs. Tremble. I think it's worth checking out this house in person, and then I can call in the local law enforcement for the arrest once we have the evidence we need." He had filled her in on his discoveries at the car rental office and at Orlando International.

"This is wonderful news, Quint. I can't believe we might have Tony back here so soon."

"So far, the cat gods have been smiling on us," he said with a gentle laugh. "I'll call you as soon as I learn anything. It might be a good idea if you and your husband stand by to come out to San Diego. The locals will want to verify my story and determine Tony's true owner before they release him. Do you think you can do that?"

"Of course. Gerry's so busy at the hotel now; I think I'll bring Kimmy. Is there anything else we can do?"

"Bring along any proof of ownership you might have—medical records, some of those photos and newspaper clippings that show you and Kimmy with the cat."

"Good idea. I'll go ahead and pack us a bag now and wait for your call."

He looked at the flight schedule on the overhead monitor. "With any luck, I'll be on surveillance outside his house at this time tomorrow. Who knows, we may have this all wrapped up by Wednesday or Thursday."

11

MCWATERS SCOOPED THE LUMPS from the litter tray and tossed them into the plastic wastebasket. He wrinkled his nose as the acrid odor assailed his nostrils, and quickly closed the lid on the container. "I've had to do a lot of distasteful things in my career, laddies," he said to the felines who were watching him warily, "but I never thought cleaning litter boxes would be part of my job description. If it was up to me, you guys would learn to clean it yourselves or live with the stink."

He shook his head and glanced at the small camera mounted in the corner of the room, smiled broadly and winked at it. "He's taking his afternoon nap now, but you never know when the old bird is watching, so don't do any funny stuff." McWaters laughed at the thought of cats doing funny stuff.

He picked up the trash container and pushed the door open. This is what it has come down to, he thought. Hauling trash and picking up after cats. He was nothing but an errand boy for a loony geek with a fetish for cats. Sure, he was a highly paid errand boy, which is better than the alternative, but it still rankled him to be ordered around like a know-nothing rookie. In his younger days he wouldn't have put up with it for a minute.

McWaters had been a second generation Chicago cop determined not to fall into the same trap that brought his father down. Chicago was a wide-open city during the '50s, and corruption was a way of life in all departments of city government, especially the police department and the Cook County Sheriff's Office. Some residents were proud of the gangster image that permeated their town, and it was an open secret that many police were on the take. Corruption was a way of life, from payoffs to shakedowns, but when eight brazen cops, who had aligned themselves with a well-known cat burglar, pulled off dozens of burglaries in the Edgewater-Uptown neighborhoods, even Mayor Daley was forced to ask for an investigation.

The Summerdale Scandals of 1960 shook up the city and brought down dozens of veteran police officers, including Captain Frank McWaters who was the ranking officer over the old Summerdale district. McWaters remembered his father seeking absolution at the bottom of a whiskey bottle, ranting against the state attorney, the Wilson Committee, and Mayor Daley. Even today, he only had to close his eyes to smell the Jamesons, see it sloshing over the glass onto his father's chin and shirt. Frank McWaters was a picture of defeat, and that picture still made him angry.

It was a sad sight, and it haunted him still. Yet, McWaters became a cop because that was all he ever wanted to do—to be like his father and serve the people of Chicago. For eight years, he carried his father's guilt on his back like an extra coat, and never thought he would put himself in a position to bring more shame on the McWaters name.

He carried the wastebasket through the back hallway and opened the door that led outside to the small fenced area next to the garage where the garbage cans were stored. Before letting the door swing closed behind him, McWaters checked to make sure he had his keys, since the paranoid von Rothmann insisted that every outside door locked automatically. He tossed the contents of the wastebasket into the trash can and replaced the lid.

The day had been warm, and the afternoon sun glowed through a curtain of wispy clouds. He reached into his shirt pocket and pulled out a Cuban Maduro, passing it under his nose and inhaling the rich aroma as he walked to the deck on the edge of the hill. Behind him, a breeze stirred the palm trees and prodded dried chaparral over the lip of the bluff.

The wooden deck had several levels leading from the side of the house to the edge of the bluff where overhead cross beams created an open arbor over half of the rectangular deck. He leaned against the railing staring at the patch of calm blue Pacific waters in the distance.

He lit the cigar and blew out a cloud of gray smoke, watching it float away in the summer breeze. An expensive cigar was one thing you could always count on to give you pleasure, he thought, studying the almost black Maduro. Smoking was a vice he had picked up while he was still on the force, and he remembered how he would stop at the upscale newsstand on his beat each morning, and Teddy, the Lebanese who owned the shop, would give him one of his better cigars.

Taking a cigar was one of the perks of being on the job in Chicago, protecting the citizens from the scum who threatened to turn the streets into their personal drug zones. He knew there were cops who did a lot worse than taking a cigar or free meal, but he would never be one of them. Or so he thought. After seven years of watching his fellow officers take enough from their shakedowns to send their kids to college or buy homes in the better neighborhoods, he finally gave in to the temptation of easy money. He exhaled a puff of smoke and saw a much younger Runyan McWaters in a Chicago alley.

McWaters leaned against the brick wall smoking one of Teddy's cigars. He rested a foot on an overturned trash can and waited patiently. The metal door to his right was closed, as it had been since he'd been waiting for the past twenty minutes. He heard the sounds of footsteps on the stairs inside and glanced at his watch. Just like clockwork. Lorenzo would be coming out this door, still high from his afternoon delight with his main girl, and make the rounds at the Robert Taylor Homes in the next block where he'd collect from his street dealers.

He had watched him for two weeks, and Lorenzo had fallen into a comfortable pattern. McWaters' CI, his confidential informant, had told him that Lorenzo's girl refused to live in public housing any longer, and he had to put her up in this apartment.

When the door swung open, he rolled the metal trash can in front of the open door and watched the tall young gangster stumble over it. He was on him in one swift move, his knee pressing into his kidney, his hand on the back of his head, flattening his face into the grimy pavement.

"Lorenzo, my man, how good of you to drop in. Did you enjoy your nooner? Please give Carla my regards when you visit her next time."

"Get off my back, or you be—"

"Or I be what? Try to show some respect for the man who's doing you a favor, Lorenzo. Not everyone would be as civil with the likes of you. You understand that, don't you?" He rolled the young gang leader onto his back and pressed his knee into his solar plexus. Holding Lorenzo by the throat, he pulled his revolver from its holster and shoved it under the gang leader's chin.

"What you want? I'm not afraid of you," Lorenzo said. But McWaters saw the fear slide into his eyes.

"You are a brave young man, I can see that." He released the boy's throat and took the cigar from his mouth, twirling it slowly in front of Lorenzo's face. Bringing it closer and closer to his eyes, brushing the ash across his eyelids.

"Get that thing away from me," Lorenzo whined, squeezing his eyes shut and twisting his head away. "You gonna cap me, go ahead, but leave my eyes alone."

"They are pretty brown eyes, Lorenzo. But I'm not here to hurt you. You need a partner who can protect you from your enemies. Someone who knows when the heat's coming down and can pass along a little inside information." He stuck the cigar in the corner of his mouth and pulled Lorenzo up to a sitting position.

"Whyn't you say so? How much you want?"

McWaters studied the traffic rounding the curve below the bluff and remembered how easy it had been to step away from his convictions. It only took one time and he joined the other corrupt cops on the take. But he was smart, not like his father. After two years, he quit and moved to California. His reputation intact and his bank account padded by forty thousand dollars. He blew out another puff of smoke and turned back toward the house.

On the Northwest face of the hill was a low outcropping covered with black sage and prickly pear cactus. Behind it, a shallow dip was eroded into the hillside, providing cover from the home on top of the bluff. Quint had laid there for hours, sweating under the afternoon sun, the dust saturating his clothes and nostrils. He was situated about forty-five degrees to the north of the home, but he had a good view of the back of the house.

He had been on many overnight surveillances, lying behind bushes, in his car, or in a cheap motel. He didn't enjoy any of them, but that was his job. McWaters had listed this address on his driver's license, but he wasn't sure he actually lived here. After checking into a hotel, he had driven north to locate the address and was surprised to find the palatial mansion sitting alone on the bluff. It didn't make any sense. Why would a man who owned such a house show up in Florida to snatch a cat from someone's backyard? Surely, he didn't pay for the house with cat ransoms?

He wasn't sure how long he lay behind that cactus, peering up at the house, and scratching ant bites. After several hours, he was thinking he should try a more direct approach, like knocking on the front door. That's when a round-faced man walked onto the deck.

Through his binoculars, he observed the man at the railing, puffing on a cigar and staring at the ocean. Ten minutes later, the man turned and walked back to the house. He didn't have to pull out the copy of the driver's license to know he had found Runyan McWaters.

Windrusher lifted his head, watching intently as the high-legged male closed the door behind him. He padded to the door and scratched at the wood frame with both front paws, then turned and sat on the sisal mat. He had been thinking about sharing Tho-hoth's message with the other cats. He wasn't sure how they might take his dream tale, but if Tho-hoth was to be believed, they needed to find a way out of this place. And soon.

He might persuade Chaser and the kitten to follow him, but he didn't think the Persian would move a whisker for him. But he had to try. As unpleasant as she was, he couldn't leave her behind and face the danger that Tho-hoth had warned him about.

Windrusher saw the other cats watching him, and decided there was only one way and that was to tell them what they must do. "We must find a way out of here," he said.

Blank Eyes approached him eagerly, attracted by the sound of his voice. She butted him softly in the side and mumbled something that sounded to him like, "Take leg, find cage." He licked the young cat on the head, wondering what she was trying to say.

"You've only just arrived," Chaser said. "This place isn't so bad. You'll see that we have everything we need and they treat us well."

"It might seem that way, but I believe we're in danger."

"Give yourself some time, Windrusher. It might not be like your other home, but this is better than living outside, scrapping for food and shelter. Better by far," Chaser added.

"Go. Me," Blank Eyes said, and this time they all understood her.

"That's right, my little friend, you'll go, too." He stared directly at Chaser, trying to assess the strength of the marmalade's conviction. Did he really believe they were better off in this strange room? He knew that most cats would take up with any Hyskos that treated it well, but he didn't think Chaser was one of those. Not from what he had heard of Chaser's story.

"Let me tell you something that may be hard to believe," he said. Chaser glanced up from the paw he had been licking, and gave him a curious look. Even Rahhna's Light cut her eyes toward him.

"You probably know of my journey. How I dreamed that I was one of the Seven Followers of Irissa-u, and she had given me the mission to locate my family." He paused and waited for any questions. When there were none, he continued. "I'm not bragging about that journey, it was dangerous and I almost lost my life. But it made me aware that as strange as it may seem, the gods are still with us."

Rahhna's Light made a snorting noise and she closed her eyes.

"I told you it would be hard to believe, but I know the difference between dreams and visits from the gods."

"The gods? You've had more than one god speak to you?" Chaser asked.

He hesitated, his tongue darting in and out as though tasting the air. "Yes. It happened before I was brought here. I dreamed I was…" he paused again, unsure of how foolish he would seem to these cats. "I dreamed I was in the Cave of Tho-hoth and the god of wisdom himself was there. He warned me that I should beware, that my life was in peril."

"You are indeed one special cat. None of us have been selected for such holy conversations," Rahhna's Light scoffed, climbing down from the couch and approaching him. "If the gods wanted to deliver a message to one of us, does it make any sense that they would speak to a common house cat like you?"

She pushed her flattened nose against Windrusher's. "And even if we were to believe your kitten's tale, where is the danger? Look around you, there is nothing to fear. Certainly, I want to return to my home and my female Hyskos, but we are too far away to consider trying to find it on our own." She sat with an audible exhalation of breath, tilting her head up as though there was nothing more to say on the subject.

"Rahhna's Light is right, though it pains me to agree with her," Chaser said.

"I admit that what I've said is confusing and fearful, but which of you can truly say that you understand the Hyskos mind? We don't know why we were brought here, why these high-legged beings act the way they do, and certainly not what they plan for us."

"Yes, but—" Chaser began.

Windrusher cut in before he finished. "Chaser, Rahhna's Light, we have been favored to be part of homes with Hyskos who cared for us. Even though we may not understand some of their language and actions, was there ever any doubt that they loved us and would never harm us?"

The two cats sat silent, heads bowed in thought.

"You know that I'm right. What happened to us is not the action of a loving Hyskos. I am certain that my family would never have been so cruel to allow this strange male to take me away without warning, without saying goodbye." He stopped and looked directly at Rahhna's Light and then at Chaser. "Don't you believe the same of your Hyskos?"

Both cats remained still, with only a nervous flick of an ear and swish of a tail to give away their agitation.

"Even without Tho-hoth's warning, I'm afraid we would soon learn that we are in peril. With the warning, it means we must act quickly to save ourselves."

Rahhna's Light lifted her head and opened her mouth.

"You were right when you said that we were far from home," he continued, thinking he knew what the Persian was about to say. "My journey was thought to be as senseless as a floppy-eared snouter by many. No cat had undertaken such a mission, but with the blessings of Irissa-u, I learned that cats can achieve the impossible."

It was Windrusher's turn to sit. He had stated his case as well as he was able, and they would either follow him and save themselves or be left behind.

Blank Eyes, who had never left his side, was the first to speak. "Go. Me. You." The young female licked Windrusher across his jaw and nuzzled even closer. There was no misunderstanding her meaning.

Chaser spoke up next. "You do make sense, Windrusher. I'm with you."

All eyes turned toward Rahhna's Light. The cream-colored Persian stared back at the other cats, her blue-green eyes cold and hard as precious stones. "If I go along on this Wetlos errand of yours, Windrusher—and I'm not saying I will—how will we get out? Will one of your gods open the door, or do you have magical powers that you've been hiding from us?"

12

AMY TREMBLE HAD INSISTED that Quint wait until she and Kimmy were there before calling the police and confronting Runyan McWaters. She wanted to see the man who had stolen Tony from their yard, but mostly, she wanted Kimmy to be able to comfort Tony when they found him.

On the flight from Orlando to San Diego, their adrenalin levels had reached the orange zone and were threatening to break through to red. They were too agitated to sleep and had spoken excitedly about bringing Tony back home with them, neither wanting to think of the alternative. Talk had given way to quiet reflection as they read or looked out the window at the clouds and landscape passing 33,000 feet below. Finally, after several hours, Kimmy had dozed off.

Amy pulled the blue blanket over Kimmy's shoulders and pushed a strand of hair from her face. She sighed quietly and was grateful for her daughter's strength. Kimmy was the one that had gone to find Tony after the terrible tornado had razed much of Belleview. Her daughter was amazing, but she certainly didn't need another crisis in her life. None of them did.

And poor Tony. What must he be going through? Amy shook her head in frustration and turned toward the window. A thick cloud bank blocked the sun, casting a shadow over the interior of the plane. Dark and dreary—that's exactly how I feel, she thought. She stared out at layers of gray clouds that reminded her of cold, dirty tundra and pictured herself walking across it, alone and lost. She shivered involuntarily and turned away.

In the past week, her personal worries had taken a backseat to her concern for Tony and Kimmy. Now, she felt fear and anxiety ooze into her mind like a black adder slipping under a door. She checked her watch and decided it was time for another pill. There was no way she would let herself slip back into the sad and hopeless baggage she had been only two weeks ago. There was too much at stake here. Too many people were depending on her.

Von Rothmann was not having a good day. His insulin hangover had left him in a foul mood, and he had taken it out on the only other person in the house. Why was the man so obnoxiously upbeat, and did he have to wear that ugly pink and black shirt? McWaters had attempted to talk him into a better humor, but this time he refused to be manipulated.

"Didn't I tell you that we needed more litter and cat food? And that room is a mess." His eyes were blazing and his surprisingly high-pitched voice was straining to reach another octave. "These are special creatures, and they have to be looked after like you would your own children."

They were standing outside the room, staring through the window at the four cats. McWaters' face was bright crimson, and his was approaching the same shade. He had one hand on the double-pane window and ran it down the glass. "I know you have no idea of how to take care of children since you used to lock them up, but pretend you're competent for something other than your shady chicanery."

He slapped his palm against the window with sudden fury. The sharp *whack* surprised McWaters, and inside the room the four cats turned toward the noise, their ears erect, eyes staring guardedly at the two men. "And clean these windows," he screamed. "They're a mess. I'm going to take a nap, and when I get up I want to see everything cleaned and new litter and food," he said and stomped off.

McWaters felt a pulse pounding on his left temple, and the tips of his ears blazed with an angry heat. He couldn't remember the last time he had been so furious. Actually, he could, and an unbidden picture of the other authority figure in his life—his father—leaped into his mind.

The honorable Captain Frank McWaters, in the days before he crashed and burned in a blaze of self-pity and alcoholism. Back then, he was respected by neighbors and friends who enjoyed his gift of the blarney, laughed at his unceasing stream of jokes, and never hesitated to buy him another shot as they gathered almost nightly at Mullaney's.

At home, he often came in late, the stench of liquor and cigar smoke clinging to him. Sometimes he'd be laughing and telling jokes, pulling Runyan and his two sisters to him and enfolding them in his huge arms. Other times, he was like another man—a black-hearted, haunted man.

For years, his mother, sweet and quiet Sheila McWaters, took the brunt of his drunken abuse. But when Runyan turned fourteen, Sheila McWaters developed pancreatic cancer, and she died in less than six months. That left Runyan as his number-one target. He only had to close his eyes to picture his father staggering in from Mullaney's.

"Did you kids leave me anything to eat?" he'd bellow, throwing open the refrigerator and pulling out a beer. He and his sisters had usually retreated to their bedroom when they heard him approach. Runyan would sit quietly reading or pretending to do his homework and hoping that tonight would be different, that the loving father would be in the kitchen waiting to hug his children.

"Did you hear me, boy? Come out here, Run-yan. Let me see if you've turned into a man yet."

He heard a chair topple and walked slowly to the kitchen. "There you are. Did you make any dinner, Run-yan?" He dragged out his name, putting the emphasis on the first syllable, pitching his voice higher, and sneering at the boy.

"We had canned stew," he replied, not looking his father in the face. "There's another can in the pantry." He kept the table between them.

"Canned stew! What kind of meal is that to feed your sisters and father? You're just worthless, aren't you? Curse your mother for giving me three girls." He stumbled toward him, but tripped over the chair he had knocked over earlier, sprawling forward on his hands and knees.

Runyan ran out of the kitchen and into his bedroom. His father seldom beat him, but he wasn't taking a chance that this would be one of those times. He slammed the door and locked it.

"That's right, Run-yan. Run away and hide. Just like a worthless little girl."

Two years later, Captain Frank McWaters had been dismissed from the Chicago Police Department, and he spent his entire day drinking, not just the evenings. Runyan thought about going off on his own, maybe talking his way into the Army or Navy. He didn't want to watch the old man drink himself to death, but he didn't want to leave his sisters alone with him. In the end, he was there to bury his father and later joined the force.

In California, Runyan landed his dream job as security chief for KVR Technologies. He enjoyed a close relationship with von Rothman, an eccentric physicist who had patented eight revolutionary processes that advanced the engineering of nanocrystalline materials. Von Rothmann asked him to stay on as his personal assistant and bodyguard and live in the mansion with him after KVR was sold.

Since the offer came with the same level of pay plus free room and board, it didn't take him long to accept and move in with the reclusive von Rothmann. KVR had paid him very well, and he and von Rothmann had an understanding that grew from his *special* assignments that usually involved his ability to uncover proprietary information on KVR's competitors. Some might look at this as industrial espionage, but he thought of it as the ability to make friends and influence people.

Even though he had been paid quite well for his work, his financial planning skills were sadly lacking, and he needed this job to keep up the standards he had set for himself since moving to California. His plan was to work for von Rothmann for seven or eight years and put the majority of his salary into the bank. Then he'd be free to go off on his own, travel, and enjoy his golden years.

Bodyguard and personal assistant was one thing. And stealing cats was another. He rather enjoyed that part of the job, but acting as a maid and babysitter to four felines was getting to be more than he could stand. He didn't believe he would last six more years without doing serious harm to the old psycho. Not if he kept acting the way he had today.

McWaters stormed into the cats' room, throwing the door back, and headed for the closest litter box. Blank Eyes scurried across the room and climbed into the carpeted tunnel at the bottom of one of the cat stands. The other three cats watched the angry Hyskos as he tossed dirty litter into the trash container, spilling it onto the tiled floor, and muttering to himself.

Windrusher sensed the fury emanating from the man like waves of heat. Each of them stayed as far away as the confinement of the room would allow, watching wide-eyed as he threw toys and pillows across the room, kicked over food bowls, and finally sat on the rattan couch with a loud exhalation of breath.

He sat there for several minutes, arms crossed over his chest, breathing heavily. Finally, he got up and went to the work counter running across one wall and pulled a vacuum cleaner from one of the storage units.

"I've got to make some noise now," he said to the cats as he plugged the upright into the wall socket. "If it bothers you, that's tough. Get used to it." He turned it on and began cleaning up the mess he had made.

After he finished and had put away the vacuum cleaner, he looked behind the doors in the storage unit checking the inventory of supplies. "Well, Maid Runyan is off to do the shopping for you kids. Is there anything special you'd like for dinner? A nice fish filet perhaps?" He glanced up at the camera and his face took on a rosy hue. The muscles in his cheeks bulged as his jaw tightened, and a lumpy lavender vein pulsed from the corner of his left eye, working its way along his temple like a worm burrowing into fresh meat.

"Your gracious host has sent me on another fool's errand while he sleeps," he spit out vehemently. McWaters grabbed the five-gallon wastebasket by the handle with one hand and picked up a nearly empty ten-pound sack of Science Diet Feline Food with the other. He twisted the door handle, flung it open, and walked down the hall.

Pausing at the door leading to the backyard, McWaters patted his pockets for the keys. "Crap," he said aloud. He started to re-enter the house, still holding the wastebasket in one hand, wrinkled his nose at the acrid odor of ammonia that permeated the corridor, and turned back to the door. Opening the door, he stepped through with his rank-smelling garbage, and carefully placed the bag of Science Diet down against the doorframe to keep the door from closing behind him.

Windrusher felt the tension leave the room along with the round-faced Hyskos. He padded toward the door, and watched through the glass panel as the high-legged being disappeared down the hall. As his footsteps receded, the big cat turned toward the others. "You asked if the gods would open the door for us, Rahhna's Light. Come and see for yourself."

He put his nose into the narrow gap between the door that was hung up on the sisal mat and pushed it open until his head was through and he was peering down the long hallway. The other three cats followed Windrusher out the door.

McWaters sucked in a deep breath of the late afternoon air. He welcomed the aroma of the fragrant frangipani flowers from the garden, but wondered how long the smell of cat urine and feces would stick to him. As though in answer to his thoughts, he looked down and saw a dark smudge on his new shirt and cursed. Dropping the wastebasket next to the oversized green garbage cans, he brushed at the spot, and when it didn't come off, spit on his finger tips and did it again.

McWaters prided himself on his appearance and even temperament. He didn't like what was happening, what von Rothmann was doing to him. He spit again, this time on the ground, and then bent to lift the wastebasket. That's when the cramp seized his calf, biting deep into the muscle and lifting his foot off the ground. He moaned loudly, his forehead furrowed as the pain ran up his leg. Extending his toe to the ground, he gingerly put his weight on the leg until his foot was flat and he was standing on both legs again.

He pressed down against the leg as though trying to transfer the pain into the pavement. Von Rothmann's image appeared in his head, and he knew that somehow he had something to do with his cramps. He never had them before he worked here, and they started to intensify after he began snatching the cats. But he didn't think it was the cats, it had to be that freaky von Rothmann.

If he didn't need the money so badly, he'd drive away and never return. He emptied the wastebasket and returned to the house for his keys. While he was there, he'd change his shirt then maybe take a drive down to Delaney's for a wee nip after the shopping. McWaters carefully stepped over the bag in the open door; telling himself he'd pick it up when he returned. He passed the open door to the guest bathroom, turned, and went directly to his bedroom.

Windrusher's whiskers brushed against the wall. Behind him, Chaser, Blank Eyes, and Rahhna's Light crept along the hallway in a single file. He smelled the odor of the high-legged being and the pungent package he had carried from their room. Pausing after a few steps to be sure the other cats were still behind him, he looked back and saw Rahhna's Light had stopped and was licking one of her paws.

"Stay together. We don't want to get separated in this big house, or we might never find our way out." He waited while the Persian padded toward them. "That's good, now stay close—"

He stopped abruptly. The sound of footsteps directly ahead riveted his attention. He turned, his eyes wide with anticipation, his tail lashing the floor nervously. It was too late to retreat to the room. Windrusher saw an opening in the corridor and scurried ahead. "In here," he called over his shoulder.

The three cats followed him across the hall into the bathroom and squeezed themselves behind the toilet bowl. They were so tightly bunched together that Windrusher felt Chaser's breath on the back of his ears. He held his own breath and closed his eyes, fearing that the high-legged being would decide to enter this small room. If he did, he might not see them hidden behind the bowl, but what if he closed the door? They would be trapped.

Windrusher, his eyes still closed, felt the pressure from Chaser and the others pushing him against the wall. For a moment, he saw the image of the Cave of Tho-hoth, he felt the rough sides of the cave threatening to squeeze the life out of him. He inhaled and opened his eyes just as the footsteps of the high-legged male approached.

Very still, stay very still, he told himself. And then the footsteps passed. They were safe, but for how long? He waited until he no longer heard any noise from the hallway and pushed his way out from under the other cats.

"Move," he commanded them. All four cats scurried from the bathroom and padded quickly down the hallway in the same direction the Hyskos had come. Within moments they came to the door propped open by the bag of cat food. Each of them, following Wind's lead, leaped over the bag and out into the backyard. Except for Blank Eyes.

Trying to mirror the leaps of the older and stronger cats, the kitten misjudged both the distance and height of the bag. Her front legs caught on the top of the food bag and she lost her balance and fell awkwardly against the door. The door inched forward, pushing the bag ahead of it and leaving Blank Eyes behind.

The other three cats watched in horror as Blank Eyes disappeared behind the closing door. Windrusher hurdled forward and bit down on the top of the bag. He pushed against it with all his strength until the door stopped its forward progress.

"Get out of there now," Chaser urged Blank Eyes. She scrambled to her feet and scrambled over Wind's head and outside to join the others. Windrusher released his grip on the bag and the door pushed the bag outside, spilling some of its contents onto the ground.

13

SLIDING, SLIPPING, AND SPRAWLING down the steep hill, the four cats scrambled away from the house. Windrusher dug his claws into the ground to slow his descent, and Blank Eyes, trailing close behind him, tripped over his legs and tumbled head over whiskers against a low tangle of deer weed and sagebrush. Dust from the parched soil rose in clouds around her head, and she lay in a ball coughing and spitting out pieces of brush.

Windrusher slid into a gulley of eroded clay and came to rest against a cluster of chaparral and cactus. He eased away from the cactus and looked at Blank Eyes lying in the sagebrush below him. The young Wetlos tried to regain her footing, slipping several times in the dirt and brush before standing unsteadily for a moment and then flopping down with her legs akimbo.

"Let's do again," the young cat said, shaking her head to dislodge a yellow flower that had attached itself to her ear. Windrusher realized that Blank Eyes was quickly learning how to communicate, and it wouldn't be long before she would be as talkative as Lil' One had become.

Down below, far, far below, he saw streaming lights of Hyskos vehicles. Darkness was rapidly enveloping them, and the sinking day globe cast an orange glow across the western sky. On the other side of a rocky outcropping it seemed that the earth was smoother, and it faded into the distance in a narrow band. Could it be a path? A path would be better than sliding headlong down the slippery hill and possibly plunging into the line of Hyskos vehicles below. He had to get them all together first. He turned and saw Chaser sitting with his rump against a large stone not far from him. The marmalade cat was licking the inside of his right front leg as though he was preparing for a nap. "Are you all right, Chaser?" he called out.

"Fine. I've been waiting for you two to stop tumbling."

"I think we're stopped. For now, anyway. Have you seen Rahhna's Light?"

"She's not far behind us. Shall I see if she needs any help?"

Windrusher craned his neck and saw the chunky Persian carefully picking her way through the steep, eroded landscape. Slowly, each paw testing the terrain to be sure she wouldn't slip, she made her way toward them. Her luxurious coat was covered with a thin film of dust, and her eyes were wide with fright.

Wind clambered out of the gully and waited with Chaser while Blank Eyes, and finally the Persian, joined them.

"That was quite an adventure," he offered.

Rahhna's Light hissed violently, her ears flattening dangerously. "An adventure? You call this an adventure?" she hissed at him. "I don't know why we're not all worm food, but it's not because of your leadership."

He ignored her outburst as best he could. "The important thing is that we're out of there and free. Now we can find our way back home." Even as he said it Wind realized how foolish the statement must sound. Four cats had been taken from four different places far distant from each other. How, by the Holy Mother, could they possibly find their way back home?

"And how do you expect us to find our way back home?" Rahhna's Light said as though she had read his thoughts.

"I'm not sure, but I have faith that Tho-hoth will help us if we try to help ourselves. That means that we have to keep moving away before they discover that we're gone and start looking for us."

"You have all the—"

"Windrusher is right," Chaser cut her off. "He found a way out of the house, and I believe he'll find a way to get us back to our homes."

Blank Eyes had quietly moved next to Rahhna's Light and began rubbing her jaw against the Persian's neck. The young tabby purred loudly, and Rahhna's Light licked the kitten across the head. "Fine. You lead and we'll follow, but spare us any more of your snouter droppings talk about the gods showing us the way."

Quint had spent two hours prowling through the county recorder's records doing a search on the house on the bluff. He found that there was no mortgage on the home and never had been. Very unusual, particularly for a house that size. The home had been built in 1999 and paid for in full. There were no liens or judgments on the property.

Nowhere in the property records did the name Runyan McWaters appear. In fact, he learned that the home was owned by a Karl von Rothmann. It's amazing what you can learn at your county courthouse, he thought.

Back in his hotel room, Quint searched the Internet for von Rothmann's name. He found several sites, including a link to this Reuters article:

KVR Technologies Sale Pending

Giant Warskeiler Global Group to add nanotechnology firm to holdings

Mon Feb 19, 2001 04:32 PM ET

SAN FRANCISCO (Reuters)- The privately held KVR Technologies, a leader in nanomaterials and nanoengineered products, has been purchased by the giant multinational conglomerate, Warskeiler Global Group for a reported $320 million in cash. The sole owner of KVR is the reclusive physicist Karl von Rothmann.

Von Rothmann built his company from a one-man research laboratory that created a platform of patented and proprietary integrated nanomaterial technologies that experts credit with substantially boosting the nascent industry. Today, KVR is the major supplier of commercial quality nanoparticles, coated nanoparticles and nanoparticle dispersions in a variety of media.

The rest of the article went on to describe the various patents KVR held and how Warskeiler planned to integrate the company into its broad holdings. Quint scratched his head. He wouldn't know a nanoparticle if it bit him on the ankle, but he understood $320 million and what it could buy. So it didn't make any sense that someone with that much money would steal a cat when he could fill up warehouses with as many cats as he wanted.

And where did McWaters fit into this picture that suddenly had become much murkier? He glanced at the clock by the bed. It was a little after eight. He had to be at the airport at 9:30 to meet Amy and Kimmy Trembles' flight. He had learned a lot today and perhaps tomorrow would provide the rest of the answers to this puzzle.

He had met with Captain Mendez of the San Diego Police Department's Northern Division while he was downtown and explained the situation. He wasn't sure if the Captain totally believed him, but he was quick to understand that a theft had occurred when he showed him the newspaper clippings.

Captain Mendez promised to have a squad car available in the morning to accompany them to the home. Quint knew they would need a warrant to go inside and search the house, but he was hoping that if they showed up with the police, von Rothmann would have to invite them in.

He ran a hand across his face and rubbed his eyes. He didn't have to look in a mirror to know they were bloodshot; the raw, stinging sensation was all the confirmation he needed. It had been more than twenty-four hours since he had slept. No wonder this thing didn't make any sense.

Quint brought Amy and her daughter to the hotel. "I told the Captain that we'd meet them at nine, so we'll have to get an early start." He smiled at Amy and Kimmy. "We're getting close. Hopefully, you and Tony will be back together tomorrow and we can return to Florida. I'll see you in the lobby at eight."

Amy nodded and thanked him. She thought he looked tired. His handsome features were taut, his eyes bloodshot.

Inside the room, she flopped on one of the double beds, while Kimmy found the television remote and turned on the set. She glanced at the clock by the bed. "Honey, it may be only 10:30 here, but our bodies are still on Florida time. We have to be up early, particularly if you want breakfast."

"I know, mom. Let me just see what's on out here then I'll turn it off," Kimmy said, clicking through the channels as fast as she could move her thumb.

Kimmy had slept for several hours on the plane, but Amy was exhausted, feeling the jet lag start to kick in. She lay back and closed her eyes. This entire experience was still unbelievable. It seemed like a bizarre nightmare that they would awaken from in the morning.

Still, she was more hopeful than ever. Quint had managed to track down the man who had stolen Tony, and it would only be a matter of hours before they were all together again. Despite her exhaustion, she sensed that she had turned the corner on her depression and was closer to her old self than she had been in months. Deep inside she knew she taken control of her life, and she was actually looking forward to going back to work.

For the second time in two weeks, she thought back to her four years of nursing school at the University of Massachusetts. This time, though, she was filled with pleasant memories remembering why she wanted to be a nurse and how proud her family had been of her. She was a good nurse, and she needed to return to her job as soon as possible.

She felt a surge of energy as her hopeful mood pushed her exhaustion aside. Yes, everything was going to work out just fine. "Okay, Kimmy, time to get ready for bed," she said. "You want to be fresh and alert for Tony, don't you?" Reaching out to the clock radio to set it for 6:30, she noticed the blinking light on the telephone for the first time. Quickly reading the instructions printed on the face of the phone, she picked up the receiver and pushed star-nine.

"Hey, honey, I hope you and Kimmy had a good flight." It was Gerry. She smiled, grateful to hear his voice and feeling once again the warmth and love for her supportive husband. "I'm sorry to leave you this message, but I was sure you'd want to know as soon as possible."

Amy's heartbeat increased, and the telephone in her hand trembled slightly.

"I got a call from Tom tonight. They've had to put your sister in the hospital."

14

THE NARROW PATH wrapped itself around the side of the hill, becoming more difficult to follow and finally disappearing in an outcropping of rocks and cactus. The four cats stumbled through the twilight. They gripped the fractured face of the hill with extended claws in an attempt to keep from sliding to the bottom.

Overhead, a few patches of stars were already visible, and they heard the noise of the Hyskos vehicles below them. Windrusher brought the group to a halt in front of the rocks. They had been picking their way along the path, struggling to keep their footing. Even with their superior eyesight, they had difficulty staying on the path, and each of them, except for the careful and slow-moving Rahna's Light, had skidded down the treacherous face of the steep hill.

"Let's rest here," he said. The other cats needed no more encouragement and sat where they were. Rahna's Light and Chaser began licking their sore paws, while Blank Eyes stared expectantly. Windrusher searched around them and saw nothing but desolation. They had left the house far behind and had seen no others while they circled the hill. In the distance were the red and yellow lights of a Hyskos village, but no signs of habitation anywhere near them. It wouldn't have been difficult to imagine that they were lost in a barren land far from any other form of life.

"We will have to be watchful, but we should reach the bottom soon." He cut his eyes toward the Persian, who had been strangely silent, and he wondered why she wasn't complaining.

Rahna's Light lay in the dirt several paces away from the other cats. This was a different cat from the perfectly groomed and confident show cat he first met in the Hyskos house. Now, her coat was matted with the brown clay that covered every inch of the hill. She held one paw to her mouth, tugging at a claw with little shakes of her head.

She looked up from her grooming and caught Wind staring at her. "Are you happy now?"

"What do you mean?"

"Are you happy that you've brought me down to the level of a filthy outdoor cat? At least it's too dark for anyone to see me, but I can't imagine what my Hyskos female would think if she ever saw me like this."

"She will love you and be happy to have you back no matter how you look," he replied.

Rahhna's Light stared at Windrusher, and then let her eyes wander past him as though she had seen something far more interesting behind him. "Why did I ever follow you out here where we're sure to die?"

Chaser jumped to his feet. "Let's continue. We still have a long way to go."

A crisp ocean breeze swept over the four cats and stirred up clouds of dust that enveloped them as they moved. With darkness pressing in on them, and the footing more treacherous than ever, they made very slow progress down the steep bluff. They were clumped together behind Windrusher, their legs stiff, muscles taut, each one trying not to lose control and slide into one of the giant boulders lining the black path carrying its deadly cargo of vehicles.

A high quavering howl suddenly split the cool night air. All of the cats froze, their ears erect, hair bushy with fright. Blank Eyes, who had been lagging back with Rahhna's Light, jumped forward, banging against the Persian, and knocking her off balance. Together, they staggered into the others, and all four cats tumbled down the hill, banging against rocks and rolling through clumps of sagebrush.

Windrusher slid down the rocky hill on his back like a hairy toboggan. His legs sliced at the air, trying desperately to right himself and regain his footing. Around him, he heard frightened yelps as the other cats plummeted in all directions followed by suffocating clouds of dust. He reached out his front legs with a supreme effort and stabbed his claws into the flaky soil. At first he thought it was too late. In his head, he saw his body slithering down the hill, scratching futilely at the scabby dirt, and finally smashing into the boulders below.

This can't be happening, he thought. With his eyes closed, he exerted every muscle in his body, driving all four claws deep into the dirt until slowly, very slowly, he halted his headlong descent. Gingerly, he regained his footing and shook his head to try to remove some of the dust and dirt clinging to him like another coat.

"Chaser. Rahhna's Light. Blank Eyes," he cried out, listening for a reply. The only reply he heard was the chirping of insects. Had the others not been able to control their fall? Would he find their crumpled bodies at the bottom of the hill?

"Here. I'm here." It was Blank Eyes.

Windrusher moved toward the sound of her voice. "Keep talking, Blank Eyes, I'm coming."

"Over here I am."

The kitten was lodged behind a rock, her legs tangled, two beneath her and two at odd angles. She meowed pitifully, but Wind could see that she wasn't hurt. "Let me help you," he said. He straddled the rock and gripped the nape of the young cat's neck, lifting her so she could regain her footing. She backed out of the narrow enclosure that had held her and sat down at Wind's feet.

She sat there breathing deeply for a few seconds, licked at a raw spot on her right foreleg, and butted Windrusher affectionately. "You saved me. You…" her voice trailed off as she struggled for the words.

"You would have worked your way out sooner or later, Blank Eyes. I only helped you along."

She opened her mouth to speak, but instead stood up and licked Windrusher under the jaw. He gratefully accepted the grooming and responded with a few licks of his own.

"Now, that's a sight I didn't expect to see."

It was Chaser. The big marmalade cat stood on top of a large rock staring down at them with a mischievous look in his eyes.

"Thanks be to Irissa-u that you were not hurt," Windrusher said.

"You're not going to tell me that was another of your adventures?"

"You're beginning to sound like Rahhna's Light. And where do you think our complaining friend is?"

Chaser's head made a ninety-degree arc, searching the barren landscape to either side of them. "I hoped that she might be with you two. I was fortunate to grasp a bush not far from here and stop my fall. You don't think she—"

"She has to be nearby," Windrusher said abruptly. "Let's find her, she may need our help. But be careful."

The three cats formed a ragged line and spread out in search of the Persian. They cautiously tested the ground as though each step might put them in contact with a poisonous snake.

"Rahhna's Light, can you hear us?" Windrusher called.

"Rahhna, where are you?" Chaser bellowed.

"Rah-rah, we find you," Blank Eyes squealed.

Carefully, they edged their way along the face of the hill, calling out for the Persian, straining their eyes in hopes of spotting her amongst the shadows. Once, twice, they slipped on loose rocks and began to slide. But unlike the last time, they kept their balance and dug in to stop the skid before sprawling out of control.

Windrusher paused. He heard something off to his right that sounded like a cough. "Over here," he yelled, and rushed toward a dark depression. Peering over the side of the eroded gully, he saw her. She was lying flat on her back, her eyes closed, each of her legs extended as though taking a nap.

"Rahhna's Light, are you hurt?" He scrambled over the side of the gulley, sliding the last few feet and kicking up clouds of dust.

The Persian opened one eye, then the other. Slowly, she rolled onto her side and pulled herself to her feet. The dust cloud settled over her, and she was seized by a series of raspy, hacking coughs. When the coughing finally ended, Rahhna's Light breathed deeply. By now, the other two cats had arrived, and they perched above the gulley, peering down at their fellow traveler. She looked up and seemed to notice the other cats for the first time. Her eyes were red and rimmed with dirt, her coat matted, and a raw abrasion on her flank oozed wet and shiny.

He spotted the open wound and moved to clean it.

"Don't you touch me," Rahhna's Light hissed. She limped forward, her eyes ablaze, teeth bared. "Haven't you done enough harm?"

"But—" Windrusher began.

"Don't but me. I don't want to hear anything you have to say," she spat out. "Why was I so senseless as to listen to you in the first place?"

"You're not being fair," Chaser interjected.

"And you're not much better than this brainless buttworm. Look at me. I'm lucky to be alive, and I take that as a sign from the gods that I've been warned not to continue this foolishness. You can follow him to your deaths, but I'm going back."

"No, you can't go back. It's not safe." Windrusher realized how foolish the statement sounded, but he knew it was the truth.

The Persian stared at him for a moment and then limped past him, struggling up the side of the shallow gulley. At the top, she turned toward the others. "Any cat with the sense of a whiskerless kitten can see that I'm right. Go with him if you wish, but I'm going back to that house where those Hyskos fed and cared for me. Where I don't have to worry about falling to my death."

The three cats watched her struggle up the hill, climbing slowly away from them until she blended into the shadows, and they lost sight of her. In the distance, they heard the howl of a hunting creature followed by a series of yips.

Von Rothmann awakened from his nap refreshed and anxious to return to his computer. Ever since he was a student at MIT, he had devoted at least four hours of every day to study and research. At heart, he was a lab rat, never happier than when he was alone in his laboratory or on his computer refining equations or conducting experiments.

Making shatterproof particles to be used for beer bottles and running boards had made him a rich man. He wasn't looking for more money and definitely not any celebrity that might come with his engineering breakthroughs. No, he kept working because he had the brains to do it, and was never happier than when he was working his way through a myriad of details.

Four hours had flowed into five, and he was surprised to see how late it was when he checked his watch. It was well after midnight. He stretched his stiff back, pushed himself up from his ergonomic chair, and decided to call it a night. But first he wanted to say goodnight to his four house guests.

McWaters was surely asleep by now. He would have cleaned the room, driven to the pet store for the food and litter, and restocked the kitty's pantry. Perhaps he was too hard on him, he thought. The man had his talents, and he was certainly useful. Still, McWaters had a way of getting under his skin.

He stopped in front of the massive wall of windows and looked out into the darkness. In the distance, he thought he saw dimly illuminated waves breaking on the beach. Lights from the cars passed below. He congratulated himself for purchasing the bluff and building his home in one of the most beautiful parts of the country. A short drive south was the lovely seaside resort town of La Jolla, and up the road was Torrey Pines State Preserve, a wild and picturesque park he'd never visited. Maybe he'd have McWaters take him there one day.

He went to the kitchen and pulled a bottle of spring water from the refrigerator. Tilting his head back, he let the cold liquid flow down his throat. He hadn't realized how parched he was. Still holding the bottle, he headed toward the glass-enclosed room housing the four cats.

He was feeling exceptionally pleased with himself tonight and whistled the opening stanza to Gilbert and Sullivan's "I Am the Very Model of a Modern Major-General" from *The Pirates of Penzance* as he rounded the corner. Not bad, he thought.

The first thing he noticed was the gap. His scientific mind took in the space between the open door and jamb and calculated it to be seven-and-a-half inches. He rushed forward, pushing the door open and quickly closing it behind him. His eyes frantically searched every corner of the room, but he knew it was too late. They were gone.

He felt his heart jump wildly in his chest. What had that idiot done? Where were his precious cats? "McWaters!" he screamed at the top of his voice. "McWaters, where are you?"

15

RUNYAN MCWATERS HAD MORE than a wee nip at Delaney's. He had soothed his wounded ego by shopping, spending several hours trying on shirts and slacks and shoes before treating himself to a steak dinner at one of his favorite restaurants, the Greystone, in the Gaslamp Quarter. Then he went to Delaney's and watched the Padres squeak by the Dodgers.

It was a quarter to one when he slipped into the big house through the back door, hoping von Rothmann was asleep. He giggled to himself as he tiptoed down the long hallway toward his bedroom, feeling like a husband hoping not to wake his sleeping wife after a night on the town.

Ahead of him he saw the lights from the *Cat House*, as he called it, and remembered the food and litter he left in his trunk. No problem, he'd take care of that in the morning. Now, he was looking forward to getting some shut-eye and not thinking about those cats for at least eight hours.

"What have you done with my cats?" Von Rothmann jumped out of the room and into the hallway. His face was the color of a ripe watermelon, his eyes wild, and his hands up near his shoulders as though he was preparing to catch a pass.

McWaters was startled, thinking von Rothmann had finally gone over the edge. The old fool had his quirks, but he had never seen him in such a state. "Hey, I'm sorry. I stopped off for a drink, but I have their food and litter in the car." He tried to calm him down, didn't want the good doctor to split a valve or throw a piston. "Don't worry, I'll go back and bring it—"

"Shut up, you fool. The cats…where are the cats?"

"Uhhh." For the first time he could remember, McWaters didn't know what to say. Stepping past von Rothmann, who was still holding his hands up but now looked like he would reach out at any minute and strangle him, he stared through the window into the cat's room. "What are you talking about, the cats are…" His voice trailed away and his mouth and lips remained open, pursed as though an invisible entity was sucking the breath from his lungs.

"Where? The cats are where?" Von Rothmann screamed at him. "Can't you see that they're gone?"

His head bobbed once, twice, and he moved jerkily through the open door. He searched the room, his eyes darting from corner to corner, peering under the couch, even opening the doors of the storage counter. He turned toward von Rothmann, who was right behind him, and scratched his head.

"I don't… They were here when I left. I promise you."

"If they were here when you left, they'd still be here, wouldn't they? As far as I know, cats haven't evolved enough to climb on one another's backs so they can reach the door knob."

"I can't explain it. They have to be here someplace."

"Do you think I'm an idiot? Of course they're someplace. I haven't had a chance to look, but I want to know how they got out. Did you let them out?"

"No. I wouldn't do that." He was struggling to remember if anything unusual had happened when he left the house.

"Then you must have left the door open. There's no other explanation, is there?"

He stared at the door, picturing himself carrying the trash pail and the bag of food, juggling them and closing the door behind him. But did he close it behind him? He tugged at the door knob, giving it a little flip of his wrist as he had earlier that night. Not too hard, and not too easy. Watching it swing in an arc toward the door frame, drag across the sisal mat, and stop inches from locking in place.

Von Rothmann was in his face, screaming, a tic working at the corner of his right eye. "You idiot. You didn't pull the door closed did you? How could you…I can't…incompetent." He was sputtering as though he had lost the ability to construct complete sentences, and droplets of spittle flew from his mouth.

Despite his three whiskeys and beer chasers, McWaters wasn't drunk. True, his left temple throbbed, but he was having a difficult time getting worked up over the missing cats. He knew they'd find them hiding under a bed or in one of the other rooms looking out the window. That's what cats did, wasn't it?

Still, something was nagging at him behind his throbbing temple. He could almost see it, but it stayed out of reach, like an itch he couldn't scratch. It would come to him eventually, but he had to find the cats now and get this maniac off his back before he did something he regretted.

It was after 2:00 A.M. when they completed searching the house. They had gone from room to room, poking their heads into every corner, behind furniture, under beds, into closets. They even went down into the basement laboratory, although they knew there was no way the cats could have entered. The lab was always locked, and von Rothmann had the only key.

The cats had simply disappeared. He didn't understand how it happened. Had someone entered the house while he was gone and stolen the cats? That didn't seem likely, but there was no doubt they were gone. The itch was still there, hidden in a dark corner of his mind. He probed, but couldn't quite pull it to the surface.

Von Rothmann had grown increasingly agitated and incoherent as their search had progressed. Moving from one room to the other, McWaters noticed the older man's hands were trembling, and a cold sweat covered his ravaged face. He seemed confused, disoriented, and, not for the first time, he wondered if the physicist was losing his mind.

It was in the basement that they both realized that he was suffering from insulin shock. "Have you eaten anything today?" he asked, grasping the trembling man's arm.

"Not since noon, I think," von Rothmann gasped. He was breathing rapidly and his eyes seemed to be going in and out of focus.

He put an arm around von Rothmann and helped him to the desk chair. He opened the small refrigerator next to the lab bench and pulled out a Snickers bar and a can of Coke. Tearing the wrapper off the candy bar, he handed it to von Rothmann who devoured it in two bites and washed it down with several swallows of the cola.

"Man, you have to take better care of yourself," he said, offering a damp paper towel to his boss. Von Rothmann took the towel and wiped his wet face. His breathing had noticeably slowed, and he closed his eyes and gulped in several deep breaths, letting the paper towel fall to the floor.

McWaters bent to pick up the towel and an image of a paper bag flashed into his head. It was lying on the ground outside the back door, and he realized that this was part of what had been nagging at him. His mind was clear now; the traces of alcohol that had addled his thinking earlier were gone. He rewound his activities from the time he left the cat's room until he drove away and played them back like an old home movie flashing on a screen behind his eyes.

There he was toting the trash can and the bag of cat food. Yes, he remembered that. He saw himself reaching for his keys and not finding them. His internal film even had a soundtrack, and he heard himself curse, then place the bag on the floor inside the house to keep the door from closing.

That was somehow important, he knew. The bag on the floor was crucial to the cat's disappearance. The movie jumped ahead, and there he was back at the door after changing his shirt and retrieving his keys. But the door was closed now, and when he opened it the bag was outside.

"The collars!" von Rothmann screamed.

"What?" McWaters was pulled back to the laboratory, the movie in his head dark and silent. He knew how the cats had left the house.

"The collars, the collars," von Rothmann repeated, slapping his hand against the arm of the chair. "How could I be so stupid?" He turned to the computer on his desk, grabbed the mouse, and clicked on a bright red icon in the shape of a satellite. Immediately, the monitor shifted to a screen divided into quarters. Each quarter of the 19-inch flat panel LCD monitor contained an aerial photo with a yellow ring. In three of the screens, the rings were moving northwest.

To the right of each screen was a block of information topped by a sentence that read exactly the same except for one word. Looking over von Rothmann's shoulder, he read the four screens, starting with the upper left screen: *Location information for Darwin*; *Location information for Murray*; *Location information for Katmandu*; and *Location information for Tony*. Below that were the time, date, and longitude and latitude readings.

"Look…look at that," von Rothman said excitedly, pointing to the screen. "How did they get over there?" He turned and glared at McWaters. "They would have had to be outside since you left early this afternoon to get that far. You let them out, didn't you?" The coloring on his face was shifting from its natural ruddiness to deep crimson. He started to rise from the chair, but slipped back.

McWaters shook his head. "No. I wouldn't do that." He might as well have carried them outside himself, but he wasn't about to admit that to von Rothmann. Still, he found it hard to believe they had made it down the hill, across eight lanes of traffic, climbed another bluff, and now were approaching the Pacific Coast Highway.

"It doesn't look like Katmandu is moving," McWaters said, pointing to the third screen containing a graphic aerial map of the bluff with von Rothmann's house. "Maybe she's hurt and they left her behind."

Von Rothmann, who was still staring at him, turned back to the monitor. Katmandu's map remained static, the latitude and longitude frozen in place. He shifted his gaze to the others with its three circles inching further west and then back to McWaters who was waiting for another outburst from his boss.

"Listen carefully to what I'm about to tell you." His high-pitched voice was lower now with a gravelly rasp as though he had been smoking all his life. His hands were no longer shaking, and his eyes bored into him. "You get down there and pick up Katmandu and bring her back here where she belongs. Do you understand?"

He nodded weakly. "As soon as it's—"

"I mean right now, not later."

He pictured himself on the side of that steep hill in the middle of the night, stumbling and breaking a leg. There was no way that he'd go out there, but what he said was, "Okay."

"And as soon as it's daylight you go and find my other three cats."
There was a dangerous edge to his voice that made McWaters nervous.
Von Rothmann reached down to the top drawer in the desk and pulled
out an electronic display unit that looked like a large Palm Pilot. After
punching several of the buttons, the screen came to life in a bright
grid with red and yellow lines. It displayed the same aerial map as the
computer monitor.

"This is a GPS receiver. That's Global Positioning System," he said
as though explaining the multiplication tables to a child. "Turn this
knob to see where each cat is. It will pinpoint their location down to ten
or fifteen feet." Von Rothmann placed the tracking device on the desk
in front of McWaters. As the former cop reached for it, von Rothmann
grabbed his wrist. "I don't care what you have to do, but don't come back
without Tony. I'd like to get all four back, but it's imperative that Tony is
returned."

He squeezed his wrist with surprising strength and speared him
with a look that sent a chill through him. "You better not foul this up
again, McWaters. Tony is my cat, and no one else will ever own him. If
you can't bring him back to me, for whatever reason, make sure that his
traveling days are over."

16

INTERSTATE 5, KNOWN SIMPLY as "the 5" to locals, is the only Interstate that runs from the Mexican to the Canadian border. The San Diego County portion of the freeway was added to the state highway system in 1909, and each day hundreds of thousands of commuters wheel over its pavement on their way to and from their jobs.

Rush hour was thankfully hours behind them by the time the three cats reached the bottom of the hill. Exhausted, but exhilarated to have made it down the steep bluff, they scrambled over the boulders and onto the emergency lane. As the first vehicle whipped by, Windrusher was immediately gripped by his old fears. He breathed deeply, recalling the black paths he had traveled and what he had learned from those experiences.

Be wary and ever watchful of the Hyskos vehicles, he told himself, but don't let fear overwhelm you. He knew the danger was real, but he had two other cats depending on him to lead them safely away from this place.

"Listen to me," he said, huddling with them against the embankment wall. "Stay close to the side, as far away from the vehicles as you can. I'll watch for a break, and then we will cross together. When I say it is time, run as if your life depended on it, because…" He didn't complete the thought although he nudged Blank Eyes to be sure the little cat was paying attention.

They set off in a tight triangle, Windrusher at its point, Chaser and Blank Eyes right behind. He had no idea how long it had been since they left the house, but the sky was completely dark, and only the glare of the vehicles illuminated their path. He used the lights to gauge the distance of the cars and trucks approaching from behind them as they traveled north.

Shadows shifted over them as the lights from the oncoming traffic in the far lanes mixed with the beams of vehicles behind them. Ahead of them, the black path curved and he saw breaks in the oncoming traffic. He stopped and turned to the others. "Remember, when I say go, don't hesitate, follow closely. I want to feel my tail brush across your face."

Blank Eyes pushed against Windrusher's tail. "Like this?" she asked.

"Yes. Like that."

Together they watched the oncoming traffic. Finally, he thought there was a large enough gap for all of them to safely make it across the four lanes. "Run!" he yelled and surged forward onto the black path. The pavement was hard and unyielding beneath his feet, and the acrid stench of the vehicles' exhaust stung his nose.

Chaser and Blank Eyes scrambled behind him, and they were quickly across the first lane and then the second, their feet barely touching the pavement. From the corner of his eye, he saw the big marmalade cat leaping with him, stride for stride, and take a position next to his right shoulder. His heart was pounding, but they were almost past the last lane.

Then it happened. A brilliant light washed over them. Windrusher spotted the vehicle approaching rapidly in their lane. "Hurry," he gasped, unsure if he could be heard above the roar of the oncoming car. He swished his tail in an arc behind him, hoping to feel Blank Eyes.

Nothing.

The light was blinding now, threatening to freeze him in its stunning glare. The throb of the motor vibrated through the pavement and up his legs. Chaser had already reached the concrete barrier in the center of the path, but where was Blank Eyes? He risked a turn and there was the kitten only a tail's length behind him, running for her young life. As he was about to turn back and join Chaser in the safety of the open lane, Blank Eyes' feet tangled and she tripped and skidded on her nose.

He didn't have time to think about what he was doing, about the very real danger that both of them would be crushed if he stopped to help the kitten. Planting his front paws into the pavement, he whirled around and swiped at the still tumbling Blank Eyes. His paw caught the young cat under the ribs and carried her forward, steadying her just enough to regain her footing. But was it too late?

It would have been, but at the last moment, the vehicle braked and swerved around them. A curtain of hot air and noise buffeted the two cats as they completed the final steps to safety.

"Are you hurt?" Chaser cried out, licking and nuzzling them.

"Thanks be to Irissa-u, that was close." Wind's legs were trembling so much that he sat down. "What about you, Lil' One?" He said the name without thinking.

"You saved me, Windrusher. I…" She paused, searching for the right words. "I would be dead if you…if you didn't come back and save me." Vehicles were racing by on each side of them, but for that moment it seemed like they were alone in the universe.

Chaser and Windrusher looked at each other then back to the small gray and white cat who was now licking Wind's neck. This was the longest and most sensible sentence they had heard from the kitten since they had been together.

"You were almost there, I only helped you along," he said. "We need to get across the rest of this black path, so don't thank me yet." They climbed to the top of the barrier and Windrusher noted that there were considerably fewer vehicles coming from the other direction. "I don't believe we'll have much trouble crossing here. What do you think, Chaser?"

The big marmalade wasn't looking at the roadway, but seemed to be studying the little cat beside him. "What I really think is that we need to find a new name for Blank Eyes."

After crossing the highway, the three cats scrambled down a steep embankment. They were almost immediately faced with another bluff. The adrenalin rush from their dash across the highway overcame the exhaustion that was seeping through their bodies. Windrusher prodded them onwards, marveling at the energy and strength of his companions as they slowly climbed the hill.

At the top, they collapsed, dirty, muscles aching, their bodies craving sleep. Wind let them nap for a time before rousing them and leading them to another roadway. This one was smaller and nearly deserted, and they ambled across it to a broad expanse of grass running parallel to the beach.

His internal compass told him he was far from his home in the land of warm waters, and moving farther away with each step. Even though Chaser had said they were traveling toward his home, the important thing in Windrusher's mind was that they were putting distance between themselves and the house from which they escaped.

Rahhna would pierce the shield of darkness before long, and another night would come to an end. Soon, he thought, they would stop and embrace the deepest of sleeps. But first, he would find them a safe haven; a place where the Hyskos would never find them.

With each step, the young kitten had been thinking about what Chaser had said: *We need to find a new name for Blank Eyes.* She had been called by another name at her first home, although she didn't understand what the high-legged beings were saying. Her mind had been a confusing jumble of images and emotions, and she wasn't certain what to think or how to react to the glare of attention she found herself under in those first few days.

She had been isolated from other cats and had no memory of her mother. She was constantly prodded and subjected to painful sticks from long needles. And when she wasn't the center of unwanted attention, she was left alone in a small cage in a cold and smelly room.

Being taken from that place was actually the best thing that had happened to her. She had never been happier than when she was introduced to Chaser and Rahhna's Light. Windrusher joined them and made it even better. For so long her head had been swirling and buzzing like it was infested with swarms of insects. No wonder they called her Blank Eyes. It was only in the past few day globes that the buzzing insects had gone away, and her head was so much clearer.

Every cat must have its own call name, and she wanted one that would be hers for life. She was no longer Blank Eyes, but what was she? She would have to give this a lot of thought.

17

WHY AM I DOING THIS? a furious Runyan McWaters asked himself.

He had been searching the side of the hill for the past hour, slipping on the dry dirt so many times he had lost count. In one hand he held a green flashlight; in the other he clutched the GPS receiver. He stopped near a rough outcropping of rocks and cactus and shined the flashlight on the display screen. It looked like he was going in the right direction, but he wasn't sure.

Damn that von Rothmann, he thought. Forcing me to go outside in the middle of the night so I can break my neck looking for a cat. He sat on one of the rocks to catch his breath, and studied the illustration of what was supposed to be the hillside seen from about five hundred feet in the air. A yellow circle remained static in the middle of the screen, just as it had for the past hour. Katmandu hadn't moved one foot since he had been out here.

"If I'm using it right, that is," he said aloud, not completely sure if he actually knew how it worked. Of course, he would never admit that to von Rothmann. He turned the knob to the next screen and the map changed to Darwin's position. Quickly, he scanned the other two cats and was relieved to see they were still together. "Your time is coming soon, my furry friends."

Switching back to Katmandu's screen, he calculated that he must be within one hundred feet of the yellow circle. He pointed the flashlight in that direction and saw more dirt, cactus, and dark shadows. His head jerked as a coyote howled from nearby, and he swung the light toward the sound. Nothing there that he could see, but a prowling coyote might explain why Katmandu hadn't moved. Too bad, he thought. He actually liked the pompous Grand Champion.

With an audible sigh, he pushed himself off the rock and checked the screen once more. He turned a half step to his right and started down the hill once again. His feet were turned sideways, and he planted his foot securely before taking the next step. Carefully, very slowly. One slip is all it would take and he could end up rolling down the hill. Maybe crashing into one of the rocks or even all the way down to the highway.

That wasn't a pretty thought and he tried to put it out of his mind and concentrate on his footing. After nearly twenty minutes he stopped again and checked the receiver. The circle was still in the same location, but now it looked like he was far to the right of it. This gadget was starting to tick him off. He felt like he would never find Katmandu in the dark, but he was damned if he would go back to the house without the cat.

He held his wrist under the beam of the flashlight: 3:30. Shaking his head in disgust, he brushed at the dirt on his shirt and pants, sending up puffs of dust. He looked again at the GPS unit and started off in that direction. His nose tickled, the dust finding its way deep into his nostrils, and he sneezed loudly. As his head involuntarily lurched forward with the sneeze, he stepped into a hole, twisting his ankle and losing his balance.

McWaters felt the pain shoot up his leg. He fell forward, landing hard on his left knee. "Ahhh," he cried in pain and surprise. Then he was rolling down the steep hill, skidding over the rough terrain as he tried to dig his right foot into the crumbling dirt.

Desperately, he grabbed at a large sagebrush. It slowed him enough so that he was able to scissor his legs out and stop himself. He lay there panting for two full minutes before he finally sat up, wincing at the pain in his knee. On his feet again, he carefully tested his leg. It hurt, but not as bad as it could have.

The good news was he still had the flashlight, but he had lost the location device in his clumsy slide down the hill. No telling how far down it could have slid. He swept the beam in a wide arc hoping to see a reflection glinting off the face of the gadget. Continuing around, he moved the beam lower. Still nothing.

Perhaps it was above him, close to where he first fell. He peered up the hill, seeing the shadows that covered the rocks and ankle-twisting holes. He didn't want to climb back up, wasn't sure he could. But he had to find it, and there was only one way to do that. He began a slow, painful ascent.

He had only climbed about twenty feet when he saw it in a shallow depression, the yellow circle still visible. Finally, some good luck; it hadn't broken in the fall.

Covered with dirt and dust, his ankle throbbing, he studied the GPS receiver and continued his search for Katmandu. He stared at the ground around him, playing the light at his feet. This had to be the spot. There was nothing but a few rocks and a clump of chaparral and cactus a few feet to his right. Down on his hands and knees, he peered into the shadows and behind the rocks. There was no Katmandu anywhere.

He looked again at the screen to be sure the circle hadn't moved. He felt like banging it a few times to be sure it was working. A little impact engineering might be what the thing needed, but he decided that might not be a good idea. His knees hurt from crawling so he stood again and limped to the chaparral and cactus. This was the only place the cat could be hiding. He pushed aside the plants with his foot, peering at the brown earth. This thing must be on the fritz, after all, he thought.

That's when he saw it laying there. Dropping to a knee, McWaters reached out and picked up the collar.

18

"She had a seizure."

Amy realized it was two in the morning in Florida, but she had to find out how Jeannie was doing. Her call had awakened Gerry, but he quickly told her everything he knew.

"Tom called me from the hospital about seven tonight and said that Jeannie had some kind of seizure."

"Oh, that poor girl." She blinked back tears as an image of her sister slipped into her mind. It was the picture of a six-year-old Jeannie Tremble wearing white lace and a mischievous grin taken at their cousin's wedding. "It has to be eclampsia," she said softly.

"Yeah, that's what Tom said. She has an excellent medical team, and they're working to get her stabilized."

She didn't want to dwell on the consequences of Jeannie's condition, but she knew that eclampsia, which had been known as toxemia for ages, was marked by seizures. Doctors had no idea what caused it or which women might progress from pre-eclampsia to eclampsia, but she knew that about one in two or three thousand pregnant women developed eclampsia.

"I wish I could be there with her. Tom must still be at the hospital, don't you think?"

"Uh huh, do you want the number?"

"Yes. But I'll wait until morning to call him." She wrote the number on the pad next to the phone. "Call me on my cell if you hear from him again, and hon…"

"Yes," he answered sleepily.

"I'm sorry I woke you."

"Don't worry about it. I had to get up to answer the phone, anyway."

She smiled at his little joke, as though she hadn't heard it a hundred times over the past twenty years. "I miss you, Gerry."

"Me, too. You and Kimmy find Tony and come on back home."

She hung up and turned toward Kimmy who had been quietly listening to the conversation.

"Aunt Jeannie has a condition called eclampsia."

"Is it serious?" Kimmy asked, trying to read her mother's face.

"The doctors have it under control," her eyes slid from her daughter's face to the telephone. She didn't know if that was true, but she didn't want to upset her. "We'll call Uncle Tom in the morning and find out how she's doing. Be sure to say a little prayer for her."

"Mom, you don't think…will she lose the baby?"

She shifted over to sit beside her daughter and draped an arm around her. "Jeannie is well into her eighth month. That means the baby is strong and they can take it if there's any real danger. I don't think you need to worry."

Kimmy slipped an arm around her mother's waist and squeezed hard. "But you're worried, aren't you?"

She gave Kimmy a tight smile. "You know me too well. She's the only sister I have, but I have to believe that she'll be fine." She disentangled herself from her daughter and gently pushed her down on the bed. "Now, we need to get some sleep. We have a rescue mission coming up in a few hours. Or have you forgotten?"

Amy slept fitfully, waking up every hour and checking the time. Finally, she sank into an exhausted sleep.

She was walking. Then she was falling, falling into a pit that seemed to close around her. From the darkness that pressed down on her, she saw clusters of sparks like a forest full of fireflies. She was lying on her back in the pit watching the spectral display until the whirling lights disappeared and darkness pressed in on her. That's when she felt tiny specks falling on her face.

She had to be dreaming, asleep in her San Diego hotel room. Her eyes were open, though, and she stared into the void, feeling the grains of…was that sand falling on her face? It seemed as though she were in a hole, buried alive. She shook her head to cast away the grim vision, and once again the darkness whirled sending off more granules of light.

Her pulse was racing now, and she tried to assure herself that she was not in a grave but asleep in bed. Before her, the lights coalesced into a magmatic paste of shifting shapes that glowed and flowed until it formed the face of her sister. Jeannie smiled, her eyes crinkling at the corners, one side of her mouth a bit higher than the other. It was the same face she had seen earlier, the Jeannie of their youth, carefree and full of life.

"Jeannie," she heard herself call out to the vision of the young girl that was now melting and evolving into another face. "Don't leave me, Jeannie. I love you." She wasn't sure she was speaking the words aloud or just dreaming them. But Jeannie must not have heard her, because she was gone, her face replaced by another. It was the face of a girl with red hair and freckles. It was Tabitha Worrell's face and it floated directly above Amy's, staring down through eyes that seemed old and sad.

She tried to speak, but no sound emerged. "What are you trying to tell me?" she wanted to ask Tabitha. "Why are you here?"

The image of Tabitha slowly shook its head, the eyes boring into her. Then her mouth moved. She was speaking, but Amy couldn't hear anything. She concentrated on the moving lips, trying to make out the words, but in her dream Tabitha's face split into three pieces and now Kimmy and Tony were part of the picture. They were looking at her with the same concern as Tabitha, the cat's eyes glowing bright green.

Tabitha's lips were still moving, and now she heard her: "The pit. Stay out of the pit."

All of the faces folded into themselves and there was only darkness once again. She awoke with a shudder, and stumbled to the bathroom where she splashed water on her perspiring face.

Staring into the mirror, Amy searched for a sign that this was something other than a bad dream. She understood why she might dream about Jeannie, Kimmy and Tony. She was anxious and concerned about her sister, and, of course, they were in the middle of a two-coast search for Tony. But she hadn't thought of Tabitha since this business with Tony, and what was it that Tabitha had said? *The pit. Stay out of the pit.*

Maybe it was her subconscious admonishing her to stay the course and not fall back into her *pit* of depression. That made as much sense as anything else. She ran a hand through her hair, turned off the bathroom light and returned to bed.

Kimmy was sleeping peacefully in the other bed. At least she hadn't disturbed her, she thought. A look at the clock told her she still had an hour before the alarm would go off. She lay back down and tried to put the dream out of her head.

The eastern horizon was aglow with soft bands of magenta and apricot when the three cats entered Torrey Pines State Reserve. Windrusher had set a brisk pace, pushing the other two cats to keep moving. He wanted to get as far away from the two Hyskos as possible before they stopped to rest. Finally, in the dim light of Rahhna's first rays, he led them past the exposed beach and they climbed into a brush covered scrubland.

They had been lucky to find an overflowing trash can earlier, and had eaten their fill from the refuse left behind by the high-legged beings. Now, they all longed for sleep, their aching bodies crying out for rest. Still, Windrusher pushed them further inland until he felt they were safe. The cats had no way of knowing that they had entered Torrey Pines State Reserve. It was here the trio found a trail leading into the park and followed it into an area dense with vegetation. "In here," Windrusher said, pushing his way through the low-lying bushes.

They collapsed in exhaustion in a small clearing beneath a scrub oak. Each of them was lost in thought, reliving the great distance they had traveled during the long day and night. Blank Eyes, who had lived in cages all of her short life, should have been the most affected by their overnight trek, but, despite her exhaustion, she was exhilarated and too excited to sleep.

Her mind was ablaze with memories of their escape from the house. Vivid pictures flashed through her head: the slide down the hill; crossing the Hyskos black path and nearly being crushed by the speeding vehicle; Windrusher prodding them on, never stopping. Like a kaleidoscope of shifting images, she saw first four cats, then three, moving steadfastly away from the two Hyskos who had imprisoned them.

As she replayed the memories there was one thing that struck her: She was not a hindrance to the other two much larger and stronger male cats. She was with them every step of the way, never falling behind, never a burden. It was all so clear to her now that she was growing and changing. She absently clawed at the collar on her neck while she thought about this. It had irritated her throughout the night, chafing her neck and stinging. She pulled at it, pushing it up higher on her neck to the base of her ears, and then let it fall back.

She stared at her paw as though she hadn't seen it before, spreading the digits like an open hand, and carefully licked between each digit. She did this unconsciously, her mind still trying to come to grips with everything that had happened to them. Now I know what it's like to be a brave and free cat, she thought. Like Windrusher. He saved my life on the black path, but, who knows, one day I might save his life. Her eyes darted towards the big orange and gray cat and she continued licking her paw.

Windrusher, who had experienced many similar hardships during his long journey to find his family, seemed exhausted. With some effort, he raised his head and studied his two partners. Chaser's head was on his paws, his eyes were nearly closed and his chest rose and fell rhythmically. Blank Eyes' tail swished nervously, and the little kitten was licking her left forepaw.

"We have gone a long distance," he said quietly.

Chaser opened one eye and looked at him without speaking.

"It wasn't that far," Blank Eyes blurted out and actually jumped to her feet. "Are we almost there?"

"Almost there? It would help if we knew where *there* was," he said. "No, we're not anywhere near our homes, if that's what you mean. We will need more than the luck of Irissa-u to help us."

Chaser had opened his eyes and now joined the conversation. "We are moving in the direction of my home, but it is still many lengths from here. But not nearly as far as your home must be," he said, nodding to Windrusher. "It must be so many night globes from here that…" His voice trailed off and he looked away.

"Yes, I fear it is even farther than my first journey." He stared into the brightening eastern sky as though deciphering a message in the clouds. "I learned a few things in my travels that should help us, but it would be best to find your home first, Chaser. It is closest, and perhaps your Hyskos will help us."

"She would. I know it," Chaser said with more enthusiasm than he had shown since they left the house. Then he turned toward the kitten. "But what about you, Blank Eyes? Do you even know where your home was?"

"That's not right," the kitten said in an adamant tone, her ears flattening in a display of annoyance.

Chaser and Windrusher looked at each other then back to Blank Eyes.

"What's not right?" Windrusher said.

"He called me Blank Eyes. That's not my name. I have my own call name, and I never want to be called by that other name." She glared at the two males, as though daring them to call her Blank Eyes again.

"That's fine. I only called you that until you named yourself," Chaser said.

They stood there waiting for her to answer, but the young cat continued staring at them, her tail slapping the ground.

"Are you going to share your new name with us?" Windrusher asked.

She had spoken her mind so abruptly that it had surprised even her. Moreover, she didn't have a name, she only knew that it wasn't Blank Eyes, and she never wanted to be called that name again. Her eyes drifted away from her two traveling companions as she searched for a name to give them. She looked down at her paw, the one she had been grooming so diligently only moments before. Her spittle was still wet on her nails, catching Rahhna's early morning rays.

She held the paw up and leveled her gaze on Chaser and Windrusher. "My name is Bright Claw," she said with a flip of her head.

"Bright Claw? Yes, that's an excellent name," Windrusher said.

"Bright Claw it is," said Chaser and licked the young cat on the top of her head.

"Now that we know each other's names, I suggest we rest," Windrusher said. "It's been a long time since any of us have slept, and we'll need our strength to continue." He paused and regarded each of them for a moment. "Let us pray that Tho-hoth will bring us wisdom while we sleep. At least, we know that the two Hyskos can never find us here."

20

"Short Shank, your wisdom is always appreciated."

Windrusher had descended quickly into the core of the Inner Ear. He continued to be surprised by the uproar his appearances provoked and that Short Shank was nearly always one of the first to greet him. Surely, this cat must do nothing but sleep.

"Are you still held prisoner by the Hyskos?" the old tom asked.

He told Short Shank what had happened to him since the last time they had communicated. It was only a few day globes ago when he soared above the ground on the Hyskos flying vehicle, but it seemed to him that so much had changed in that time.

The Inner Ear was relatively quiet during his retelling, then the voices swamped him. Thousands of questions were thrown at him, opinions offered. Well-meaning expressions of dismay were mixed with tangential and irrelevant statements.

Short Shank cut through the bedlam with his deep, gravely voice. "Windrusher, my adventurous friend, it seems that you are in the land of Sobeknut, where Rahhna falls into the great waters to sleep. You may follow your instincts to avoid danger, but you know that you are far from the land of warm waters of your home?"

"My concern is keeping us safe until we find Chaser's home," Windrusher replied. If we do, then I may be able to eventually return to my own home. If not—"

"I'm familiar with the land of Sobeknut where you and the other two cats are hiding," a new voice cut in. The voice identified itself as belonging to Bent Ear, a cat that had been on its own since being abandoned by two young, male high-legged beings in the same wilderness area where Windrusher now slept. "It is a wild place filled with steep hills and treacherous paths that can toss you into the water below if you're not careful. And beyond that, if you continue to travel in the same direction, you will find more black paths filled with as many Hyskos vehicles as there are hairs on every cat's body."

"We crossed one black path that was like—"

"Whatever you saw was nothing compared to what lies ahead. Imagine if every high-legged being you've ever seen was in a vehicle on the same black path. That's what awaits you if you are fortunate enough to approach Chaser's home."

That wasn't the kind of information he had hoped to hear, but at least it was a fair warning. "Thank you, we will be careful."

After a few more questions, he found it difficult to concentrate, and felt the insistent tug of Hwrt-Heru pulling him down another path. He excused himself and departed the Akhen-et-u. His sleeping mind drifted for a time; renewing the energy and spirit that he had lost during the many hours he had been awake.

Deeper, he floated, following ancient channels until his mind was still, all concerns vanquished.

He heard the splashing sounds first. Water? Perhaps, but more solid, as though feet were tramping through a muddy field. Then he felt the pull of the mud on his feet. His feet?

Opening his eyes, Windrusher saw a bog surrounded by a thick growth of overhanging trees. Swamp grass covered the bog, and scattered through it were the rotted carcasses of unrecognizable animals. A stench of death filled the air. How did he come to be in the middle of this nightmare scene?

Humidity pressed down on him and covered his body with a greasy layer of sweat. The dense mat of intertwining branches trapped Rahhna's rays and cast a shadow of gloom over the swamp. Shaking sweat from his eyes and nostrils, he walked cautiously across the boggy surface. Muck covered each paw, and with each step there was a wet *plop* as he pulled his leg from the mire.

Mud oozed between his toes and coated his legs. Straining to keep moving, heaving his shoulders forward with each torturous step, he caught movement out of the corner of his eye. A large object passed in front of a slash of light that had cut through the tangled branches of black gums and giant tupelos.

Tho-hoth stood on a narrow islet of land thrust out of the swamp, the silvery rays playing off his broad, dark shoulders. He turned toward him, and the light caught the blood red Stone of Life. Sparks seemed to shoot from it, and Windrusher understood that he was back with the ancient god. But where was he? This was certainly not the Cave of Tho-hoth where he had first encountered the great god of wisdom.

Questions bounced in his head, but he needed to reach solid ground. To claw his way out of this swamp and… He wasn't moving forward any more. The ooze had reached his belly and he was having difficulty lifting his legs. It felt as though the muck had hardened around each leg, and a fist was grasping his limbs and pulling him down.

"Tho-hoth," he cried in panic. "Help me."

Tho-hoth raised his shaggy head, and Windrusher saw the fine white tufts of hair in the great god's ears quiver with the movement. His tongue shot out and seemed to taste the air before retreating.

Had he heard him? Surely he could see him struggling, sinking deeper and deeper in the bog. Why didn't he save him? Then he remembered that this was only a dream. A very real dream, but it wasn't possible that he was actually in a swamp with Tho-hoth looking on as he was about to disappear in the muck and mud. Yet, what if it was real?

"Windrusher." The sound of his name washed over him and through him. The deep voice of Tho-hoth was a revelation that moved him even more than it had the first time he heard it. "Windrusher, you have done well to escape the perils of the Hyskos home. But more remains to be accomplished." Tho-hoth paused and looked away.

The murky water had reached Windrusher's chin, and he was struggling to keep his head up. He was closer to the spit of land where Tho-hoth stood, but he wasn't sure he would make it. A loud splash behind him sent a shiver coursing through his body. Even if he could, he didn't want to turn around and see what caused the splash.

"You must remain vigilant, Windrusher. Recall what I said. *The fate of others will depend on you.* Prepare yourself for the danger that will soon be upon you. And even when you believe you have survived the worst of it, remember that danger is always with you."

Slimy muck, smelling of sulfur and long-dead creatures, oozed into the corner of his mouth. He craned his neck, spitting out mud and gasping for air. "But how can I…" The blackness covered his nose.

"The answer is there, but you must beware of the…"

21

As Captain Mendez promised, there was a squad car and a team of officers waiting for them when they arrived at the San Diego Police Department's Northern Division office. Quint shook hands with the two officers, a personable young man named Lawson who obviously did some serious weight training, and an equally young Latina, Officer Torres, with a somber face and skeptical eyes.

After introducing Amy and Kimmy Tremble, he reviewed the situation beginning with the disappearance of Tony from his Florida yard. He caught the exchange of glances between the two officers when he mentioned that Tony was a high-profile cat who had received a lot of press after apparently finding his way from Connecticut to Florida. He ignored it and told them how he had traced Runyan McWaters to San Diego and later spotted him in the backyard of the house on the bluff.

"And that's where you come in."

"Captain Mendez explained that you wanted us to pay a visit and inquire if they know anything about the missing cat. Is that right?" Lawson asked.

"We don't have a warrant, of course, but I thought that if we showed up and brandished the colors," he nodded toward the two officers with a quick smile, "they might be inclined to invite us in to look around."

"And if they don't?" This was Torres, eying him as though sizing him up for a pair of handcuffs.

He shrugged. "We're not talking about a capital offense here. But we're hoping to learn something even if they don't let us in. Maybe they'll give enough away that we'll be able to obtain a warrant to search the house." He paused and waited for the two officers to speak. When they didn't, he continued.

"I don't know what the penalty is for transporting stolen property across state lines, but maybe you can lean on this guy enough to put a scare into him."

Lawson and Torres exchanged looks again before Lawson said, "What do you know about the owner of the house?"

"Not much. It's a big house sitting alone on a bluff on what has to be very pricy real estate. From what I pulled off the Internet, he's a former physicist who sold his high-tech company for millions. Now retired and doing….." He held out a hand palm up and gave them a *who knows* look. "His name is Karl von Rothmann, and he apparently likes cats. That's about it."

Amy opened her mouth as though to speak, but closed it again. Quint noticed the lines appear on her forehead and a slight tightening of her jaw. She was obviously taking this hard. Of course, her sister was on her mind, too. That didn't help matters. Amy had told him about it on the way to meet Torres and Lawson.

"Okay, here's the way it's going down. We're in charge, and you let us do all the talking." Torres gave him another hard look. "You understand?"

"That's fine with me. I'm just along for the ride. You may want to introduce Mrs. Tremble and Kimmy and explain that their cat was stolen and—"

"We're not rookies," Lawson cut him off. "Don't you think we know what we're doing?"

Quint held his palms up and backed off.

Amy spoke up. "I want to tell him that we won't press charges, we just want Tony back with us."

"Hmm," Lawson scratched his chin, as if mulling this last statement. "I'm not sure that's a good idea, Mrs. Tremble. But let's see how it works out." He turned back to Quint. "If he lets us look around and we don't find anything, then we end up with egg on our face. A cat's not very big and he could hide it anywhere."

"If he has it at all," Torres added.

Quint smiled at the two uniforms. He eyed Lawson's bulging biceps under his tight short-sleeve shirt, and thought that he would hate to go up against him mano y mano. "Like you said, let's see how it works out."

The sun had only been up for a few hours when McWaters entered Torrey Pines State Reserve. He paid his four dollar parking fee and found a space in the nearly empty lot. Getting out of the car, he noticed the sign with its list of *no-no's*: No smoking or fires; No dogs or horses; No picnics; No bicycles or motorcycles.

He smiled and noted that there was nothing in the list of prohibitions about the taking of cats. A cool breeze blew through the parking lot, and he was glad he had brought a windbreaker with him. He knew that it would heat up nicely as the sun climbed, but he hoped that he wouldn't be here that long. Reaching into the car, he pulled out three pillow cases and stuffed them under his jacket. Then he patted his right pocket and felt the reassuring rigidity of the Buck knife. He had carried the law enforcement model folding knife since his days in Chicago, and it had never let him down. It weighed less than six ounces and had a four-inch blade that he could open with one hand with a flick of his wrist.

He pulled the GPS device from his pocket and quickly scanned the three screens. All of the cats were together in virtually the same place. They had been there for the past hour, and he assumed they were asleep. He hiked down the closest trail until he was about a hundred yards from the cats.

He hoped he had better luck with these three than he did with Katmandu. The old man certainly wasn't pleased when he showed him Katmandu's collar. Von Rothmann had held the collar between his thumb and index finger, and raised it up close to eye level. His middle finger seemed to caress the underside of the collar, and he eyed it through half-closed lids like it was a long lost family heirloom.

"And there was no sign of the cat anywhere near the collar?"

"Like I said, there was nothing around, but I heard a coyote and it was close enough to raise the hairs on the back of my neck. It could have carried the cat away."

Von Rothmann shook his head very slowly. "I think we would have found blood or fur or something that indicated that poor Katmandu had come to a violent end."

"Not necessarily. She probably lost the collar while they were struggling and then the coyote carried the cat somewhere else for the dinner party." He didn't understand why they were spending so much time on this cat. He said he wanted the cat back or to make sure the cat never returned to its old home. Mission accomplished. There was no way this cat was going anywhere, unless cats really do have nine lives.

Von Rothmann turned his malevolent gaze fully on him. "You've lost me one of my precious cats, Mr. McWaters. I do hope you have better luck with the others." He stood and stepped menacingly toward McWaters.

"I meant what I said. Bring me back Tony and the other cats. The only two options I'll accept is that our feline friends have joined their Persian companion in the afterlife, or…" he paused dramatically and stuck a fleshy finger into his chest, "or that you are no longer among the living."

22

LAWSON AND TORRES STOOD side by side on the top step of the portico. Lawson hitched his belt and rose up on the balls of his feet several times as though preparing to leap through the door. Torres stood impassively. They had rung von Rothmann's doorbell three times in the last ninety seconds. Torres looked back toward Amy, Kimmy, and Quint who stood watching them from the walkway.

"Doesn't look like anyone's home," Torres said.

"It's a big house," Quint answered, craning his neck to stare at the massive glass wall that formed one side of the house. "If he's in the back or down in the basement it would take him some time to get here. Give him a few more minutes."

Kimmy tightened her grip on her mother's hand and gave her a nervous smile. "I hope Tony's here, don't you, Mom?"

Amy nodded and put an arm around her daughter. They had come such a long way, and the girl had been upbeat the entire time, convinced they were going to find Tony and take him home. Of course, twelve-year-olds have every reason to be optimistic, to expect the best in life. She hoped that this was one of those times when her expectations were fulfilled, and her daughter wouldn't have to learn a cruel lesson about the realities of life.

Her mind was a jumble of thoughts, like a collapsed wall of dominos. Maybe she should have let Quint handle the whole thing. At least then, she would have been free to be with her sister in Connecticut.

"Knock on the door." It was Quint, now displaying as much impatience as the rest of them.

Lawson shrugged and made a fist with his right hand. As he raised it, the door swung open away from them.

"Can I help you?"

The two police officers effectively blocked the doorway and Amy couldn't see the person speaking from where she was. She stepped forward onto the first step to get a better view, but Quint grabbed her arm and pulled her back. He shook his head at her and gave her a look that she took to mean *not yet, let the police handle it.*

"Yes sir. I'm Officer Lawson of the San Diego Police Department and this is Officer Torres. Are you Karl von Rothmann?"

"Yes. Yes, I am. Is anything wrong?"

"Well, we're not sure, sir, but we'd like to ask you a few questions about a missing…a missing item of personal property."

"And you believe I can help you locate this… uhmm… item of personal property?"

"It's possible," Torres said. "Certain evidence suggests that this property may have been brought to your home." Torres let her eyes slide away from von Rothmann and toward her partner.

"I see," von Rothmann said. "Can you tell me what exactly it is you're looking for and maybe I can be of help?"

"It's a cat, sir," Torres said. "A cat named Tony, to be exact. Tony was allegedly stolen from his home in Florida and flown here by a man named…" She flipped a page on her notebook. "Runyan McWaters. Does that name mean anything to you?"

"Oh dear," von Rothmann said, his ruddy face turning a shade darker.

Both of the police were staring at the red haired man in the doorway. "Do you know him, sir?" Lawson asked with a hard edge to his voice.

"He used to work for me, but I had to fire him. Found out he was stealing from me." He shook his head as though it had pained him greatly, although it wasn't clear if it was because he fired him or because McWaters had stolen from him.

"Mr. von Rothmann, do you have a cat in your house?" Torres took a half step toward the door as she asked the question.

"No, not now. I'm sorry, where are my manners? Would you like to come in?"

"If we may, sir," Lawson said and stepped to one side on the large portico so that von Rothmann could see the other three people below them. "Let me introduce you to Mrs. Tremble and her daughter Kimmy. They're the owners of the missing cat. And Mr. Mitchell, who is helping them locate Tony."

Von Rothmann stepped between the two uniformed police and smiled down at them as though they were guests arriving for a holiday party. "Please, all of you, come in. I seldom have any company these days."

He stepped aside as the two officers walked in followed by Quint and then Kimmy. Amy had pushed her daughter ahead of her so she would be the last one through the door. She searched his face with questioning eyes then quickly looked away and stepped into the foyer. She felt a touch on her arm and looked up. Von Rothmann had turned his back to the others waiting in the foyer and was leaning in toward her. His voice was nearly inaudible, and she was sure no one else heard his words: "So nice to see you again, Amy."

Von Rothmann turned to the five people standing in a foyer the size of an office building's lobby. "Please, come in," he said, leading the way around a cypress and mahogany partition to a seating area in front of the vast expanse of windows. He pointed at the angular, leather-covered chairs and sat down.

The look on her face was incredible, he thought. He took her totally by surprise, although he couldn't believe that she would have come all this way and had no idea of who lived here. And how did they trace Tony to his house? McWaters was obviously not the consummate professional he liked to think that he was. Another thought flitted through his mind. *Maybe I should thank him for letting the cats escape. If they were here when the police arrived I wouldn't have been able to invite them in, and how would that look?*

"You were saying that Mr. McWaters used to work for you."

"That's right, Officer...I'm sorry, I've forgotten your name."

"It's Lawson, sir. And this is Officer Torres."

"Yes, thank you. Well, Mr. McWaters was my security chief before I sold my company, and I kept him with me as a personal aide. Help me run the house, that sort of thing."

"And he stayed here?"

"Yes, he had a room, but he was out a lot. And now he's gone."

"Tell us why you fired him," Officer Torres asked.

"As I said, I caught the man stealing from me. I trusted him to pay bills, make household purchases, but he got too greedy and was putting a lot of it in his pocket." He paused and made eye contact with each of them in turn, stopping at Amy last. "It wasn't the money. I'm a very wealthy man, and I won't miss it. It's the lack of integrity, I can't abide."

"When you were asked if you had a cat here, you said—" Quint began before being cut off by Lawson.

"You said that you no longer had a cat in the house, is that right?" He gave Quint a look that even von Rothmann recognized as a reprimand. There were territorial rights at work here.

He nodded affirmatively at the officer. "Mr. McWaters went away for a few days, said he had some personal errands to take care of, and when he came back he had this rather handsome cat with him. I didn't mind, in fact I am planning to open a shelter to house some of the poor abandoned and homeless cats in our community."

Torres looked up from her notebook where she had been writing notes as he spoke. "A shelter?"

"Yes, a shelter. As I mentioned, I have a great deal of money and no one to spend it on. I'm quite a compassionate person and when I learned that nearly six million unwanted cats are put down each year, I felt I had to do something." He made a gesture with his hand indicating that it wasn't much but at least he was doing something.

"So, I formed a non-profit corporation to help pay for spay-neuter procedures, assist organizations that are trying to find homes for our feline friends, and I'll use a part of my home to temporarily house some of these cats until they find more permanent homes." He glanced at Amy again. "I call it the Bluto Foundation. Very childish, I know, but it's named after a pet I knew many years ago that meant a great deal to me."

"That's very good of you, Mr. von Rothmann. Tell me, was this cat that McWaters brought home named Tony, by any chance?" Officer Lawson asked.

He was quiet for a moment. He looked at the muscle-bound policeman and said, "No, he called him Buster, I think. Not very original, is it?"

"Didn't you think it was strange when he showed up with this cat?" Torres followed up.

"Not really. He knew about the foundation, and even helped me set up the shelter. He said the cat was a stray he picked up, and it could be the first one to use our shelter. I'll be happy to show it to you before you leave, if you'd like."

"Yes, we'd like that," Lawson said.

Quint pulled a folded sheet of paper from his pocket. "Did the cat look like this?" he asked and started to hand it to von Rothmann, but passed it to Lawson instead when he caught the look the young policeman gave him.

Lawson unfolded it, glanced at it and handed it to von Rothmann. He took the color copy of Tony and held it at arms length. Squinting at the picture, he tilted it to the left, then the right before giving it back to Lawson. "It could be. The coloring's right, but I can't be sure."

"And McWaters took the cat with him when he left?" Torres asked.

"That's right. I guess he became attached to the poor thing. That happens, doesn't it," he said looking at the girl.

Lawson stood up. "Can we take a look at the house, now?"

"Certainly, I have nothing to hide."

He showed them his basement laboratory first, explaining that he still conducted research on nanoparticle dispersion, which he described in highly technical terms. It was clear that they had no idea what he was talking about.

Upstairs, they went from room to room taking in everything, occasionally asking him to open a closed door. Finally, they came to the large room with the glass wall and the tree growing inside. "And this is my cat shelter," he said proudly. "As you can see, everything is ready. All we need are the cats. But there's no shortage of cats, is there?"

He turned his back on the room and began walking toward the

front of the house. "I'm sorry that you didn't show up yesterday, before Mr. McWaters left with the cat," he said without turning around to see if they were following him.

In the foyer, he opened the door and held it open for them. "I'll be sure to get in touch if Mr. McWaters shows up here again, but I don't think that will happen. He left in quite a huff."

Lawson handed him a card. "If you think of anything, please call."

"Of course. You know, he's originally from Chicago, and still has a sister there, I believe. He might have gone back."

They thanked him for his time and said good bye. Before closing the door, he nodded toward Kimmy. "Young lady, I certainly hope you find your kitty. I can't imagine how much you must miss him."

23

THE TWO POLICE OFFICERS had left them after a cursory conversation in which they said they would keep the file active in case McWaters or the cat showed up. By the looks on their faces, Amy saw that they had already moved on and put this behind them.

Quint was driving them back to the hotel. Kimmy in the back seat, her arms folded, eyes closed. She sat up front with Mitchell staring out the window as he offered them his perspective on the situation. "It's obvious this guy is lying. He said they had set up that room to take in unwanted cats—the Bluto Foundation—who's going to believe that?"

She didn't answer. She was still in a state of shock from seeing Karl von Rothmann after all these years. What did this maniac want from her? Was it all some kind of sick game he was playing? Would he actually steal Tony to get back at her for some perceived slight from…what was it…twenty-five years ago?

Her mind was reeling and she recalled the first time she met von Rothmann. He was a graduate student at MIT and she was in her final year at the UMass Boston College of Nursing. She and a few girlfriends from the School of Nursing were eating breakfast at an all-night diner after a marathon study session for their mid-terms.

At a nearby booth, three older male students sat drinking coffee. Two of them were talking loudly, obviously trying to be noticed, the third was busy writing in a notebook that was stuffed with scraps of paper. Tania, Amy's former roommate, turned to look at them and waved. Turning back, she bent toward Amy and whispered, "That's the guy I told you about, Jack, the MIT graduate student. Very smart, and good looking, isn't he?"

"What are they doing here?" she asked.

"Jack's parents have a big house nearby," Tania answered, "and they're in Europe this summer. So…" Her voice trailed off and she blushed. "I guess he brought his roommates with him this time."

Amy looked at the three men, not sure which one Tania was referring to. One of them smiled at her and waved, the other gave him a shove on the shoulder and giggled. Did he actually giggle? These couldn't be MIT students. They were both pretty good looking guys, and she assumed that the one that waved was Jack. Then she noticed the third man in the booth. He had his head down, and was writing in a notebook that was perched precariously on a stack of text books. It didn't look as though he even noticed his two companions were there, much less the girls in the booth next to them.

He had a full head of rusty-colored hair, and just as she was thinking that she'd like to see what his face looked like he glanced up and caught her eye. His face was round and smooth, slightly ruddy to match his hair. He immediately looked down at his notebook. Jack got up and approached the three nursing students. He said hello to Tania, who introduced him to Amy and Eileen, Tania's current roommate.

Jack slipped into the booth next to Tania and gestured to the other student who had been watching them expectantly. Jack introduced his friend, Gary something, and tossed an arm toward the solitary figure sitting alone in the booth. He lowered his voice and winked at the three girls. "That stooge over there is Karl von Rothmann. He's a bit of a weird duck."

Gary something, who was standing next to Amy, cackled and said, "As if you're not."

"No, I mean it," Jack replied. "He's all brains and not much else. Shares a room with my geeky friend here who is about to flunk his Fluid Physics course. Karl aced it, like he does everything, so Gary is paying the guy to get him through the mid-terms."

They all turned to look at von Rothmann, who seemed to be oblivious to everything except whatever he was writing in his notebook. Amy had always been impressed by men with brains and she instantly felt sorry for this outcast. Eileen bumped her knee and she turned back to see that Gary was trying to squeeze into the booth with the two of them.

"Wait," she said, "there's not enough room for all three of us here." She slid out of the booth and walked to the next booth. Karl hadn't noticed her or was pretending not to. "Do you mind if I sit down? Your friends seem to have pushed me out."

He finally looked up from his notebook and Amy saw the remoteness in his eyes soften and his mouth attempting to shape itself into a smile. She realized he was painfully shy, and again felt sorry for him, imagining a boy growing up looking like he did, having to shoulder the double curse of superior intelligence and no social skills. Had to be tough on him.

The memories of the few weeks she had spent being a friend to Karl flashed back to her. She realized that he had put more importance on their few dates than she had. He was so quiet, so tense, as though he had never been with a girl before. And he probably never had. She didn't want to hurt his feelings since she was his only friend, and even invited him to her apartment once where she made them macaroni and cheese and he attempted to explain Bernoulli's theorem to her.

It was at that dinner that she introduced him to the pet she had brought with her from home, an enormous tabby cat she had named Bluto after the character in the Popeye cartoons. How obvious could he be? She could tell that he hadn't really liked her cat, although he grinned at it and tentatively stuck a finger out like he thought the cat might take it off at the first knuckle.

She remembered how uncomfortable she'd been throughout that evening and had made up her mind to let him down gently. As he said goodnight to her in the doorway, he awkwardly kissed her, a glancing kiss that skipped across her nose onto her lips. She was so surprised she didn't have time to react before he was out the door and down the steps.

"What do you think, Amy? You haven't said a word." It was Quint yanking her back to the present.

"I'm sorry. This has been so confusing that I don't know what to think." She turned to look at Kimmy. "Honey, I'm so sorry we didn't find Tony, but don't give up, I just know he's somewhere close by."

Kimmy gave her a nod and a half-hearted smile, but said nothing.

"I agree with you, Quint, von Rothmann is lying to us. McWaters must have been acting on von Rothmann's orders."

"That's how I see it. The only question is why."

She didn't answer, letting her eyes stray to the side of the road and her mind back to the memories of twenty-five years ago.

She had told Karl that she had a boyfriend back home and was sorry, but she didn't think they should see each other again. She remembered that they were in the same diner where they had originally met. He was sitting across from her, both hands on the table, the omnipresent stack of books next to him. He didn't respond to her statement, but looked down at his hands, which he held tightly as though he feared what they might do. When he looked at her, she saw that his face had reddened considerably and that there was moisture in the corner of one eye.

She was moved by his pain and put a hand on his arm, but he jerked away. Those eyes that had reflected human emotion only moments before became cold and lifeless, like she was looking into the eyes of a snake. He grabbed his books and left without saying a word.

That wasn't the last time she had seen Karl von Rothmann. She saw him once lurking outside her apartment building. It was late; she had just returned from the hospital where she was interning and parked across the street. She took two steps toward the four-story walk-up when she remembered the bag of groceries in the back seat. Turning, she caught a glimpse of a figure ducking into an alley. Later she told herself that it was dark and it could have been anyone. But there was a nearby street light, and in the glow it seemed to her that whoever it was had red hair.

Then there was the time, shortly before she graduated, that she came back to her apartment and had an eerie sensation that someone had been there. It was nothing that she could put her finger on. Nothing had been moved or was missing, that she noticed, but still something hung in the air that didn't feel right.

It spooked her enough to have a chain lock installed on her door, and she pushed a chair under the handle each night before she went to bed. It wasn't until later, after she'd graduated and she was packing to move, that she found the cross missing. The small silver cross had been her grandmother's, and she kept it in the jewelry box with a few other pieces, some of which were much more valuable. Amy searched everywhere, but never found it.

Back at the hotel, Quint discussed the possible options. "I know this is adding up to more than you expected to pay, so we can either wrap it up and let the San Diego police handle it, or I can give it another couple of days and see if we catch a break. Either way, you and Kimmy might want to fly back to Florida."

She wanted to tell Quint about von Rothmann, but it didn't make any sense to her, and if she didn't understand it, then Quint would think she was as crazy as von Rothmann. She trusted Quint, but she thought she might be able to use their past relationship to convince von Rothmann to give up Tony. No, she couldn't take a chance on Tony getting hurt. She'd tell Quint everything—after she spoke with von Rothmann.

"Quint, don't worry about the money. You stay on the case and find Tony for us. I have to believe that we're very close." She put an arm around her daughter and pulled her against her. "Kimmy and I will stay here for a few more days and then we'll go home—with Tony."

24

WINDRUSHER AWOKE from the dream with a start. He stared wildly at the brush around him, expecting to find himself up to his ears in oozing slime, the muck forcing its way into his nostrils and mouth. Instead, he was curled up on a sandy patch of dirt in the midst of a thicket of windswept brush.

He pushed himself up on his front legs and thanked whatever gods had saved him from drowning in that murky bog. He saw the two other cats and remembered where they were. But what was he to make of the dream? Tho-hoth had given him another warning that sounded even more ominous than the last one. It seemed to mean that there was danger everywhere. Maybe even here. The first two dreams had taken him to the Cave of Tho-hoth, but this one was different. He had been in a fetid swamp, sinking below the surface. What did it all mean?

He scratched at a nagging itch near his right ear, trying to recall Tho-hoth's last words. *Even when you believe you have survived the worst of it, remember that danger is always with you.*

And he remembered that Tho-hoth had a last warning to beware, but beware of what? His tail swished spasmodically reflecting his frustrations. He had to believe Tho-hoth's warning. They were still not safe, and that meant they had to keep moving.

Rising on all four legs, he stretched as well as he could in the confined space and sniffed the clean, crisp morning air. Rahhna's rays were strong, piercing through the bushes, and the sky above was clear except for wisps of white clouds. The temperature was cool, but not uncomfortable, and he thought that this was going to a good day to travel.

Chaser, who was rolled into a ball, his head tucked along his body with his legs crossed to form an x, opened his eyes. He rolled over against Bright Claw and both of them struggled to their feet, stretching and yawning. "It's not as soft as the pillows we had in the Hyskos house, but I've slept in worse places," Chaser said, giving the little cat a friendly lick along her neck.

Bright Claw responded with a loud purr and head butt to Chaser's ample belly. "I slept like a kitten with—"

They all heard the snapping of the twig and froze. Windrusher's nose caught a strong scent and immediately knew that the noisy high-legged being was nearby. It didn't seem possible that he could track them all this distance, but somehow he had. Was this the danger that Tho-hoth had warned him about?

Without another sound, he burrowed through the bushes and the others followed behind him. He pushed between the scrub oak and weeds until he found a narrow trail and increased his speed. Behind him he heard the unmistakable sounds of the Hyskos male crashing through the brush.

"Hurry," he shouted over his shoulder. "The Hyskos is right behind us. We may have to scatter and go in different directions. Surely, he can't track all of us."

Bright Claw and Chaser were on his tail as they cut one way on the rocky soil and then another. They broke through the undergrowth and found themselves on a well-worn trail winding through a grove of pines. Windrusher followed the trail around a bend, and saw it rising steeper in the distance. There was space to run at top speed here, and he was accelerating when he heard Chaser's cry.

Wind turned to see the Hyskos man bent over, struggling to hold Chaser. He had him by the neck, and the large marmalade was fighting, trying to twist out of the man's grasp. Windrusher growled and stepped forward, about to throw himself against the high-legged being. Another sound stopped him before he had taken two steps. It was the Hyskos screaming as he released Chaser and grabbed his hand.

That's when he saw Bright Claw, clinging to the man's wrist, drop to the ground and run off. Chaser was nowhere to be seen either, and he decided that it was past time for him to disappear, as well.

The cat bit him. McWaters couldn't believe it. He squeezed his wrist and a few drops of blood popped to the surface. The puncture wounds weren't very deep, but he knew he would have to get it tended to when he got back. Cat bites, he'd heard, could lead to nasty infections.

He wiped away the blood and pulled out the GPS receiver. Now, he had to track them down again, and he was getting tired of this game. He switched over to Tony's screen. It's you and me, big boy, he thought. The other two can run into the ocean for all I care, but you are coming back with me—one way or the other.

The circle on the screen was moving steadily away from him. He pulled the sheet of paper out of his back pocket and unfolded it. It was a map of the various trails in Torrey Pines State Reserve that he had taken from the rack in the parking lot. He studied the wavy lines that marked the six trails, then the GPS screen, then back again. It looked like the cat was following the Razor Point Trail. McWaters had been here before and knew that it was a winding, picturesque climb ending at Razor Point, a steep bluff overlooking the eroded badlands. He also knew it was a dead end.

The bite on his wrist was beginning to throb and he sucked at the wound. Someone was going to pay for this, he thought, patting the Buck knife in his jacket pocket. And it might have to be Tony. He consulted the receiver once more to be sure he was still moving along the same trail, and then began trotting after him.

Fear and desperation pumped through Windrusher, and he ran for his life up the steep trail. Plants and trees rushed by in a frenzied blur. Manzanita and mountain mahogany, deer weed and bladderpod. To Windrusher, they were only flashes of green and brown but he smelled the pungent odors of the plants as he whipped past.

He was focused on only one thing—putting as much distance between the high-legged being and himself as possible. An image of

Bright Claw hanging from the man's wrist slid into his mind and he felt a surge of pride and incredulousness that this Wetlos kitten had come to Chaser's defense.

Ahead of him, he saw another path intersecting and made a running turn onto the sandy trail. He followed it into a dark tunnel of overhanging bushes and stopped, his chest heaving, tongue lolling like a floppy-eared snouter. His sensitive ears swiveled to hear any sounds from behind him, his nose sniffed for the man's scent.

For a moment, he thought he had finally lost the Hyskos, but then he heard those insistent footsteps thudding along the trail again. It seemed impossible that he had found them after they traveled so far from the house, but even now, running through the thick undergrowth, he stayed right behind him as though he was leaving an invisible trail.

Digging deeper into his reserves of energy, he ran through the tunnel of bushes, accelerating as the path opened up again. He needed to find someplace to hide. Someplace where this Hyskos couldn't find him. Even as he ran, he heard footfalls behind him and the sounds of someone pushing through the bushes.

Windrusher turned abruptly as the trail switched back, passed over a little wooden bridge onto a rugged landscape with low-lying plants and dead trees. He decided that he was making it too easy for the man to follow him and cut to his left, through a cluster of laurel sumac and yucca.

A bleached skeleton of a dead tree rose before him, ghostly branches reaching out with splintery fingers. At the base of the tree was a small mound of twisted branches, weathered and shining in the bright sunlight. The gnarled branches were intertwined like silver worms, but he burrowed into them, hoping that the sharp branches might deter a tender-skinned Hyskos. Of course, with any luck, he would never suspect that he was hiding there.

The point of one branch poked him in the side, but Windrusher remained motionless, holding his breath and trying to still the pounding of his heart. His right ear fluttered as though it had a life of its own, and he felt an infuriating tickle that moved from the inside tip down into the center. He realized that something was crawling in his ear.

Windrusher remained silent. It took a mighty effort to combat the urge to claw at his ear, possibly upsetting the dead limbs balanced on his back. In the distance, he heard the padding of footsteps moving closer. The insect was still moving along the delicate tissues of his inner ear. Whatever it was had more legs than a cat, and it felt as though each of its legs was stroking the sensitive hairs on the inside of his ear.

He tried to put the insect out of his mind and concentrated on the footsteps. They were much louder now, very near, and he wondered how fast he could escape from this twisted pile of sticks if the Hyskos came for him. A puzzling silence surrounded him, and he realized that the footsteps had stopped. The only sounds he heard were the breeze rustling through the bushes and a bird calling for its mate from the branches of the dead tree. He tensed his thigh muscles, prepared to run for his life once again. Instead, the footsteps started to move away from him.

The Hyskos was leaving. He waited quietly, listening to the sound of the footfalls receding into the distance until the only sounds were his own shallow breathing. After he felt it was safe to leave his splintery lair, he poked his nose tentatively through the branches and sniffed the air. He was finally alone. Easing his way out from under the gnarled branches, he surveyed the empty trail, staring back in the direction he heard the footsteps retreating, and turned and ran the other way.

Steel cables running through posts lined each side of the path, dangerously close to the edges of steep, rocky bluffs. He followed the well-worn trail past a signpost with an arrow that said *Razor Point*. He couldn't read the sign, but he scurried off in the direction of the arrow. A direction he hoped offered safety and protection from the relentless Hyskos intent on finding him.

McWaters knew exactly where the big orange and gray cat was hiding. He stood on the path, the GPS device in his hand, and studied the tangled heap of bleached branches. They looked like old bones, twisted and curling under the weather after countless years. Their sharp tips reached out to the dead tree as though reminding it that they were once a single living entity.

He wasn't about to go thrashing through that snaggle of pointed sticks or risk another cat bite. If that brainless little clone of a cat could chomp on his hand the way it did, he knew what Tony's big teeth would do to him. No, there was a better way. Let the cat think he was gone and continue on his way to Razor Point. Once there, he'd have no place to run, except to him.

25

THE RAZOR POINT TRAIL WEAVED through scrublands toward crumbling slopes of eroded sandstone. Windrusher scurried along the sandy trail. Ahead of him was a wooden observation deck that overlooked the red-hued coastal bluffs.

At the end of the trail, he stepped on to the wooden deck jutting over the rugged beach. He stopped and studied the sandy trail behind him. It was clear and he heard nothing out of the ordinary. Finally, the high-legged being was gone. He could only hope that Chaser and Bright Claw were as fortunate and hadn't been captured by the tenacious Hyskos.

For the first time, he noticed his surroundings. The day globe was not yet to its highest point, and its sharp rays intersected with the surging waves below. His eyes traced the rock-strewn shore and drifted out to sea. Each of the waves seemed to explode with flashes of light from Rahhna's rays. It was a beautiful sight, and, sucking in the clean salt air, he felt momentarily at peace.

But only momentarily. He walked to the narrow t-shaped overlook flanked on each side by wooden planks. A deep gorge covered with angular boulders dropped away on either side of the overlook. It was a cold and frightening drop and he instinctively stepped back.

He closed his eyes and Kimmy's face appeared, and he heard her soft voice calling his name. Where was his female Hyskos, was she looking for him? He had only been gone for a short time, but he realized now how much he missed his old life, how much he wanted to be back with that Hyskos family. The loud cries of a seagull soaring overhead broke through his daydream. He had to find his way back to that family, and he wasn't going to do it sitting here.

There was only one way down from the overlook, and it was the same way he had arrived. He padded across the deck to the trail. Walking carefully along the steep path, so intent on where he placed each paw, he didn't see the Hyskos until he nearly stepped on his shoe.

McWaters straddled the narrow trail, blocking the cat's escape. He was sure that cats couldn't think, certainly not like people do, but he could swear he recognized a flash of surprise in Tony's eyes. It was almost funny to watch the fear and panic in those green eyes and then see him turn tail and run back to the wooden overlook. He was so excited about finally finishing this job that he hardly noticed the throbbing in his wrist. With each step, the sun glinted off the four-inch blade of the open knife he clutched behind his back.

The cat backed away from him, moving to the middle of the fenced overlook. McWaters licked his lips and smiled warmly at the cat. "Tony, you poor thing. I'm so sorry you had to spend the night outside," he said. His voice was low and compelling, reaching out to soothe and sway his listener.

He moved slowly toward Tony, who stood stiffly, staring up at him. When the cat stepped back, he stopped and leaned toward him, his right hand still behind his back. "You must be so tired and hungry. Let me take you back home and feed you. Mr. von Rothmann misses you deeply and was hurt when you left him." He took another step forward, a broad smile on his face, his left hand out in a gesture of friendship.

Tony edged away, his rump nearly touching the lowest plank of the protective rails. He moved to his right and McWaters moved with him, closing the distance between them by another step. He kept his voice friendly, his body language neutral, but made sure he blocked the exit.

"This is a wild and beautiful place, isn't it?" He made a small gesture toward the breaking waves and looked down at the beach. Below him, he saw a young man carrying a bright yellow kayak on his head.

Turning back to Tony, he said, "I guess if you have to spend the night somewhere, this is as good a place as any. But surely you miss the comforts of home and the companionship of your friends."

He was less than a yard from Tony and squatted, keeping the incandescent smile on his face and his finger pointing out at the cat. There was no doubt that the cat was buying his act. Its tail was down and he was staring at him with what McWaters interpreted as trust, sniffing his finger then backing up again.

"That's right, my beauty. Remember when you and I met back there in the Florida sun? I only wanted what was best for you then, to take you where you would be treated like the heroic cat that you are." The sun was overhead now, casting a shadow at his feet. He was careful to keep his right hand tucked behind him, and he waited for Tony to take another step forward. He felt a sharp stitch in his right calf, and eased himself upright to straighten the leg and put some weight on it. The pain receded and he bent over again, smiling his Hollywood smile.

"What if I can talk Mr. von Rothmann into letting me take you back to your Kimmy in Florida?"

The cat's ears perked up when he said "Kimmy," and he continued, his voice consoling as though he were comforting someone who had suffered a painful loss. "Kimmy must be very sad, don't you think? She misses you, and I know that you miss her, so why don't we do the right thing and get you two back together again."

He moved a step closer to Tony. Just a little closer, he thought. Take another step and I'll have you by your furry neck before you know what hit you. And if you don't cooperate, then von Rothmann will have to be satisfied with your head in his trophy case.

As if sensing his intentions, Tony slid under the lower rail and onto the narrow ledge surrounding the overlook. Before McWaters could react, Tony was running along the outside edge of the wooden deck and was back on the trail.

"Tony, why are you running from me," he yelled out, a note of hurt and disappointment in his voice.

The cat stopped and made eye contact with him, and McWaters thought he sensed indecision in Tony's green eyes. Tony turned back toward the trail and took several hesitant steps away from the overlook, hugging the edge of the path close to the protective cables.

"Please, Tony, I only want to help you. Don't run away." McWaters said plaintively. Tony stopped again and McWaters thought he had another chance to win the cat's trust.

He slowly approached Tony until he was within two feet. The cat watched him warily, his tail swishing nervously, but he didn't run. That was the important thing; he didn't run. He had stopped at a bend in the trail with prickly pear cactus growing on both sides and stood looking up at him.

"I know you're frightened, Tony, but you have to trust me." McWaters was smiling again, his voice low and confident. "Look at me. I'm your friend and only want to help you." He squatted again, his hand just inches from Tony who began meowing softly. His index finger gently caressed the cat's nose and he edged forward so that he was just able to reach the top of Tony's head. The wrenching pain grabbed his calf again, but he bit on his cheek and sucked in a mouthful of air, waiting for it to pass. He scratched Tony's head and was rewarded by a low purr that bubbled up from deep inside the cat.

"You do trust me, don't you, Tony? You and I are old friends, and old friends may have their disagreements from time to time, but it's all about trust." He gripped the knife tighter with his right hand. With his left, he stroked the cat's neck, and he thought that it was too bad this creature was so trusting.

The cat lifted his head and stared into McWaters' eyes. He saw the trust there, the longing to be taken home and fed and pampered like the spoiled cat he was. It was time to act while he still had his trust. He lunged out with both arms, his left grasping for the cat's neck, the right brandishing the deadly blade.

It should have been so easy, but when he reached out, the cat wasn't there. It had jumped not away from him, but toward him, clawing three deep ruts in his forearm and running through his outspread legs. He jerked back in shock. "Christ," he screamed, grabbing his forearm and feeling the slick dampness of blood on his hand.

"You're a sneaky underhanded animal, Tony," he growled menacingly at the cat who was watching him warily. The knife was in front of him about waist high and he moved it slowly in small circles.

"And now you've made me mad."

Still squatting, he tried to stand, and a stabbing pain bit deeply into his calf. Gasping in agony, he rose tenderly to his feet, his forearm bleeding, the searing cramp in his calf growing more intense by the second.

"No. You're not getting away with this, you malicious creature." He was screaming madly at the cat, but somewhere in his head he knew he was also screaming at his cramp. He lurched toward Tony, each step driving hot spears through his leg.

Tony had edged away from him to the other side of the path, his back near the low steel cable that curved sharply around the bend in the trail. A fleeting thought flickered through McWaters' roiling mind—why hadn't the cat bolted instead of waiting quietly for him to approach?

"I tried to be nice to you. Tried to be your friend. Only you turned on me." He thrust his bleeding arm out, and limped forward until he was standing over the frightened cat. Tony had backed himself into a corner and didn't have anyplace to go—except into the rocky gorge that fell away precipitously just inches from the trail's edge.

They stood staring at each other for a moment, drops of blood spattering the dirt at his feet. He forced another smile and with an immense effort brought his breathing under control. "Last chance to make your choice, old buddy. Think carefully on it, Tony, because your life may depend on it. What will it be, a life of luxury in von Rothmann's mansion or..." He was so close to putting an end to this charade.

"Come on now, let's be friends again." His voice rumbled, deep and compelling. "Tony, believe me, I only want—" The pain slashed through his leg again, and he jerked forward involuntarily, his cramped muscles twisted in agony.

"Not again," he screamed, his eyes closed against the pain. He felt something brush against his leg and saw the cat scooting past him as his calf muscle contracted. He pivoted toward Tony on his good leg and saw the cat standing on the other side of the path, green eyes boring in on him. The cramp bit deeper and he bounced on the leg like a maniacal marionette, shifting backwards in tiny, awkward hops. He felt something hard hit him on the calf, and he was momentarily puzzled. The cat didn't return, did it? He stared dumbly down and saw it was the cable lining the trail, and he was leaning back over it, his center of gravity shifting dangerously.

He pushed desperately on his cramped leg but it wouldn't respond, and he felt his body tilting precariously over the gorge. His arms whirled out trying to regain his balance, hands grabbing at the air as though he could grip it and pull himself upright. He lunged for the cable as the sky slipped past him, but it was too late. He saw the lovely cerulean blue of the sky shift over his head, and he caught a brief view of the Pacific Ocean and the yellow kayak in the distance. His feet were above him now and he toppled head first over the side.

Just before his head slipped below the edge, he glimpsed the cat standing on the trail staring at him with those intelligent green eyes. Everything had been moving in slow motion, and he was aware of the warmth of the sun on his face, the crisp sea breeze whipping up from the beach, and the cramp in his leg that felt like someone had pounded a fiery spike into him.

The last thing he saw was a huge jagged boulder speeding toward him. The air exploded violently from his chest and he was aware of a grinding pain in his head.

Then the pain was gone.

26

Thanks to Charla, his office manager, Quint had stayed on the telephone all morning. On a hunch, she had used the Internet to research missing cats and found three other notable felines that had disappeared under mysterious circumstances.

Quint read through the articles that Charla had emailed him before calling the owners to see if they knew anything that might help him with his case. After a half-dozen calls, he was able to reach the lab director at Texas A & M University. Dr. Kurtis had a whining voice that faded at the end of his sentences as though he had lost his train of thought. He was a bit defensive at first, telling Quint that he didn't know what happened to Darwin, but it wasn't anything that he did.

When he told him that he was looking into a similar case of a missing cat, and might have a lead, there was no response. "Dr. Kurtis, are you still there," he said.

"Yes, but I really must return to my duties. To tell you the truth, Mr. Mitchum—"

"Mitchell."

"Sorry, what I was trying to say is that it wouldn't be in Darwin's best interest to come back here, if you know what I mean. She was the first of our test subjects, and since she's been missing so long, we can't be assured that proper protocol was upheld. Our team would need to put her through some *very rigorous* testing." He stressed the words *very rigorous* like they were a contagious disease.

"You don't mean they'd kill—"

"I can't say anything, but use your own imagination. Wherever she is now, she's a lot happier than she'd be back here with us. Let's leave it at that."

He spent more time trying to track down Iona Wager. He left messages at her home, with the network that aired *Larry's Life*, and the production studios where the sitcom was produced. He didn't hear back from her until after he had spoken with Katmandu's owner.

Esther Corcoran was a brusque woman who thought he was with the police department. "Well, it's about time. I've been trying to get some action from you people since my Katmandu was stolen. Did you find her yet?"

"I'm sorry, Ms. Corcoran, I'm not with the police, I'm trying to locate another stolen cat, and I thought there might be a connection."

"Do you mean to tell me that someone is stealing other show cats?"

"No, not exactly show cats, but there seems to be a common thread running through these abductions."

"That's terrible. Do you have any information about my poor Katmandu, anything at all?"

"The connection seems to be that they were all taken by the same person. I believe that the man that took your cat might have taken Tony, that's the cat I'm looking for, and several others. Can you tell me anything about the man who took Katmandu?"

Her voice softened slightly. "He said his name was John Morrow and he seemed to be such a nice man. So caring and sensitive. And you should have heard his voice.

"His voice?"

"Yes, if you don't mind a mixed metaphor, I'd compare it to honey dripping from a sugar cone. I'd never heard anything like it." She paused and Quint heard an intake of breath. "How could I have been so foolish," she said in a deflated voice.

"Ms. Corcoran, can you describe Mr. Morrow for me?"

"I'll never forget that face. It was round and slightly florid with rubbery jowls that kind of jiggled when he talked. But the most striking thing, aside from his voice, was his smile."

"What about his smile?"

"It lit up the room. You had to see it to believe how bright and wide it was, with these perfect teeth. And when he talked, he had a way of sucking you in, touching you like you were the only one in the world that mattered."

He sensed that Esther Corcoran was nearly as shaken by the loss of Morrow as her cat.

"I don't know how he did it…got the lights to go out like that. But one minute we were talking, and Katmandu was lying on my arm. She's a Grand Champion, and we were about to go to the judging ring where I know she was going to break another record."

"Yes, I read about her. She was—is a magnificent cat."

"Oh, God, my life has been turned upside down." He heard her suck in and expel a breath across the receiver and guessed that she was smoking.

"I have three other lovely Persians. Adore them all, of course, but none of them are Katmandu. She captivated the judges and if she ever got less than a perfect score, which she hadn't for a very long time, she would go into a funk. Tell me cats don't know what this is all about."

"Ms. Corcoran, the man you described sounds very much like someone named Runyan McWaters. I've tracked him to San Diego after my client's cat disappeared."

"Do you think Katmandu might be there?" Her voice seemed to jump out of the phone.

"I don't know for sure, but there's a chance. I've alerted the police, and I'm still investigating."

"Well, I hope that you're better than the police here," she spit out. "They've been less than worthless. I've posted a generous reward of $5,000, Mr. Mitchell, and I'm hoping that you'll be the one to collect it and bring her back to me." Her voice trailed off with an audible gasp and Quint heard her sobbing.

After a moment she spoke again. "People don't understand that Katmandu and I are a team. Her ribbons and trophies don't mean a thing if I can't have her back. She…"

"She's probably with Tony," he said gently. "When I find him, I'll find Katmandu."

"I'm sorry, Mr. Mitchell, but this has been a dreadful experience."

"I understand."

Quint had been watching the noon news when the phone rang. He muted the TV and picked up the phone. It was Iona Wager. She didn't have much to add other than confirming that her cat, Murray, had disappeared from the hotel room when she went downstairs to sign for a special delivery package. Arriving at the front desk, she learned that there was no special delivery, and back in the room she found Murray gone.

He thanked her and told her he'd let her know if anything turned up. He studied the notes he had taken, leaning back in the desk chair. It didn't make a lot of sense, but it looked like McWaters and von Rothmann were stealing high-profile cats. But why? Ransom? No, there had been no ransom demands. And if there was one thing that von Rothmann didn't need, it was money.

He had no proof, but his gut told him that all four of those cats were in that house at one time or another. Possibly all together. He fingered the small scar on his chin and looked up at the mirror over the desk. "This is a real puzzler," he said aloud to his reflection. "Where are those cats now?"

The truth was that he liked puzzles. There could be any number of answers to his question. Maybe they were keeping the cats somewhere else besides von Rothmann's home. But why build that cat palace? He thought of the glass-enclosed room and remembered seeing the bowls—four bowls—lined up like place settings against one wall.

No, those cats were there, and not too long ago. He wondered if McWaters might have seen him from the deck, told von Rothmann and they panicked. Moved the cats, or… Or what? Or let them go. Or dropped them off at a nearby shelter or humane society.

Would they have done that after going to all that trouble and expense to snatch them in the first place? He didn't have any idea because none of it made any sense to him. It was like trying to get inside the brain of an alien creature to learn what made him tick. He wouldn't have taken them to a shelter because they might ask too many questions.

Quint believed in following hunches and he had little patience for sitting still and letting things work themselves out. He pulled out his map of Southern California and studied the area. If he was trying to get rid of the cats without being seen, he'd drop them off at a park and get out of Dodge. He started scribbling on the hotel pad by the phone. Torrey Pines State Reserve was the closest to von Rothmann's house, but there was also Sessions Park and Marion Bear Park. A longer drive would take them to Tecolote Canyon Natural Park and Mission Trails Regional Park.

He found an area telephone directory in the drawer and hunted for the phone numbers. After he had located a number for each park, he found the numbers for both a shelter and the Humane Society in San Diego.

He had been sitting for too long, and as he got up and stretched, a scene on the muted TV caught his eye. Finding the remote he clicked on the sound and heard the end of the segment. "That's it for this week's Pet Friends. If you're interested in adopting Chloe, call the San Diego Humane Society at the number on the screen, and remember that good people need Pet Friends. I'm Denise Waters and I'll see you tomorrow on the TV-8 News at Noon. Have a nice day."

The camera zoomed past the smiling Denise Waters to a chunky calico cat that appeared to be sleeping in her lap. "Hmm," he said, and wrote *Denise Waters/Pet Friends/TV-8* in his notebook.

Realizing he hadn't eaten since last night, he decided to see if the Trembles were interested in grabbing a burger. He'd let them know what he'd learned from his conversations with the other owners and what he planned to do after they returned to the hotel. If they were lucky, something would break for them. But it would have to wait until after lunch.

27

WINDRUSHER WAS IN a state of shock. He had just watched the angry Hyskos plunge over the side and disappear. Pulling himself out of his paralysis, he padded to the edge of the trail and stared down at the crumpled body of the man. It was wedged between two sharp rocks, one leg sticking up as though he was trying to climb out of a hole.

He stood motionless studying the body, his tail swishing in agitation. He had recognized that this was the same high-legged being that had originally stolen him from his home, had chased him down the long corridors before carrying him on the Hyskos flying vehicle, and had been chasing them ever since they had escaped.

There was no doubt in his mind it was the same being. His smell was all over him, but he was marked even more by the flood of words that tumbled out of him like a never-ending flow of water. Windrusher closed his eyes to shut out the horror on the rocks and remembered the man's voice. It was so friendly and comforting that every fiber in his being had wanted to trust the man, to let him touch him, and hold him.

He realized the man was reaching out to him, trying to befriend him. Yet, he knew from past experience that he shouldn't trust this high-legged being, no matter how soothing and coaxing his voice might sound. The Hyskos had used the same voice and the same comforting words the first time he saw him and Windrusher had been mesmerized by it. He had dropped his normal wariness and let the man, with his soothing voice and friendly smile, caress him and hold him.

As much as he had been tempted to trust this male, he understood that there were some high-legged beings that should never be trusted no matter how friendly they seemed to be. This Hyskos was not his friend;

he had meant him harm, and he knew he had to protect himself.

Yet, he never expected it to end like this.

Turning away from the awful scene, he forced his legs into action. Slowly at first, then faster, he ran from the hill of death, down the trail. His immediate mission may have changed, he no longer had to worry about the vicious male who had been chasing them, but he was still determined to find a way home.

Below the overlook, the trail split off and he veered to the right. There was less vegetation here and it wasn't long before he saw the beach directly before him. He realized that this wasn't the same path he had taken earlier but was pulled along by the beauty of the scene and the steepness of the trail.

Before long he was on a narrow path leading across the face of a sandstone cliff. He had to be very careful here, the erosion that had been relentless for the last forty-five million years was still acting on the cliff face and the footing was treacherous. But the view was staggering. Even as he made his way across the eroded sandstone layers, Windrusher was moved by the majesty of the scene below him.

Huge waves broke on the large flat rocks and shot out geysers of spray. Birds flew in circles above the surf and sand searching for food. He listened to their pleading calls, heard the thunderous slaps of the waves, and was suddenly engulfed by a feeling of loneliness and vulnerability. It was like he had been transported to another time, before the Hyskos had arrived on these shores. Looking around him, the rugged terrain seemed to match his mood.

The end of the trail came abruptly and he found himself on the sandy beach. Now, he had to decide which way to continue his journey. The gods had put him upon this Path for a reason. They would surely help, but it was up to him to find his way home. He climbed on one of the flat, smooth rocks that lined the shore and scanned the turbulent sea. He breathed in the salty air and squinted at the waves glistening in the afternoon sun. Rahhna was high in the sky, and her rays scattered across the water in countless points of light.

Wind became aware that he wasn't alone. He heard Hyskos voices and saw groups of them walking along the narrow band of beach and others on the cliff trail behind him. Turning back to the water, he saw a small yellow vessel bobbing in the surf, and could just make out the high-legged being sitting atop it paddling through the waves. Above him gulls dived into the water and he thought how strange it must be to have to search for your meal in this way. Still, he had to admire the freedom of the winged creatures soaring above the earth.

Looking at his own earthbound feet, he was struck with the nearly impossible challenge ahead of him. How many Night Globes from home was he this time? He wasn't sure he could survive another journey like the last one. And what had become of Chaser, Bright Claw, and Rahhna's Light? He hoped that they were safe, and he felt pangs of guilt that he wasn't able to lead them home.

Home was where he intended to go, but for the first time, his instinctive sense of direction failed him. More than anything he wanted to turn his body toward his home and know that he had a goal in sight. If he plodded on long enough, had the good fortune of the gods behind him, and the help of some kind Hyskos, then he would eventually return to the family that cared for him.

But for some reason he felt confused and helpless. Maybe it was the huge body of water that covered everything as far as he could see. Or perhaps it was the massive ochery cliff face behind him. Whatever the reason, he was left to guess about the direction.

What he needed was sleep. He closed his eyes and hoped that Tho-hoth would appear to him once again. Surely, Tho-hoth would assist him since he had selected him for this mission. Hadn't Tho-hoth helped them escape from the house? He thought about their crossing of the treacherous black path with its swarm of vehicles, and even the close escape from the Hyskos who had tried to harm him.

Reciting these accomplishments lifted his sagging spirits, and the journey ahead of him didn't seem quite so daunting. He drew in a large breath of fresh air—and water. The crashing wave took him completely by surprise, first smashing him against the rock and then sucking him backwards. He scratched blindly; trying desperately to dig his claws into the boulder, but the immense power of the wave dragged him off the rock, across the rough beach, and swept him out to sea.

28

THE KNOCK ON THE DOOR startled Amy and she rose from the chair where she had been sitting, wondering how to confront von Rothmann.

"It's Quint," the investigator called out.

She opened the door and smiled expectantly, hoping that Quint had unearthed more information. He had and told her about his conversations with the other cat owners.

"I think this shows a pattern of thefts that tie directly to Runyan McWaters." He leaned his lanky body against the door frame. "Unfortunately, we still don't have a motive or a direct link to von Rothmann. I thought we could talk about it over lunch. I don't know about you, but I'm hungry enough to eat a triple burger with fries and a chocolate shake. How about you two?" he said, gesturing toward Amy and Kimmy.

The truth was that she was hungry, too. Hungry for the truth, craving answers to this horrible von Rothmann riddle. "Quint, I have a headache and I was just about to lie down and take a nap. Why don't you and Kimmy go get that burger, and I'll eat later."

"No, I'll stay here with you, Mom," Kimmy said with a look of concern on her face.

"Really, Kimmy, I'm fine. Nothing a little sleep won't help." She hugged her daughter and eased her toward Mitchell. "Get yourself some lunch, and then if Quint doesn't mind, maybe you could go to the Gaslamp District for a little shopping."

Kimmy brightened and gazed expectantly at Quint who had raised his eyebrows. "Do you think we could?" she asked, pulling on his arm.

"Maybe for a little while, but I have a lot of follow-up calls to make this afternoon."

"Great," she said, pulling some money from her purse and giving it to Kimmy. "You might check out the clothes since it looks like we're going to be here for a few more days. We'll go back later this afternoon or tonight and you can show me what you found. Okay?"

Five minutes after they left, she called the front desk to request a taxi cab.

She asked the cabbie to wait. She didn't expect this would take long, but she had to find out once and for all what von Rothmann was up to. Clutching her purse tightly like a protective amulet, she climbed the front steps of von Rothmann's pretentious house and rang the doorbell.

Inside, von Rothmann had been frantically attempting to contact McWaters on his cell phone. Every few minutes he called and each time it was the same. The phone rang and an infuriating voice informed him that *the cellular customer you are trying to reach is unavailable.*

That damn fool probably turned it off, he thought. Why is it that I have to do everything myself? He was still boiling over the visit by the police that morning. And, of course, there was Amy. The shock of seeing her was almost more than he could take, but he thought he handled it well. After the immediate surprise, he rather liked the thought that she was here in California and that she knew he was involved with her cat's disappearance.

Amy, you thought you were so high and mighty. Too good for the likes of me. But I guess I showed you, didn't I? He smirked and actually smacked his lips thinking about the look on her face when she saw him. He hadn't counted on seeing her again. He only wanted to take something from her that she couldn't replace. Something that would hurt her the way she had hurt him.

Still, seeing her again brought back the old feelings, and he wondered if he might somehow… No, he was fantasizing again. He needed to talk with McWaters and tell him not to come back to the house. He was their only link to him, and without the talkative

Irishman, there was no way they could tie him to any of this. They didn't have any evidence or they would have come with a search warrant.

He called once more with the same results, cursed, and started toward his laboratory to check on the cats' whereabouts. That's when the doorbell rang.

Amy stood tensely waiting for the door to open. She wasn't sure what she was going to say to this madman, but she had to find out what had motivated him to do something so hurtful. And maybe, just maybe, she could prevail on him to return Tony. She remembered that von Rothmann often seemed to be more machine than human being, but she had found there was a softer side to the intense engineering student. Perhaps, if he hadn't grown so callused that human emotion no longer touched him, she might be able to reconnect with him on some level.

She heard the click of the lock and the door swung open. She found herself stepping back, away from the man with the pumpkin shaped head leering at her from the doorway.

"Amy, how nice to see you again." His voice seemed strained, and it was obvious that this time he was the one who was surprised. He stepped onto the landing and reached out a hand for her as though he expected her to shake hands with him. She ignored it, and he peered past her to the long driveway. "Are you alone?"

"I thought it would be best for us to talk without the distractions of the police."

"Good, come on in. Please." He stepped aside and she walked past him into the foyer.

"I don't have long, but I wanted to ask you, as an old friend, if you can help me find Tony." She forced her anger into some hidden recess of her mind, and turned to her years of professional nursing experience dealing with difficult patients. She touched his forearm briefly to demonstrate that there was no hostility toward him.

"I...I d-d-don't know..." he stammered, his eyes on the spot where Amy's hand had been. He looked at her and seemed to gather his thoughts. "As much as I'd like to help you, Amy, I told you that Mr.

McWaters took Tony with him. I really have no idea where your poor cat might be."

She stared into those watery green eyes that wouldn't meet hers and knew he was lying. The anger she felt burbled to the surface and she felt her cheeks growing red. Careful, she told herself, this guy could be dangerous. "That's what you said, Karl, but I have a feeling that you know more than you're telling us." Her words had a harsh edge to them and it was obvious they had an impact on von Rothmann.

His mouth was open as though he had been stopped in mid-sentence. He closed his mouth, blinked rapidly several times and swallowed before turning away from her. Over his shoulder, he called out "Let's sit in here for a moment."

She followed him into the same sitting area they had been in that morning, but instead of sitting down, she remained standing, staring coldly at von Rothmann. "Sit down, please," he pleaded, pointing to the chair across from his.

"No, thanks, I don't plan to be here that long since it doesn't look like you're going to tell me the truth."

"Amy, please don't—"

"Don't what," she spit out. "Don't forget that you are a rich and powerful man who apparently doesn't need to obey the law? Or don't I realize that you're a heartless soul intent on causing pain? What is it you don't want me to do?"

Her fury hit him like a physical slap, pushing him back in the leather chair. She sensed that she may have gone too far as von Rothmann's eyes went wide with alarm and shock. Yet she couldn't help feeling satisfaction that her attack had apparently hit home.

He gulped several times like a goldfish out of its bowl, his eyes bulging and his face a fiery shade of crimson, and she thought for a moment that she might have to perform CPR on him. She watched him breathe deeply, struggling to control himself, and then he rose from the chair to confront her face to face.

"You have this all wrong, Amy. I had no idea that was your cat McWaters had." He paused and bit his lip, his eyes slipping past hers. "Why would I want to hurt you? We were once very close."

Amy stood with her arms folded across her chest, her jaw tight. How pathetic could a human being be, she thought, but remained quiet.

"If there's one good thing that's come of this unfortunate incident it's that it has brought the two of us together again." He offered her a slight shrug and lifted a hand, palm up, as though to say that God moves in mysterious ways.

She still didn't respond, and she could see that it was having an effect on his shaky confidence.

He licked his lips, his eyes cutting from her face to some unseen point behind her and back again. "I know that you are upset, and I'm very sorry. If there was only some way that we..." he paused and wiped his forehead which had become moist with perspiration despite the air conditioning. "What I mean is that we were so close at one time, and maybe there's a way we can..." He pulled a handkerchief from his back pocket and mopped his face.

His discomfort was tugging on Amy's sympathies, and she remembered why she had felt so sorry for the awkward young doctoral student. "Go ahead," she said, her voice much softer this time.

He sat down again, and this time she joined him. Von Rothmann twisted the handkerchief as though he were trying to wring out a coherent thought. "You're right to be angry, Amy. I would be, too, if I lost something that I loved, but this might be a stroke of good fortune, don't you see?"

"How do you mean?"

He suddenly popped up from the chair and began pacing in front of her. "Yes, this is how it can work, how we can solve this problem." He was talking rapidly, as though working through a complex calculation in his head, discarding the various options, and settling on the precise solution.

"You're right that I am a rich man, and I may be able to use my resources to find Tony and reunite us. I mean you, Kimmy, and Tony."

She didn't know what to make of his rantings, but she was encouraged that he seemed to be saying that he might be able to find Tony. "Do you think it's possible?" she asked hopefully.

Von Rothmann stopped pacing and faced her, and she saw

determination and self-confidence flash in his eyes for the first time.

"Of course, anything's possible where there's the will and the resources available to make it happen." His eyes were shining and he fixed her with one of his frightening grimaces that was his way of smiling.

"Kimmy and I would be most appreciative if you could help," she said quietly, thinking that something good might actually come from this visit. Perhaps she had been wrong about him, after all. She returned his smile, stood, and put a hand on his arm.

His face bloomed like a spring flower, and he grasped her hand in his. "Oh, Amy, you don't know how much I've thought of you over the years. How I've missed your warmth and passion for life."

For a horrible moment, she was afraid he was going to kiss her, but he continued on in a breathless gush. "We're both older and wiser people, wouldn't you say? I have too much money and time on my hands, and I need someone to remind me of the human side of life. You and me—"

"There is no you and me, Karl. I'm a married woman with a life of my own, and—"

"Yes, yes," he cut her off. "What I'm trying to say is that maybe we can…can take a step back and make up for lost time. Because…" he paused, hunting for the proper words and stared longingly into her eyes. "Because I've always loved you," he blurted out, running one scaly hand up her arm and onto her neck. His stubby fingers, with the nails bitten to the quick, moved over her throat and down.

She jerked away from him and stepped back, nearly tripping over the chair behind her. Her face twisted in revulsion as she steadied herself and backed toward the door. "You really are delusional, aren't you? There is no lost time and there will be no making up because we were never close. Do you understand, Karl?" She spat out the words like machine gun bullets.

"We were friends for a few weeks because I felt sorry for you. That's right, sorry for a social misfit with no friends and who obviously has psychological problems." She stopped at the front door, her chest heaving. She was sorry she had lost her temper. It wasn't like her to knowingly cause pain, but this vulgar, insane bug of a man had pushed her over the edge.

She slammed the door shut behind her and hurried to the waiting taxi.

Von Rothmann stared at the closed door, the sound of her last words reverberating in his head—*sorry for a social misfit with no friends and who obviously has psychological problems.* Raising his hands, he saw that they were shaking uncontrollably. He clasped them together, intertwining his fingers, and squeezed, bringing them up to his chin as though he were praying, and waited for the throbbing in his head to subside.

He heard the taxi drive away, and, breathing deeply, he slowly brought his careening emotions under control. If this is the way she wants it, he thought, then...he let the thought trail off as he crossed the room to a mahogany wall unit. Reaching behind a massive bronze sculpture of an eagle in flight, he found the recessed panel and withdrew the Colt Series 70 pistol. McWaters had given it to him as a gift after he had moved into the house with him.

He had only held the Colt once before and never thought he would ever use it. He raised it up, pointing it at the door, and noticed that his hand wasn't shaking anymore.

29

COUGHING AND SPITTING, Windrusher popped through the churning waves. His chest was heaving, lungs aching, and he gasped for air. He had no idea how long he had been below the surface, bouncing against the rocky bottom like a toy ball.

He paddled furiously just to stay afloat, and when a wave lifted him he caught sight of the sandstone cliffs lining the shore. How did he get so far from the beach in such a short time? he wondered. He plunged back into a trough and lost sight of the cliff in a struggle against the force that pulled him from below. Again, a wave carried him up and he was aware of the gulls flying overhead, their bleating cries echoing plaintively like a plea for help.

He kept paddling, but exhaustion was seeping through him, and he realized he wasn't making any headway against the tide. A hard wind was blowing inland, but instead of moving closer to the shore, he saw the cliffs moving away into the distance. Below him, the retreating waves churned through a narrow gap in a sandbar, creating a tide of such force that nothing could resist it.

His legs felt like heavy weights had been tied to them and he had difficulty keeping his head above the water. How long could he fight against the strong current that was pulling him out to sea? His lungs ached and he gasped air through his nose to avoid swallowing more water.

Is this how it's going to end? he thought. After all he'd been through. Being stolen from his home, meeting Chaser, Bright Claw, and Rahhna's Light, and escaping from the vicious Hyskos. This can't be the end, he thought, and then remembered the terrible dream where he nearly drowned in the fetid swamp.

He meowed pitifully, and a rush of water filled his throat. Choking, he thought: Where are you now, Tho-hoth? Where are you when I need you? His legs were no longer moving and his body felt like it was encased in stone. Slowly, he sank below the surface, and his mind wandered to the time when Lil' One fell into the lake and nearly drowned. Lil' One. Even in his last moments his thoughts were on his old friend and he wondered if he was happy with his new family.

He hit the bottom, and willed his spent legs to kick off and hoped he had enough strength to reach the surface one more time. One last look at Rahhna, that's all he wanted, to see the sky and feel the breeze on his face. Hadn't he survived more than his share of danger? Maybe now it was his time to meet the gods. Still, his legs propelled him upwards until his head emerged from the water. He sucked in the precious air, his eyes closed, barely breathing. He was so tired and thought if he could only sleep, everything would be fine.

The water was his bed now and he settled into it, no longer conscious of the world around him. An image of his female Hyskos appeared, and he saw her calling for him, begging him to come home. He would miss her and the family that cared so deeply for him.

Sinking below the surface again, he was unaware of the hand grabbing his collar and lifting him out of the water. He was on the edge of unconsciousness, not sure if he was dreaming or was already dead and the gods were taking him away.

He choked, water spewing from his lungs, and opened his eyes. A young Hyskos male was holding him tightly against his chest, talking to him in soft, comforting tones. The man was sitting inside a bright yellow craft that bobbed atop the waves. He lay him across his legs, grabbed the paddle, and headed toward the beach.

30

QUINT WONDERED if he should bill the Trembles for three hours of baby-sitting. As he had feared, after lunch Kimmy had dragged him through almost every one of the 140 stores in the Horton Plaza shopping mall. It was after 4:30 when they got back to the hotel.

Tired and a little annoyed at how his day had turned out, he sat down at the small desk and started making his calls. He left a message for Denise Waters at the TV station and spoke to several people at the state parks without learning anything. It was almost 5:00 P.M. when he called Torrey Pines State Reserve, and after the phone rang six or seven times he figured they had already closed.

"Hello," a breathless voice answered.

"Hi, is this the Torrey Pines State Reserve office?" Mitchell asked.

"Actually, I'm in the gift shop. The office closed early and all the rangers are busy with….with something that came up unexpectedly." It was the voice of a youngish woman, nineteen or twenty, he guessed, and she still sounded like she was out of breath.

"I wonder if I could leave a message for the supervising ranger to call me in the morning. It's about an investigation I'm conducting."

"An investigation? Are you with the police?"

She sounded shocked and puzzled, and he wondered if there was any kind of turf problems between the police and State Park Rangers. "No, nothing like that. I'm actually a private investigator from Florida and I need to ask him about a missing cat that may have wandered into the park." He thought that sounded both innocuous and a bit intriguing. Hopefully, the ranger would be curious enough to call back.

"Oh, a cat." She said it with a certain disappointment that told him that she was definitely not a cat person. He gave her both his hotel phone number and his cell phone number, and asked again for the ranger to call him in the morning.

"I know Ranger Eddy will be very busy in the morning, but I'll put the message on his desk before I leave."

Did she really call him Ranger Eddie? Who were the other rangers on his staff? Ranger Skippy and Ranger Timmy? "Can you give me the ranger's full name, please?"

"It's Nelson Eddy."

"You're kidding."

"What do you mean?" She sounded genuinely bewildered.

"Nelson Eddy, like the singer."

"There's a singer named Nelson Eddy? I didn't know that. What band is he with?"

Quint closed his eyes and shook his head. "Never mind, I guess he was a little before your time. Thanks for your help."

He made a note to call Ranger Nelson Eddy if he hadn't heard from him by mid-morning, but he didn't hold out a lot of hope. By now, it was too late to call the shelters and he tossed his pencil on the desk in disgust. An entire day shot to hell. Determined not to let it be a complete waste, he called Charla to see what was happening back in Jacksonville Beach.

The ringing phone brought Quint fully awake. His body was still on East Coast time, and he had awakened several times since 4:00 A.M. even though he'd stayed up watching *The Big Sleep* with Humphrey Bogart and Lauren Bacall before finally falling asleep around 1:30 or two in the morning.

He grabbed the phone, noting that it was only 6:45. "Hello," he said wondering who was calling so early.

"Mr. Mitchell?" a wide-awake voice asked.

"That's right."

"I'm sorry to call so early. This is Ranger Eddy at Torrey Pines State Reserve. You asked me to call you."

"Ranger Eddy, yes, thanks for calling. I didn't expect to hear from you so soon."

"We get an early start out here—particularly this morning. Your message said something about looking for a missing cat. That caught my eye, and considering everything that happened yesterday, I thought I should contact you right away."

He had Quint's full attention. "Do you know something about a missing cat?"

"Why don't you tell me your story first," he answered cautiously.

"That's fair. It's rather convoluted and a little bizarre, but the short form goes something like this: A guy has been stealing celebrity-type cats and apparently bringing them to a home in San Diego County. I was hired to find one of the cats and tracked him to the house, but he's gone and so are the cats. I just called you and some of the parks in the area in case he had dropped them off." There was silence on the other end.

"I told you it was bizarre."

"Do you know the name of the man, by any chance?"

"Sure do, it's McWaters, Runyan McWaters. Why?"

The line was quiet for a moment before the ranger spoke. "Did you see the news last night, Mr. Mitchell?"

"No, I was watching a movie. Did I miss something?"

"We found the body of a man in the gorge below Razor Point yesterday afternoon. Apparently, he lost his balance and toppled over the edge. At least that's what it looks like to us and the police."

"That's a shame." He wasn't sure what this had to do with him, but it explained why the girl sounded so hassled when he called yesterday.

"Mr. Mitchell, the man's driver's license identified him as Runyan McWaters."

"Oh, crap."

"That about sums it up. But there's a little more to it, including the two cats that were picked up in the park by one of our Ranger Cadets, and the cat prints found on the trail near where Mr. McWaters was found. I guess you understand why your message intrigued me."

"Can I meet with you this morning?"

"The park opens at eight, how soon can you be here?"

After a quick shower and a cup of coffee, Quint headed north in the rented Buick. On the way, he called Amy and told her about his conversation with the ranger. She seemed a bit out of sorts that he hadn't brought her along, but he said he had to move quickly and he'd call her from the park. To be honest, he wanted to learn more about McWaters' death and study the scene and that was easier to do without Amy and Kimmy tagging along.

His next call was to KFMB and Denise Waters. To his surprise, she picked up on the second ring, and when he told her there might be a break in the case involving the body that was found at Torrey Pines State Reserve, he could feel her interest level shoot up.

"My boss will want us all over this. Do me a favor; please don't give this to another station before I've had a chance to interview you. Promise?"

He promised.

"Good, I'm calling him at home as soon as we hang up. Then I'm going to find a cameraman and meet you out there."

"I may be busy for a while, why don't you meet me at ten."

"No problem, that will give me time to do a little research on the story."

It was almost exactly 8:00 A.M. when he drove into the park, paid his four dollars parking fee, and found Ranger Eddy in the office of the adobe building. The ranger was about forty, he guessed, maybe a few years older. He had a deep tan and the high cheekbones associated with Native Americans.

"Ranger Eddy, I'm Quint Mitchell," he said, sticking out his hand.

The ranger gripped him with one of the largest hands Quint had ever seen on a man that wasn't wearing a Laker's jersey. Eddy held it perhaps a few seconds longer than necessary and stared curiously at him, as though he might find the answer to McWaters' death in Mitchell's eyes.

"Thanks for coming over so quickly, Mr. Mitchell—"

"Please, call me Quint."

"Okay, Quint, and you can call me Ranger Eddy." His brown eyes danced, and he smiled broadly.

"Not Nelson Eddy?" Mitchell countered.

"Oh, Rina must have told you," he said sheepishly. "I plead guilty, but you have to blame my mother for that. I guess I'm just lucky she didn't name me Jeannette MacDonald."

Quint laughed along with the ranger, who had probably told the same joke a thousand times. "You said that you found cats in the park yesterday."

"That's right, two of them. And a third was plucked out of the surf by a kayaker who apparently took it home with him. It was the damndest day I've had since I've been here."

"What happened to the two cats?"

"I had the cadet take them to the Humane Society in Encinitas. It's not too far from here."

"I'm going to want to check them out, maybe one of them is the cat I've been looking for. Can I see where they found McWaters' body?"

"Sure, I was going to suggest we take a walk. The police are supposed to be back this morning. I hope you don't mind, but I called them after we spoke to let them know you would be here." He grabbed his hat and motioned for him to follow.

Outside, they crossed the narrow walkway that led to the parking lot, and Ranger Eddy took the lead on a well-worn path. Quint picked up the thread of their conversation. "I was in touch with the police earlier in the week, and they had a report so they eventually would have put it together and called me. I thought you guys did your own investigative work."

"We're all sworn peace officers and trained to conduct criminal investigations," Eddy said. "We can make arrests, if we have to, but obviously we work closely with the local law."

They finally climbed the rise to Razor Point overlook. A length of yellow crime scene tape blocked the trail but Quint followed Eddy's lead and stepped over it. "I'm not sure this is technically a crime scene, since it looks like an accident," Eddy said. "But the knife really got their attention."

"They found a knife?"

"Yeah, one of the team climbed down into the gorge to put a sling under the body, and when they lifted it, they spotted the knife in the rocks."

"And they think it belonged to McWaters?"

"Fingerprints will tell them one way or the other, but it wasn't an old, rusty blade so it was probably his."

They walked to the edge of the overlook and Eddy pointed into the deep ravine. "That's where we found him. Actually, a young couple on their honeymoon spotted him around three o'clock yesterday. They ran to the office to tell us."

"That had to be a shock. Guess they'll never forget their honeymoon."

"Yeah. Here are his footprints next to the cable, probably lost his balance somehow and fell over. Maybe now the Service will give me the money to build a real fence so this doesn't happen again."

Quint's eyes slid from the cable, which was just below knee level, to the gorge, and he shook his head slightly. "It's hard to miss that cable. Something must have distracted him. Was there anything unusual about the body?"

Eddy removed his hat and ran his fingers through his thick, black hair. "The ME will do an autopsy to see if he had a heart attack, but I did see fresh scratches on his arm. Pretty deep ones."

"Could they have come from his fall?"

"No, I don't think so. These were more like a small animal clawed him. Maybe a cat."

"Huh."

Eddy pointed out the cat tracks in the dirt. "I don't know if this is your cat, but if not, it's a hell of a coincidence."

They were soon joined by a pair of detectives from the San Diego Police Department, and Quint spent nearly an hour telling them about Tony, McWaters, and von Rothmann. They left after they had asked all their questions, leaving Quint and Eddy alone.

"You said on the phone that a cat had been pulled out of the surf by a kayaker. Did anyone get a look at the cat?"

"Sure, there were people on the beach, but we didn't get their names."

"And the guy in the kayak?"

"Sorry, we don't know who he is, but some young guy in a yellow kayak comes up here four or five times a month. Probably the same one. We'll keep an eye out for him."

"Thanks. Oh, Denise Waters from one of the TV stations is on her way here to do an interview with me, if that's okay. I thought the publicity might help us find Tony. She'll probably want to talk with you, too."

"Thanks for the heads-up. They were buzzing all around here yesterday. Don't know how they found out so soon, like buzzards circling over a corpse."

Denise Waters had short brown hair, bright caramel-colored eyes and a saucy smile that Quint found hard to resist. She asked a lot of questions about the search for Tony and the other missing cats before they began taping. He gave her a copy of Tony's picture, and she promised to include it in the broadcast.

It was 11:15 when Quint finally finished with Denise and said goodbye to Ranger Eddy. Next on his schedule was a visit to the Humane Society shelter in Encinitas, but he thought he'd better contact Amy. He knew she'd insist on going to the shelter with him, and she had every right. But it was a forty-five minute drive back to the hotel and only about twenty minutes to the shelter. He'd lose almost two hours on the road by returning to the hotel to pick up Amy and Kimmy then driving to Encinitas.

He considered his options and decided that it was only fair that the Trembles accompany him to the shelter. This was their case and their cat, and if Tony was in the shelter, they should be there to take him home. He called her on the way back and told her to get ready.

The Rancho Coastal Humane Society was a sprawling series of one-story structures that looked like a modest yellow ranch house that had attempted to clone itself with mixed results. They headed toward the building marked Visitors Entrance, and inside the combination gift shop and lobby they were welcomed by a young woman with laughing eyes and a wide mouth who reminded Quint of Reese Witherspoon—if Reese Witherspoon had favored spiked red hair.

He noted that her name badge identified her as Libby. "Hi, Libby," he said with a winning smile, trying not to stare at the demure silver stud in her left nostril.

"Hi back at ya," the girl said flashing a broad grin.

"We're looking for a cat named Tony that may have been brought in yesterday. I understand that two cats arrived from Torrey Pines."

"Oh, you mean the two with the collars? We've named them the Captain and Tennille."

Kimmy and Amy exchanged glances. "Tony didn't have a collar when we last saw him," Amy said, "but I guess someone could have put one on him."

"These were rather interesting collars. Our director has them now, but they didn't have any names or addresses on them. What did your cat look like?" She glanced from Quint to Amy, apparently not sure whose cat it was.

"He's a large orange and gray tabby," Amy replied.

He handed her a color copy of Tony's photograph. "This is Tony."

"Good looking! But he's not one of the two they brought in. I'm sorry." She started to give the photo back to him, but he shook his head.

"No, you keep it in case he shows up. My name and phone number are on the back along with a description of Tony."

She put the photo on the counter, and he continued. "Can we see the two cats? There were some other cats that went missing and maybe we can help find their owners."

"Sure, they're in the cattery." She paged through a log on the counter. "The Captain is in seven and Tennille, she's the little crooner, is next to him in eight. Right next door, can't miss it."

The cattery was a small room painted the same shade of pale yellow as the outside walls and stacked with a dozen stainless steel cages. Two young tabbies named Ben and Jerry were napping in the first cage, and a pair of sleek black longhairs peered out at them from inside a tall cage by a padlocked storage cabinet. As they walked past, the friendlier ones pushed against the doors, meowing loudly, some poking a paw through the enclosure.

Kimmy was taken by a fluffy gray and white cat with one blue eye and one green eye. "You're a cutie pie," she said, scratching the cat's head through the mesh cage. She looked at the cat's name on the card in the slot on the door. "Gus. Well, Gus, you're a friendly guy, aren't you. I'm sure someone is going to come along and snatch you up."

Quint and Amy found cages seven and eight, and Amy's face fell. "I know she said that he wasn't one of the cats they brought in, but I still hoped she was wrong."

"I understand," he said, "but these are two of the other cats that McWaters stole." He pulled out a half-dozen sheets of paper from his notebook. "I had the owners email these photos to me yesterday after I spoke to them."

He sorted through the copies and selected two of them. "See, this is Murray, and the other is Darwin. They're both rather well-known cats, so Tony was in good company."

Kimmy ran to the cage excitedly. "That's Murray. He's on that television show, *Larry's Life*. We've seen him on those cat food commercials, Mom."

The marmalade cat had been lying quietly on a towel draped over the top of a box within the cage, but his ears perked up at the sound of his name, and he lifted his head and stared out at the three people.

Quint nodded to Kimmy. "Right. I'm surprised no one here recognized him, but I guess they see a lot of cats that look alike."

Amy, who had been scanning the rows of cages, looked back. "What about the Persian, the one from the cat show?"

He flipped through the cat's pictures and found the champion Persian. Holding it out for Amy and Kimmy to see. "I don't think Katmandu would last long in a shelter. She'd be adopted before she had a chance to use the litter box." He eyed the rows of cages to be sure. "Murray's trainer will be ecstatic when I tell her we found him. That's the good news. Katmandu's owner is another story. I'm dreading talking with her."

Darwin, the cat that had been renamed Tennille, butted the cage door and meowed loudly. "Aww," Kimmy said, rubbing the cat's head.

"What about this one, are you going to call her owner?"

He hesitated before answering. "Darwin is a special case. I'm not sure exactly what to do with her," he said. "I'll tell you about it later, but she will be better off if they can find her a nice home out here."

Libby walked in with the photo of Tony in her hand. "I see you found the Captain and Tennille."

"Actually, Captain here is a pretty important feline," he said, gesturing toward the cage. "I want you to meet Murray. And this is his friend…Dudley," he improvised. He didn't want anyone calling the University until he figured out what to do about the cloned cat.

The girl's eyes grew wide and her mouth dropped open. "Murray! Omigod, you mean from TV? No way." She gave Quint a push on the shoulder to emphasize her surprise.

"The one and only. I'm going to call his trainer, Iona Wager. She lives in L.A. and will want to come down and get him as soon as possible. Hold on to Dudley, for me, though. I'll let you know what to do with her." He put his hand up to the cage and let Darwin nuzzle his fingers. "Don't let anything happen to her until I get back to you, okay?"

"Oh, man, this is like the most exciting thing that's ever happened here. Mr. Menefee will go nuts. He's our director. Oh, I almost forgot, I'm going to tape Tony's picture in here so our volunteers will see it when the cats are brought in." She held the picture up, studying it and then walked to the wall across from the cages. "Right here, don't you think?" She held it against the wall, and then pulled a small roll of tape from her jeans pocket.

Quint walked over and held the picture while she taped it. "Here," he said, handing her the photo of Katmandu. "This is another one of our missing cats. Her name is Katmandu, a Grand Champion Persian. There's a chance she may show up, too."

As expected, Iona Wager was thrilled to hear the news about Murray. She said she was driving down from Los Angeles immediately and couldn't wait to see her cat.

The conversation with Esther Corcoran wasn't nearly as pleasant.

31

QUINT WASN'T SURE if Esther Corcoran was already in a foul mood when she picked up the telephone or perhaps it was hearing his voice that did it. He knew he had that effect on some people.

"Ms. Corcoran, I'm sorry I don't have any news about Katmandu, but I thought you'd want to know that two of the other missing cats have been found and—"

"Did you find the cat those people hired you to find?"

"Uh, not yet, but I think we're getting close."

"Isn't that what you told me the last time you called? I'm happy for those other people who will get their cats back, Mr. Mitchell, but I want my Katmandu home with me where she belongs."

He heard the tremor in her voice and knew she was about to break down again. "I know this is difficult for you, Ms. Corcoran, but a lot of people are looking for your cat. I've alerted the San Diego Police and the area shelters. I think it's just a matter of time." He was trying to sound as positive as possible.

A sharp snorting sound came from the phone and then nothing. "Are you still there, Ms. Corcoran?"

"Katmandu is different than those other cats you're looking for. I've coddled her like she was my own baby. Given her the most expensive food, the best care money could buy. I combed and groomed her every day like the champion that she is. Don't you understand, she only knows one way to live and can't survive on her own?"

"You know your cat better than I do, but most of them are a lot more resourceful than we give them credit for. Look at Tony—"

"No, you look at Tony." She was practically screaming into the phone, and then grew silent. "I'm sorry. I tend to get a bit hysterical when I think of Katmandu alone, only God knows where. Please, I need you to find her. Tell me, where is my Katmandu?"

The shopping plaza was nestled against a patch of heavy woods not far from Interstate 5. A person with a sharp eye might notice the narrow path circling behind the thickly matted bushes, around the scrub oak, through the low-hanging vines and disappearing into the darkness. But they would have to be looking for it.

Walter Johnson didn't have to look for the path; he knew it as well as he knew the way to the rescue mission. In a clearing at the end of the path was the GE refrigerator carton that served as his home. He wore two t-shirts, neither of which had been washed in the past month, and a pair of faded jeans torn at the knees. They would have fit perfectly on a size thirty-eight waist, but Walter weighed only 129 pounds and the jeans were bunched around his waist with a belt he had picked up at the mission during his last visit.

He bent over the open can of beef stew sitting atop the makeshift grate and stirred it with his only spoon. He inhaled the warm fragrance of vegetables and meat and closed his eyes. That smells heavenly, he thought, licking the spoon and then using it to scratch a sudden itch on his cheek which was covered with a heavy beard.

He picked his nose, examined his fingers, and wiped his hand across his shirt. "This is gonna be one tasty dinner," he said aloud, seemingly speaking to the can of stew. "Yessiree, Bob. Let me tell you, there's nothing like a mouthful of stew to make the old taste buds sit up and take notice."

He stuck the spoon into the can again and selected a smidgen of potato. "Here's how you can tell if it's ready. Get yourself a piece of potato, and if it's hot to the core, then you're ready for some good eating." He popped the potato into his mouth, chewed it slowly and rolled it from cheek to cheek as though he was savoring an expensive wine.

"Just a mite more for Dinty Moore." He laughed loudly, a cackle that jackknifed out of his mouth like the braying of a mule.

Shadows had blanketed the small clearing in a dark gray cloak. Walter turned toward the refrigerator carton, his face catching the uneven glow from the flickering flames. "I'm telling you, we're lucky to have this. It's getting harder and harder to get those stingy people to part with a few coins."

He squinted into the darkness, reached down by his feet, and picked up a half-empty quart bottle of beer. Walter sucked in a long swallow, wiped his mouth with the back of his hand, and carefully put the bottle back down. "I remember when I could bring in ten dollars or more in an afternoon. Maybe it's the economy. Do you think that's it?"

His mouth twisted in disgust, and he answered his own question. "Nah, it's the government. They're trying to put all of us in the crazy house, deny us our American rights. But it's not going to work."

He turned suddenly back toward the fire as though he had forgotten it was there. "Uhmm, smells like its ready." He dipped the spoon into the bubbling can and lifted the gravy to his lips. "Oh, that's good. I'll bet you're hungry." He spooned several scoops of the stew onto a paper plate, blew on it, and held it toward the refrigerator carton. "It's chow time, Queenie."

Walter set the plate of stew on the floor of the carton in front of a grimy, long-haired cat. Two bright eyes flashed from the cat's flattened face as she examined the stew, and then stared up at him as though questioning whether it was okay to eat. He laughed and ran a hand through the cat's matted fur. "Go ahead and eat," he said kindly.

The cat lowered her head and greedily lapped up the gravy and the hunks of beef and vegetables. "Queenie, you are one hungry cat, aren't you? You and me may not have all the refineries of life, but don't you worry, Walter will always find us something to eat. You're my queen-bee now, and I'll take good care of you. Better believe it."

He gently stroked the cat's neck, fingering the muscles and delicate bones. "Aren't you glad I took that nasty collar off you?"

Katmandu purred loudly and rubbed against his arm. Walter reached a hand under the purring cat and lifted her up until she was looking into his grimy face. "We may be two lost and ugly old cats, but we've got each other now. What more could we want?"

32

BRAD SHERMAN WAS LUCKY to have found the small house on Manchester Avenue. The elderly owner was tired of cleaning up after a succession of students from the nearby Mira Costa College. After six months or a year, they left a house that looked more like a garbage dump than the rustic three room bungalow he had built with his own hands in the 1950s.

Brad was young, too, but he had a maturity that may have come from living on his own for the past nine years. After moving from Florida to California, following the waves, as he put it, and living out his dream as a professional surfer, he was ready to get on with his life. The twenty-six-year-old knew he couldn't afford to buy a home in Encinitas, but this was where he wanted to live and work. He convinced the owner that he was here for the long run and would treat the house like it was his own. He even agreed to take care of the mongrel that the last two guys left behind when they departed three months earlier.

The softhearted owner knew the dog would probably be put down if he brought it to the Humane Society and continued to feed it and let it sleep in the tool shed. He was so delighted that Brad agreed to take the dog, that he reduced his rent by one hundred dollars. The first thing Brad did after moving in was to wash the dog, which smelled like it had spent weeks marinating in the runoff from a landfill.

Brad had laughed out loud when he first saw the dog standing on the small patio in the backyard, tail wagging, rheumy eyes signaling the dog's need for affection. He thought it would take a team of genealogists working for years to track the parentage of the animal. It had the classic Heinz 57 pedigree, and Brad recognized traces of the Greyhound in the slim, sleek hips, but with the short stubby legs of a Bassett hound. He could only guess at the combination of genes that gave this dog a head that provided a different perspective when viewed from different angles. There was more than a hint of Schnauzer in the blunt muzzle and thick whiskers, and definitely some Boston terrier in the black and white coloring and large, dark eyes.

The dog cocked its head inquisitively to study him, and Brad mirrored the dog's movement, giving it a playful pat on the head. The owner had called the dog Stinky, but Brad renamed him Camel, since he reminded him of that old saying that a camel was a horse designed by a committee. Camel was in the living room when Brad introduced him to the orange and gray tabby.

Windrusher stared at the strange floppy-eared snouter with the whiskery face and alert but watery eyes. It sat in the middle of the tiny living room effectively blocking his path into the house. Wind stood motionless, his ears back, pupils dilated, waiting to see what the snouter would do. The young male Hyskos kneeled next to the dog, one arm over its back, the other beckoning him to come closer.

The snouter let out a raspy bark along with a wet spray of drool. The young male spoke to the animal and rubbed its muzzle, and the snouter lay down at his feet. The Hyskos continued talking and Wind moved closer until he was next to the man who had saved his life. The high-legged being scratched him gently on the top of his head, and he instinctively knew he could be trusted.

Windrusher closed his eyes and enjoyed the soft strokes on his head and neck and was surprised to feel something like a wet sponge slime his face. He shook his head and opened his eyes to see the snouter leaning over him. The dog lapped him again with a soggy tongue, its tail shaking so excitedly that its slim hips moved in a nervous rhythm.

He remembered the snouter that lived with them at his home in the land of warm waters. This one did not resemble the other in any way that he could see, but both of them seemed friendly enough, at least for a floppy-eared snouter. He relaxed, and padded past the dog, inquisitive about his new home.

It didn't take long since it was small, containing only three rooms. He returned to the living room and leaped onto the back of the couch, gazing through the window into a yard filled with bushes and fruit trees. A large storage shed hugged one side of the yard, and beyond that was a chain link fence through which he saw a black path with an occasional Hyskos vehicle passing by. He stored away this information for future use, but his attention was drawn to what looked like a vast marshy area on the other side of the path.

Windrusher liked what he saw, and realized that he was situated in a good location whenever he decided to continue his travels. For now, though, this was as good a home to live in as he had found since he was taken from his own family. Certainly, this one was smaller than the one he and the other cats had been taken to, but this one contained an ingredient that was essential to all cats: It came with a Hyskos that he trusted. This high-legged being obviously wanted him here since he had saved his life and made him a part of his family.

Brad still surfed almost every day, and he made his living by designing and making boards for other surfers. He had worked part-time at a San Diego surf shop after he first moved to the coast and quickly learned the craft of shaping the boards from the foam blanks. Experimenting with his own designs, he would shape them, and then carefully sand the bottom of the blanks for maximum strength and performance. The glassing process came next and then more sanding and several weeks of curing.

It took him months of work and dozens of boards before he settled on a design that was what he called his *magic* board. It was fast in the small waves, yet held the big waves, allowing him to be more aggressive and respond to the shifting pocket of water. When other surfers began asking him to make them one of his magic boards, he knew he had found his calling. Today, Brad's Bluebirds were carried in four area shops, and he was making ten to fifteen a month with the help of an assistant. This not only provided a steady income, but allowed him time to surf at Swami's Beach, and kayak at nearby Torrey Pines once or twice a week.

It was a good life for a former surf bum with few responsibilities. Of course, he now had another mouth to feed, but he didn't mind having Wipe Out in the house. That's what he named the cat that was going under for the second and probably last time before he plucked him out of the surf.

He was glad to see that Camel and Wipe Out were getting along. That made it a lot easier to leave them alone together while he worked on the boards. In the afternoon, he usually unwound by taking Camel for a walk along the trails of the San Elijo lagoon across the street. There were five miles of trails surrounding the shallow-water estuary, and he and Camel enjoyed walking a different trail almost every afternoon. The ecological reserve was alive with birds and flowers, a surprise around each bend in the trail. Pets had to be on a leash, and he wondered how Wipe Out would take to a leash when he brought one home the next day.

He had disposed of the bulky collar soon after rescuing Wipe Out; afraid the sodden leather would constrict the cat's airflow. He attached the new collar and leash, and took Wipe Out into the backyard. The cat sat motionless for a few moments and then ran toward a butterfly hovering over a frangipani flower. He trotted along behind the cat, which seemed unconcerned about the leash or the man running behind him, then waited while it sniffed at the plant and dug in the rich brown soil.

He let Wipe Out wander a bit and then tugged gently on the leash to get his attention. The cat stared at him, his green eyes so focused that Brad believed it was actually thinking through this new situation with the leash and understood what was expected of him. Wipe Out walked over and stood in front of him as though waiting for him to take the next step. When Brad started toward the shed in the southeast corner of the yard, Wipe Out loped off ahead of him.

He smiled and called encouragingly to the cat. "Good boy, Wipe Out. You are one smart feline." He felt funny talking to the cat the way he usually talked to Camel, but there was something quite un-cat-like about Wipe Out. He always thought cats were so independent they could never be trained. Maybe he was wrong.

Walking back to the house, he retrieved the old dog, and the three of them headed toward the San Elijo Lagoon Ecological Reserve.

Windrusher was exhilarated by the walk he had taken with the Hyskos and the floppy-eared snouter. The leash had surprised him, but he had quickly become accustomed to it, and allowed the young Hyskos to guide him through the marshy flatlands. The area was alive with strange plants and insects, and large birds floated in the lakes. He chased some of the skittering lizards and explored trees whose branches drooped to the ground like they were too tired to stay erect.

Back at the house, he found a soft spot on the couch, sniffed the cushion, and wasn't surprised to find that the snouter had been there before him. He turned several times before settling down and looked forward to a long nap. Like all cats, Windrusher had his pre-nap grooming rituals and began with his front paws. Licking first between each of his toes, he then cleansed the callused pads, wiped them across his head, and repeated the process. The familiar routine relaxed him and before he realized that he had closed his eyes, he was asleep.

He waited until the mass of voices subsided, and merged his mind with the others. Following the ancient code, he quickly identified himself. "I am called Pferusha-ulis, Windrusher, Son of Nefer-iss-tu. My voice, alone, is small and weak, but joined with Akhen-et-u, we become one and unbreakable."

A swirl of voices whipped around him from all directions as soon as he had introduced himself. Some were insistent, others more timid, but all wanted to know more about his travels. Questions flew at him as they probed him for details, each cat hoping to be the first one acknowledged by the legendary Windrusher. It had been overwhelming the first few times after he returned to his own family, and the story of his miraculous journey spread though Akhen-et-u. Now, he took it in stride and let the voices talk themselves out before proceeding. He told them of his recent experiences with the violent Hyskos, the man's tumble into the gorge, of his near-drowning and rescue. "I believe I'm safe with this young male, but I'm worried about my two friends, Chaser and Bright Claw. Did they get away or did the Hyskos find them before he tried to attack me?"

Noise rebounded around his unconscious in response to his question. He caught a word here, a phrase there, an occasional question asking for more information on the two cats. Wind had received valuable assistance through the Inner Ear in the past. He had also wasted time with trivialities and petty bickering, but there was always a slim chance, he thought, that Chaser or Katmandu might be plugged into the Akhen-et-u. As it turned out, he was right.

"Thanks be to Irissa-u that we are all safe." The familiar voice sliced through the din. "Chaser, is that you?"

"Yes, and I'm back with my female Hyskos in my own home. I heard your story, and it sounds like the smiling one came to the end of his Path. You were fortunate to escape with your whiskers intact."

"I'm pleased to hear that you are back home, of course, but how did you get there so quickly." Windrusher was truly amazed.

Chaser told him about being picked up by the uniformed Hyskos and taken, along with Bright Claw, to the room full of cages. "Cats were stuffed inside every one, many begging to be released."

Wind thought about Chaser's earlier experience as a young cat, hunted and held against his will until he was rescued by his female Hyskos. "You must have felt that you were reliving a bad dream," he said.

"I knew what to expect, but Bright Claw was very frightened."

"I'm sure she was, but you're both out of there now."

"No. Bright Claw is still there, as far as I know."

"What happened?"

Chaser told him about staying in the cage overnight, about a morning visit by a family of Hyskos who seemed to be quite interested in them, and then his female entering the room some time later and taking him home. "She was very happy to see me, and I was just as happy to be out of that place. But sorry we had to leave the little one behind."

"There's always a chance that another kind Hyskos will want her," Wind offered hopefully.

"True, the Wetlos doesn't deserve to live in a cage, and—" Chaser stopped abruptly, and Windrusher thought that perhaps his friend had awakened and was no longed plugged into the Akhen-et-u.

"I nearly forgot," the marmalade cat said. "When the family was there, standing in front of our cages, another female came to us and she held your likeness."

"My likeness?" Wind was puzzled.

"You know that the Hyskos are fond of capturing our likenesses and putting them on their walls, in their homes."

He did know that. Many had flashed his likeness after he escaped from the dark force and from Bolt, and been reunited with his female Hyskos. Some had even wanted to be standing with him when the small boxes flashed.

"Are your sure it was *my* likeness?"

"You are an unmistakable cat, Windrusher. She was holding it very close to our cages, and then she put it on the wall across from us so we had to turn away to avoid looking at it."

"I'm sorry if it made you uncomfortable." He was curious about why they had his likeness and who these other high-legged beings might be. "Chaser, tell me about this Hyskos family that was there."

"What can you say about the Hyskos, they all look alike, don't they?"

There was a lot of truth in what Chaser said, but Windrusher knew there were differences in ages and sizes. "You said it was a family of high-legged beings. Were they old or young, female or male?"

He noted that the Inner Ear had grown strangely quiet while he waited for Chaser to answer him.

"There was an adult male and female and younger female who spoke kindly to us and stroked Bright Claw."

Windrusher listened closely hoping that something Chaser said made sense. He had an image in his mind of his young female, her eyes shining brightly, holding him in her lap. His family had an older male and female, plus a younger male. But there were more two-legged beings than cats had hairs in their coats, and he realized that it was unlikely that these Hyskos were part of his family. Still, they had his likeness so they may have been looking for him.

"There's one more thing," Chaser added. "The young female, she also had a likeness of you on an ornament she wore on her false fur."

"An ornament?"

"What would you call it? I've seen these high-legged females decorate themselves with shiny ornaments, but this one held your likeness and that of a young Hyskos."

"The likeness of the young Hyskos, could it have been the same female that wore the ornament?" He had seen her wearing such a thing after he had returned to his home in the land of warm waters.

"Perhaps," Chaser said. "As I said, they do look alike, but it could have been the same female."

It was true; she was here. His family had come looking for him, to take him home. His young female had found him once before and now she had found him again. But how? He knew that cats had the uncanny ability to find their way over long distances, but he was constantly amazed at the instincts these beings possessed. Just when he was convinced that they had less sense than a hairless kitten, they surprised him by doing something like this.

"By the gods, that is my female," he said excitedly. "She has come for me as yours did for you, Chaser."

"Your story will have a good ending, then, my friend." Chaser paused before continuing. "But…"

"What? But what?"

"But you're not in the room with the cat cages where I left Bright Claw. How will she find you?"

Chaser was right. His sense of exhilaration evaporated as quickly as it had appeared. She had no way of knowing that he was with another Hyskos, living with him and a floppy-eared snouter in this small home. He would have to leave here and find her before she gave up and returned to the land of warm waters.

"Thank you, Chaser. You have been a good friend. I wish you well, but now I must find my female Hyskos."

"May Irissa-u lead your way and Tho-hoth walk with you." The usually flippant marmalade had grown serious, and Windrusher sensed concern in his voice.

The strain of forcing his consciousness to remain focused even while he was in deep sleep was wearing him down. Quickly, he excused himself from the Inner Ear and drifted into the welcoming arms of Hwrt-Heru, the holy mother of sleep.

33

AMY TOSSED AND TURNED, caught in her own waves of restlessness and agitation. She had checked on her sister after returning to the room and was overjoyed to learn that Jeannie was stabilized and doing much better. That was some much-needed good news amidst the disappointments and disasters of the past few days. She missed Gerry and G.T. and wanted to return home, but Quint insisted that they were very close to finding Tony.

She gazed at her daughter sleeping soundly in the next bed, and knew it wouldn't be fair to Kimmy to leave without her cat. Not when she felt it was her fault that Tony was stolen. She thought that everything would have been different if not for her depression-filled days and nights. That included watching Tony more closely and preventing his cat-napping. Of course, she was ignoring the fact that if she hadn't suffered her bout with depression she would have been at work and Tony would have been alone anyway.

Still, she was wracked with guilt. Guilt for Tony's predicament, guilt for what she was putting Kimmy and the rest of the family through. And guilt for not telling Gerry or Quint about von Rothmann. What was the problem, she asked herself? Was she afraid they would blame her for Tony's disappearance? That they might believe she and von Rothmann had a much deeper relationship than they actually did?

It was preposterous. She hadn't thought of Karl von Rothmann in more than twenty years, not until she heard his name yesterday. Yesterday? It seemed like weeks had passed since she and Kimmy arrived in San Diego, but it had only been a few days. It's time to act like a grown-up, she told herself. Time to accept responsibility for your actions.

She decided that tomorrow she would tell Quint everything. That was the last conscious thought she remembered before falling into a troubled sleep.

He heard the rumbling first. It came as from a great distance, far under his feet and suddenly emerging from the ground, enveloping him with violent vibrations that made his chest hurt. Windrusher slipped into a sandy pit, the earth giving way under his feet, and he saw rocks tumble from a cliff and roll past him.

Was this disturbing vision another dream? He struggled against the dirt covering his legs and then his body. This can't be happening. He cried out in his sleep, as the image of his own body twisted and fought to dig its way out of the rapidly filling pit. In the dream, he stretched his neck above the sand and rocks searching for a way out, hoping for a sign that Tho-hoth was near and willing to save him.

There, on top of the cliff, he saw the great god of wisdom, apparently unmoved by the violent forces around him. "Windrusher, hear me, my brave friend." His voice thundered out and over him, matching the energy of the crashing rocks.

Sand was clinging to every hair, scratching at his eyes and ears, yet he was aware of Tho-hoth calling to him. "You have proven yourself worthy of the trust we have put in you. Now, you must prove yourself again and save not only your own life, but that of your Hyskos female and her mother."

The voice rang inside his head, and he struggled to understand. He squeezed his eyes shut against the rising layers of sand, fought against the terrible panic that consumed him, hoping that this nightmare would pass.

"It is time for you to complete your mission, Pferusha-ulis."

He listened, wanting to hear words of hope, a declaration that a safe return awaited him. Tho-hoth's voice penetrated the layers of sand settling over his head, and cut through him like a vicious claw.

"Go find your family, Windrusher, but beware that dangerous forces may swallow you and end your days forever."

34

No matter how many times von Rothmann fussed with the GPS receiver trying to find Tony, the results were the same. Nothing. Absolutely nothing. He had tracked the other two cats to a location adjoining Encinitas Boulevard that he learned was the local Humane Society. At first he thought that perhaps Tony was there with them. That was before he saw the news report on the strange happenings at Torrey Pines State Reserve involving the death of a visitor and an unknown orange and gray cat plucked from the surf by a kayaker.

That had to be Tony. And it explained why the satellite positioning device was no longer tracking the feline; it must have been damaged by Tony's swim in the Pacific. McWaters' death tied up a lot of loose ends, and he should have been satisfied with the way it turned out. But all he could think about was Amy Trembles' last words, and how satisfying it would be to make her eat them and truly suffer for her cruelty.

He had convinced himself that Tony was not too far away, and would eventually turn up. This was an about face for an engineer who had spent his career immersed in the scientific method, researching and evaluating data and making decisions of precise calculations that left no room for error. His analytical mind didn't dwell on the tremendous odds against finding Tony, instead he thought about what he would do to the cat when he found it, and he only hoped that Amy Tremble was there to watch.

The other two cats, Murray and Darwin, didn't mean anything to him anymore. They were simply a pleasant diversion, and they could stay at the shelter until they rotted as far as he was concerned. No, he would wait—and somehow he knew it wouldn't be a long wait—for

Tony to emerge from hiding once again.

"It's Ranger Eddy," Quint whispered to Amy and Kimmy, his cell phone to his ear. They were having breakfast together in the hotel coffee shop, and the phone had rung as they were discussing plans to distribute Tony's picture to area newspapers.

"Are you sure it's him?" he asked into the phone. He nodded several times, listening to the ranger, before smiling broadly. "That's great," he said excitedly, and gave Amy and Kimmy a thumbs-up gesture. "Yes, we definitely want to talk with him. Don't let him go anywhere; we'll be there in thirty minutes."

Quint folded the phone. "The kayaker returned, and Eddy has him in the office."

Amy and Kimmy sat mutely, waiting for him to share the rest of the conversation. "And he has Tony."

The Tremble women both let out a whoop that drew stares from the other patrons. "Is Tony there with him?" Kimmy asked.

"No, but he lives in Encinitas, close to the Humane Society shelter we visited yesterday, and Tony's at his house." He grabbed the bill and pushed his chair back. "I knew we were close, but not this close. It looks like you and Tony will be back together before the morning's over."

Quint shook Brad Sherman's hand and introduced Amy and Kimmy Tremble to the young man in the wetsuit. Brad had never heard of Tony, but said he would be happy to return the cat to its rightful owner. "That's a smart cat you have there, Kimmy," he said to the girl. "I wasn't sure what would happen when I put the leash on him."

"You had Tony on a leash?" Kimmy asked in amazement.

"Yep, we went for walks around the lagoon next to my house. Me and Tony and Camel, my dog."

Quint spoke up, "As you can imagine, Mrs. Tremble and Kimmy are anxious to return to Florida with Tony. Do you mind taking us to him?"

"Sure, I've already loaded the kayak on my car. Why don't you follow me, it's not far." Brad gave them his address in case they got separated, and after thanking Ranger Eddy, they drove out of the park.

Quint followed Brad's Dodge Stratus to I-5, and pulled out his phone. "I'm going to give the reporter from Channel 8 a heads-up on this. I promised that she would be the first to know when we found Tony."

He tracked down Denise Waters and brought her up to date on Brad Sherman.

"Brad Sherman, not the surfer?" He was surprised that she seemed to know him.

"I guess he's a surfer, looks like one. About twenty-five or so, slim with a surfer cut. He lives in Encinitas, that's about all I know right now."

"A friend of mine was dating him back when I was in college," Denise said. "He had just turned pro, and was tearing up the regionals. He makes surfboards now, and he works and lives in Encinitas. Has to be him."

"Well, Brad is the hero of your story. He's the one who rescued Tony from drowning and took him home with him. We're on the way there now to pick him up. Do you want to meet us there?"

"What do you think? I need to round up a cameraman, and maybe I can talk the producer into letting me do a live cut-in from Brad's house. I should be there in, say, forty-five minutes. Wait for me, okay?"

Quint gave her the address, and folded up his phone. He smiled sheepishly at Amy. "It never hurts to get a little good publicity, does it? And we all can use more good news these days."

They parked in the driveway directly behind Brad's Dodge and followed him into the modest house. Amy was thankful this was coming to an end, and she didn't have to tell Quint of her involvement with von Rothmann. She took Kimmy's hand in hers as they walked up to the door behind Brad and Quint. "Honey, I don't know when I've been so excited," she told her daughter. "I can't imagine how you must feel."

Kimmy pulled her mother toward her and buried her head against her arm. "I just knew we'd find him, Mom. Just knew it," she said with a slight tremor in her voice and a glint in her eyes.

"You heard what Brad said: Tony is one smart cat. But we knew that already, didn't we?"

Brad opened the screen door and unlocked the door. He held it open for the others, and called, "Wipe Out, Camel, come and say hello to our visitors."

They stood inside a small living room that gave way to an even smaller kitchen. There was a sliding glass door to their right leading to a patio and a large backyard. In front of them was a wood-paneled hallway leading, Amy assumed, to the bedroom. She heard a scraping noise from the other room, the sound of claws clicking on the wooden flooring, and then a raspy bark as a dog of mysterious parentage appeared. The dog ambled slowly toward them and sat at Brad's feet. It cocked its head, staring inquisitively through watery eyes.

"This is Camel," Brad said, squatting in front of the dog and grasping its head in his hands affectionately. "He kind of came with the house."

"Interesting-looking dog," Kimmy said while gazing over Camel's head, her mind obviously not on the dog.

"Where's Wipe Out, boy. Is he sleeping on the bed?" Brad said to the dog. He turned and gave them a reassuring smile, then walked into the dark and narrow hallway with Kimmy, Amy and Quint directly behind him.

The bedroom was surprisingly roomy, with a double bed, wardrobe and window seats. The wood paneled walls had been stained a dark mahogany when Brad moved in, like the rest of the house, but he had painted them white to lighten the room. Two framed surfing posters were the only decorations on the wall, and the sun shining through one of the windows reflected off the glass and onto the unmade bed. Outside, they saw a well-tended garden with fruit trees, cactus, and flowers. They surveyed the room, the posters on the wall, the Mexican style wardrobe, and the bed.

There was nothing surprising about the room, except for the fact that Tony was not in it.

"Hmm," Brad said, scratching his head. "Guess he's in the yard."

Amy and Kimmy exchanged concerned glances, and Kimmy yelled her cat's name. "Tony. It's me, Tony, we're here to take you home." She paused, listening, waiting to see her cat running toward her.

They went back into the living room and Brad stepped toward the sliding door. For the first time, Amy noticed that it was open about seven or eight inches, a cut-off broom stick in the track to keep it from being opened from the outside. He removed the stick and pushed the door open.

"Camel needs to go outside to take care of his business, so I usually leave this door open for him. Tony's probably out here chasing a lizard." They walked outside, the bright morning sun etching radiant pools amidst the shadows cast by the many trees in the yard.

"Tony, are you out here? It's Kimmy, where are you?" Kimmy ran to her left where rows of fruits and vegetables were growing behind a low stone fence. Bell peppers and pole beans were intermingled with strawberries and plum trees. She quickly ran down the length of the garden, calling for Tony, and then ran across the yard to the storage shed.

"Could he be inside there?" she called back to Brad.

"I don't think so, but let's see. Be careful. It's a bit of a mess." He unlatched the door and pulled it open. It was obvious that this was a catch-all, and Brad had either inherited the mess or had created it.

"He has to be out here," Brad said, closing the shed door. Amy and Quint stood next to him, staring toward the back of the yard.

"What's that over there? Amy asked, pointing to the undeveloped property that fell away from the yard.

"That's the lagoon, where we walked yesterday."

A chain link fence bordered the lot, and the attractive mixture of tropical foliage, grass, and trees that surrounded the home gave way to sparse patches of weeds and grass along the back edges of the property. A gate was built into the fence, and Kimmy ran toward it.

"Kimmy, wait for us," Amy yelled.

They quickly joined Kimmy by the closed gate. "I'm pretty careful to keep the gate closed," Brad said. "But you can see the lagoon from here. We cross the road and we're right there. Tony had a great time wandering around there yesterday, but—"

"Look at this," Quint said, a note of urgency in his voice. He had moved along the fence line, and was staring down at the bare ground.

"What is it?" Amy asked.

His finger traced a trail from the edge of the grass across a wide expanse of rust-colored dirt. There was no doubt they were cat tracks.

"Tony was out here, wasn't he? Kimmy said.

"Sure. He came out several times yesterday, so I'm not surprised to see his tracks," Brad added.

"That's not it," Quint said, still staring at the tracks. "See how they are cut into the dirt here? As they approach the fence, they're deeper, and look where they stop." He pointed to a spot about thirty inches from the fence.

Amy saw it immediately and put an arm around her daughter. She caught Brad's eye, and she saw that he understood what Quint was showing them. They were so close, she thought. So damn close. How could this keep happening to them?

"What is it," Kimmy asked. "Where's Tony?"

Quint looked from the ground to the fence, then at Kimmy and Amy. The girl's eyes were brimming with tears, and he let his gaze drift away from her to the lagoon. Turning back, he pointed toward the ground and then the fence. "I'm sorry, Kimmy. But it looks like Tony jumped on to the fence and escaped."

35

FROM THE MOMENT WINDRUSHER scrambled over the fence and across the road, he had only one thought in mind: find his female Hyskos. Chaser's news had both energized and alarmed him. He had no idea how she could have followed him so far from their home, but it confirmed his feelings that she loved him and wanted him back.

He slid down a steep embankment and into a habitat dotted with shrubs and trees. Stepping with care past mountain mahogany and flowering gooseberry, he again noted the beauty of the landscape and the fragrant scents that tickled his nose. He followed a well-worn path around a great marsh covered with feathered creatures bobbing lazily.

A welcome breeze blew in from the shore and he lifted his head to let it cool his face. He took in the mixture of salty and sour aromas rising from the marsh and wondered about the strange brew. Windrusher had passed through the western basin of the reserve and was approaching the dry coastal slopes along the southwestern border. Biologists had labeled it the coastal sage scrub community.

Keeping the image of his female before him, he broke into a run.

"Maybe he's in one of the other yards," Kimmy said hopefully. They had exited the yard through the back gate, and were standing at the edge of the property. Kimmy surveyed the other lots, but her eyes kept drifting back to the wide expanse of wilderness on the other side of the street.

"I don't know," Brad said dubiously. "I have a feeling that he's in the estuary, where I took him and Camel yesterday."

"He can't have gone too far," Quint said. Amy knew he was trying to keep up a brave front for Kimmy's sake. He stared intensely over the terrain as though he could penetrate the thousand acres and zero in on one small cat like a heat-seeking missile.

"Maybe he's on the same trail you and the dog walked," he said.

Brad was shaking his head. "Maybe. But there are over five miles of trails, and there's no guarantee he'll stay on the trail, is there? Let me call a few of my friends who hike there all the time."

He opened the gate and held it for them. Kimmy didn't want to go back inside and pulled at her mother's arm. "Let's go on ahead while he's calling," she said. "I know I can find him."

Amy kneeled in front of her daughter and held her shoulders. "Listen, baby," she said, giving Kimmy a slight shake to get her attention. "It will only take a few minutes for Brad to make his calls. He's right, the more people we have with us, people who know this park, the better chance we'll find Tony."

Reluctantly, Kimmy followed her mother and the others into the yard and back into the house.

Brad had only made one call when there was a knock on the front door. Camel barked once and looked at his owner. "It's okay, Camel," Brad said, striding toward the door and pulling it open.

"Brad Sherman?"

"Oh, hi," Brad said, his voice taking on a noticeably lighter tone. "You're the reporter from Channel Eight."

"Denise Waters, glad to meet you."

They shook hands and he stepped aside to let her in. Quint stepped forward to greet her, and introduced her to Amy and Kimmy. She was an attractive brunette in her late twenties with one of those perky personalities that are often found on network co-hosts. Now, Amy understood why Quint had been eager to stay in touch with her.

"I'm afraid we don't have the happy ending I promised you," Quint said. He quickly told her about Tony's escape from the backyard, and that they were going to search for him in the estuary.

Denise gnawed at her lower lip while Quint related this. She went to the window, and pointed to a van parked out front. "Look, my engineer is setting up the microwave shot, and we're live on the Noon News in twenty minutes. How about if I interview Brad about the rescue and one of you can bring everyone up to date on this situation? We could probably get a lot of people out here to help."

Amy raised an eyebrow and looked at Quint. "What do you think?"

"We can use the help. That's a huge piece of land to search by ourselves."

Denise Waters turned to the camera with a look that mixed amazement and concern. "As you just heard from Mrs. Tremble, Tony is a cat with more than nine lives, and a record of incredible adventures that are stranger than fiction." The camera zoomed past Amy and Brad to a medium shot of the reporter.

"Unfortunately, this fairy tale doesn't yet have a happy ending since Tony disappeared this morning. He's thought to be somewhere in the sprawling San Elijo Lagoon Reserve, and they'll be searching for him all afternoon. Here's his picture again. If you have any information, please call us at Channel Eight News." On the monitor at her feet, a phone number appeared below the photograph of Tony before the picture returned to her standing with Brad, Amy, and Kimmy.

"We've been following this story from the beginning, and it has taken some mysterious twists that include cat-snatching, the unsolved death at Torrey Pines, Brad's heroic rescue, and now the cat that started it all is again missing." The camera zoomed to a close-up.

"We'll continue following this story to what everyone hopes is a happy ending. This is Denise Waters reporting for the Noon News on Channel Eight."

"We're clear," the engineer yelled from the open door of the van.

Denise made them promise to let her know what happened and invited them to bring Tony on the morning show when they found him. After she drove away, Brad said he'd finish making his telephone calls.

"Look at the time. We've lost nearly an hour that we could have been searching for Tony." Amy was clearly concerned. She hadn't wanted to do the interview in the first place, but Quint had made her understand that it was important and could help them find Tony. But now she was worried that Tony might get away from them while they waited for Brad to call his friends.

"I'll tell you what," Quint said, looking first at Amy then at Brad. "Go ahead and make your calls. We're going to start looking for Tony, and you can catch up with us."

36

THE WHITE-TAILED KITE PERCHED on the top branch of a long-dead and faded cottonwood, its orange eyes alert for any movement among the sagebrush and buckwheat. It lifted its handsome head, spread its black wings, and flew high above the estuary. Hovering over the marsh with yellow feet and black tail dangling, the kite glided silently awaiting a movement from below that would send it on a death dive toward an unsuspecting field mouse or frog

Windrusher scurried off the trail, past the spiny rush, through the deer weed and wild cucumber. He continued running until his sides hurt and plunged into the higher grass surrounding a sprawling eucalyptus tree. Far above him, the raptor circled. It had already made the mental calculations necessary to swoop down on the cat, but determined that this prey was too large to carry away and swallow. With a sad croaking cry, the kite continued its hunt.

Wind scrambled over a fallen log and squatted behind it, his eyes watching the winged creature high above him gliding into the distance. His heart was pounding and he sniffed the air, picking up the saline aroma from the western basin. Was he getting any closer to his female Hyskos he wondered? He had no way of knowing, but his innate sense of direction had guided him this far, and he knew that he should trust his instincts.

At this moment, however, his senses were telling him that although everything seemed peaceful, it was not as it seemed. There was something definitely wrong, and he felt the hair on the back of his neck stir. The feeling had first hit him by the pond, and he had dashed from the path, seeking cover. He rose from behind the log and slowly moved to the base of the tree. His ears swiveled like two radar dishes, alert to any movement, any sense of danger. He jerked as a gust of wind shook the branches above his head and the gray shadows at his feet shifted like a ghostly apparition.

What was it? He felt like a hairless kitten, afraid of his own tail, running from the shadows of tree branches. He wasn't sure if he heard it first or felt it. A high whistle-like vibration swept across the marsh, growing in intensity until it became a physical force that rumbled inside his chest. Behind him, the mallards and gadwalls floating in the lagoon suddenly rose and flapped away honking noisily. As he spun around to watch the ducks, he was startled by a flock of chirping red-winged blackbirds rising from the eucalyptus tree.

All around him, winged creatures were taking flight. He was confused and frightened, but he didn't know why. Should he follow the lead of these other creatures and flee, or should he find a bush to hide under? He was suddenly overwhelmed by a growing sense of helplessness.

He searched desperately for someplace to hide, his gaze wavering between the eucalyptus tree and the sandstone cliffs in the distance. He had decided on the tree because it was closer and was running toward it when he heard a sharp thud, like two mammoth rocks colliding. His eyes grew wide with fear, and a low whimper escaped from him.

The first ground wave rolled across the surface of the estuary, through the salt marsh and coastal strand, and over the clearing where he stood terror-stricken until the tremor knocked him off his feet. He struggled to regain his footing, but the ground convulsed beneath him like an angry serpent. All of his involuntary survival instincts had kicked in, elevating his hormonal levels, pushing him to protect himself. Overcome by anxiety, he stopped struggling and rode the bucking surface.

In the background, a familiar sound tried to intrude itself through the whistling vibrations and his own hammering heart beat. Taking a deep breath, he commanded himself to regain control of his quivering body. That's when the noise formed itself into a one-word cry that instantly grabbed him, and offered him hope that he might survive this freakish calamity that was shaking the earth beneath him.

The sound originated from a point near the salt marsh and floated above the vibrations rumbling across the reserve. Windrusher's heart leaped as he recognized the voice calling to him, calling his Hyskos name.

"Tony!"

Quint never considered himself much of a tracker, not of the outdoor variety, anyway. But the cat's footprints were hard to miss in the soft dirt. He spotted them almost immediately near the top of the muddy slope leading down into the reserve, and followed them onto the path winding through the low scrub country skirting the lagoon. He felt a little silly bent over the small paw prints, like a man playing cowboys and Indians, but the excitement that always overtook him when he was nearing the end of a case had returned.

Amy and Kimmy had caught his sense of excitement, and their dark mood from that morning had lightened to match the beauty of the afternoon.

"He's here, isn't he?" Kimmy said, running ahead of them.

"Careful, don't step on his tracks," Quint called out.

"Tony, where are you? Tony!" Kimmy yelled as though expecting the cat to answer her.

Quint knew that the cat had at least an hour's head start on them. Still, how fast can cats travel? They had made good time following Tony's meandering trail through the clusters of Mohave yucca and laurel sumac. They had to be gaining on him, he thought.

The afternoon sun was beating down, and he wiped the sweat from his forehead. He wished he had thought to bring a hat with him. Still, it felt good to be outside and finally closing in on the elusive Tony. This time, he wouldn't get away. At least he hoped that was the case.

Amy walked beside him on the trail, keeping an eye on Kimmy who was about twenty feet ahead of them. She stopped and turned, staring behind them, a quizzical look on her face.

"What's that noise?" she asked.

He didn't know what she was talking about. All he heard was the chirping of birds and insects. "What noise?"

"Don't you hear it? Like a high-pitched whistle."

"I don't hear anything, but my hearing isn't that good." He turned back to the trail, following the cat's tracks around a small bend next to a large shrub with pointed shafts rising from its core like the spines of a porcupine.

"Wait!" Quint stood and stared off to his left. "Tony left the trail here. It looks like he's headed—"

A loud thud cut off the rest of his sentence. He recoiled as though someone had shot at him. "What the hell was that?"

As if in answer to his question, the landscape began to twist and roll in a wave that made their legs feel like they had liquefied.

"Kimmy," Amy screamed, as her daughter's legs were knocked out from under her.

"Earthquake," Quint blurted out, throwing his arms around Amy and dropping to the ground.

A low rumbling vibration swept across the reserve. He didn't know much about earthquakes, but this didn't seem to be a major one. But it still scared the hell out of him, and as he listened to the rumbling that moved the earth beneath them, he became aware of Kimmy's screams.

She cried out her cat's name over and over. "Tony, Tony, Tony."

37

KARL VON ROTHMANN'S HOUSE was only twenty minutes from the San Elijo Lagoon. He had hovered near his television set since Amy's visit, waiting with confident patience for the news that Tony had been found. He had not slept in nearly twenty-four hours, but his skin tingled with nervous energy and his eyes glowed with such fierceness that sleep found no welcome there.

He had always prided himself on his stamina, remembering those euphoric days of discovery working for seventy-two hours at a time, fueled by coffee and an inexhaustible drive to succeed. He put down the technical journal he was reading when Denise Waters came on the air. The news that Tony was thought to be in the reserve brought a smile to his face and he grabbed his car keys and dashed to the garage.

On his way to the nature preserve he thought that it was only a matter of time. With any luck, he'd not only find Tony, but Amy as well. Then we'll see who the real losers are. He cast a glance into the mirror and noted that his ruddy face was more flushed than normal. Had he remembered to take his medication? He couldn't be bothered with that now; he had to find them before they got away.

He ran his tongue over his parched lips, thinking back to his last encounter with Amy Tremble. The image of her berating him caused him to wince. Why had he let her see him grovel like that? He had forgotten the painful lessons learned as a boy living with a loveless mother. He was only eight-years-old when he discovered the secrets for avoiding pain: First, never let yourself care about other people, they were only things to be used to accomplish his goals; and second, he learned to construct mental walls around his own feelings, isolating him from all emotional entanglements.

Reason, intellect, and logic were his primary tools for coping with the outside world, and he had proved to be a master of them all. There was no room for emotion in his life. Emotions, he knew, could only lead to vulnerability and weakness.

Only one other time had he let himself feel something for a woman, and the results had been the same—with the same woman. Stupid! He felt like hitting his head against the steering wheel, but settled for banging his palm against it instead. She could have had anything her heart desired. He would have given her the world if she…

That's enough self-pity, he told himself. It's over and done with. He had learned his lesson, and now he was going to make her pay for the pain she had caused him. He reached down to his belt and ran his fingers over the Colt's double diamond walnut grip. He felt a spark of electricity run from his fingers, up his arm, and course through his body.

Windrusher was literally shaking. The ground beneath him seemed to be rolling; the eucalyptus tree over his head swayed as though reacting to the rhythms of an inaudible syncopation. He was too frightened to move, even if he could, and closed his eyes to shut out the incomprehensible havoc that was taking place around him.

Was this what Tho-hoth had warned him about? The great god of wisdom had been right that there was danger in his future, but there was no way he could have prepared himself for such a thing. He flattened himself against the ground, his tail fluffed out in fear, his ears twitching apprehensively. Finally, the bucking earth slowed, and he stopped bouncing. For the first time he thought that he might survive this nightmare.

Breathe deeply, he told himself, pulling in great gulps of air, as though he had been holding his breath all this time. He would never know what caused the ground to shake like it had, but relief flooded through him. He was still alive and could resume his journey to find—Then he remembered that she had been there calling his name when the bedlam had driven the memory of her voice from his head.

The voice had come amidst the rumbling noises as though from a great distance, but he was sure that it was the voice of his female Hyskos. He pulled himself erect, testing his legs against the now tranquil earth. His ears still twitched nervously, but he felt more confident knowing that she was nearby.

All seemed to be right with his world once again. For the first time he noticed the worn path leading past the tree and toward a beige-colored bluff. The sandstone cliff formed a sterile wedge in the otherwise verdant landscape as though a giant had gouged the earth, piling up layers of loose brown dirt.

There was something about the slopes that reminded him of his first visit to the Cave of Tho-hoth. He moved toward the cliff, and then stopped when he heard her calling again. "Tony!" The voice was unmistakable, and it was much closer this time. Whirling around, he saw three high-legged beings moving swiftly toward him.

"Tony, it's me, Kimmy. Don't be afraid, we're coming to get you. To take you home."

His heart pumped wildly. It was true. She was here, and she had come for him. After all he had been through, it was almost too much to hope that they'd find each other, but there she was running toward him with the older female behind her. A two-legged male that he didn't recognize was with them, and they were waving at him. He would be going home after all.

The surface wave took him completely by surprise. There were no warning vibrations this time, only a sudden surge of energy whipping through the earth's crust, racing along the fault line with enough strength to knock the legs out from under any living creature in the vicinity. The three Hyskos dropped as though an invisible hand had swatted them. He was tossed to the ground, and he rolled over several times.

Frantically, he scratched at the roiling terrain, gripped by a depth of fear he had never known. In his panic, he only thought of his survival and began crawling away looking for a refuge from this nightmare. There had to be a safe haven, but where?

Fighting against the twisting and rolling ground beneath his feet, as well as the terror that nearly paralyzed him, he lurched forward. Step by agonizing step, scraping across the bucking landscape toward his safe haven—the Cave of Tho-hoth.

38

THE ONLY ACCURATE PREDICTION scientists can make about earthquakes is that there will be one today. On any given day, thousands of earthquakes trigger seismographs tracing the ground oscillations beneath them, but most are too small to be felt. On this afternoon the compressional wave that traveled through the San Elijo Ecological Reserve originated more than sixty miles away along the Elsinore Fault Zone. Scientists would later classify this disturbance as having a Richter value of 5.4, but because it originated in the relatively unpopulated area near Quail Valley and Canyon Lake, the damage was light.

While it broke dishes and windows in those towns and toppled chimneys and signs in Wildomar, the primary or "P" wave was felt as far away as Las Vegas and Baja California. Among its many other attributes, Southern California straddles the boundary between the Pacific and North American plates. These are large sections of the earth's crust that slide past each other at glacial speeds. The fastest moving of these faults, up to two inches a year, are found in Southern California (San Andreas, San Jacinto, Elsinore, and Imperial Faults) and account for half of the significant earthquakes in the region.

The stress and strain along the Elsinore Fault had been building for decades. Like titanic Sumo wrestlers locked in a death grip, the forces acting upon these blocks of the earth's crust grasped one another in massive head locks, bending, twisting, and finally breaking. On this day, they snapped to a new position and caused the vibrations felt by Windrusher in the estuary.

The P wave raced from the Elsinore Fault at the speed of four miles per second, breaking through the surface of the earth and causing the thud heard by Windrusher and the others. Coming behind it, the slower shear wave set off surface waves that made the earth seem like it was rolling.

He left the shaking eucalyptus tree behind, stumbling blindly away from the furies that were wreaking havoc on his world. He followed the path beneath him through the grass, over the rocks, and along a rocky ridge to the sandstone bluff. He was too panicked to see the grotesque faces carved along the cliff walls by creative young people over the years. The earth was still quivering, and he pushed forward, climbing the crumbling slope until he reached a sandy ledge beneath the cliffs that rose above him on two sides. He scrambled over a large rock and found what he had been looking for—a shallow gulley running from the edge of the cliff face down into the lower slopes he'd just climbed.

It was no more than a few inches wide at the lowest edge of the slope and fanned out to four or five feet nearest the cliff face where years of erosion had eaten it away. He stood staring into the pie-shaped ditch, remembering the opening in the cliff wall from his dream of Tho-hoth. The gash in the earth dropped back into the shadows, and he had no idea how deep it was. But it had to be deep enough to offer him protection from the shaking earth.

Another shock wave spread across the estuary, vibrating through his entire body. He was sure he was about to die, that this invisible force that had set the earth to wobbling would squash him unless he found his safe haven. Eyes wide with fright, blood throbbing through his veins with such velocity that he heard his pulse drumming in his temples, Windrusher dived into the gulley.

Amy's heartbeat was nearly back to normal now that the vibrations had slowed. She put an arm around her daughter and pulled her to her feet, "Are you all right, honey?"

Color was returning to Kimmy's pale face. "I'm fine, but we have to find Tony," she said breathlessly.

"I know, baby. We will." She hugged Kimmy like she had been lost for days. They had lived through one of the most stressful experiences that she had ever encountered, and she told herself that she would never complain about the unfairness of life or feel self-pity again. Please, give me boredom anytime.

"He was over by the tree," Quint said, pointing to the eucalyptus.

"I know, and I think he heard me," Kimmy answered. "I saw him turn, then the other quake came and he ran away toward those cliffs."

"He must be so frightened," Amy said, thinking that he wasn't half as frightened as she was.

"Hopefully, that's the end of the aftershocks. Let's find him and get back to the house," Quint said.

Amy nodded her agreement. Kimmy pulled out of her arms and ran toward the sandstone cliffs. "Wait for us, Kimmy," she yelled. She wasn't sure if her legs were up to running yet.

With some impatience, Kimmy slowed and let the others catch up to her. Together, they walked briskly past the eucalyptus tree and followed the path toward the bluff.

Quint took the lead as they approached the sandy slope of the bluff. "Be careful where you step, there are a lot of stones here, and that path doesn't look all that stable."

This time it was Amy's turn to play Indian guide. "Look, he came this way." She pointed to the tracks scratched into the sand spilling from the ledge. Kimmy released her mother's hand and scrabbled up the slope.

"Tony, where are you?"

She was on the large rock screaming his name into the pale notch of sandstone. She turned back frantically. "He's not here. Where could he have gone?"

They all heard the plaintive meow from the other side of the rock. Quint climbed on the rock and Amy and Kimmy stepped around and stared into the gulley. "There," Kimmy yelled, pointing at a shadowy form. "There he is."

Tony was curled into a tense ball huddled in a pit nearly five feet deep. He saw them and lifted his head to meow again. His ears twitched as though they were still vibrating to the earthquake's oscillations, and Amy realized the poor thing was so frightened that he was shaking uncontrollably.

"Tony, are you all right?" Kimmy cried. "Do you think he's hurt?" She was close to tears and looked from her mother to Quint and back to her cat.

"I think he's just scared. We may have to help him out of there," Amy said.

Kimmy stepped carefully into the ditch calling to Tony who was making an effort to stand. Without warning, Quint pushed Amy roughly aside. She tumbled backwards off the edge, thinking that he had lost his mind. She saw him lunge forward and grab Kimmy by the shoulder.

"No, don't," he shouted hoarsely. He yanked her back and tumbled with her down the sloping path next to Amy. Kimmy screamed as a crumbling block of the bluff slid in a rush of sand and rocks down the cliff face and onto Tony.

39

BURIED ALIVE. Beneath a pile of dirt and rocks, Windrusher slept. Maybe one of the rocks knocked him unconscious, or perhaps this was his way of coping with the unthinkable. Either way, still curled into a ball, in a pocket of air that had formed around him, he spiraled deeper into sleep.

Everything was black and hot. He moaned in pain, in fear. Instead of the renewing embrace of Hwrt-Heru, this sleep was tortured. A form emerged far away in a circle of light, as though at the far end of a tunnel. It moved closer, the light growing brighter until he saw that it was Lil' One—Lil' One, his old traveling companion left behind at the dairy farm.

"Lil' One, is that really you?" he asked in his dream.

The image expanded until Lil' One's face peered down on him as though from a massive movie screen. "You've looked better, you old tail chaser," the image said in Lil' One's voice. "I've missed you, Windrusher. Missed our adventures together."

"And I've missed you, Lil' One," he replied. An aura of colors swirled around Lil' One's head, lending the dream a surreal quality.

"Do you remember our run down the mountain?"

"It was only a hill."

"And Scowl Down's complaining? Our ride in the moving room with the young female? Do you remember what we meant to one another?" Lil' One's questions peppered him accusingly.

"Of course I remember. I remember it all and think of you often, my little friend."

"Keep me with you, Windrusher. Maybe one day we will see each other again."

Then he was gone. "Lil' One," he called out. But the image had faded away and only blackness remained. Then his mental movie screen flickered, and he saw another familiar figure. It was the old woman he had lived with before the black fury had flung him into the night. They were sitting together, as they had done on many nights, she in her easy chair, he lying on her ample lap.

She smiled at him, one hand gently brushing his coat. "Crackers, you are one lucky cat."

He remembered that she had called him Crackers, and he was amazed that he understood the Hyskos speech in his dream. It was as though her words popped into his brain as complete thoughts and not the nonsensical babble he usually heard with his ears. How much he had loved this woman. She had taken him in when he was in pain and nursed him back to health. He purred loudly in his dream.

She continued petting him, running her nails through his fur like the tines of a fork. "Here we are again," she said, "even if it's only in a dream. You can understand me, can't you?"

He purred again.

"Good, because I want you to listen carefully. We don't have much time. You don't have much time. You've slept long enough, you need to wake up and get on with it."

What was she talking about, he wondered? It's true that these high-legged beings made little sense, but she was talking in circles like a whiskerless kitten. In his dream, he rubbed his head against her thigh and purred again.

"The time for sleeping is over, Pferusha-ulis. Get on with it," she repeated.

How was it possible for her to know his feline call name? He squirmed in the elderly woman's lap, the heat from her body making him sweat. Windrusher gasped for air, his chest felt tight and it hurt to breathe. Why was he having these dreams? He didn't need the pain that came from revisiting these old ghosts from his past. Why couldn't they let him sleep in peace?

With a great effort, he turned to look at the old Hyskos woman. Her wide, gentle face with its broad smile seemed to melt before his eyes and he found himself staring up at Tho-hoth. The great god of wisdom was standing on top of the sandstone cliff. Dirt sifted down the side of the bluff in little flurries, but he stood erect, his collar with the blood red Stone of Life throwing off sparks.

He waited expectantly for Tho-hoth to explain this strange series of dreams. A luminous nimbus enveloped Tho-hoth, who finally turned his great head and looked directly at him. "Here you are, Pferusha-ulis, trapped in the very pit of death I warned you about."

The words erupted in his head in molten bursts of heat, and he felt pressure building in his brain. He squeezed his eyes shut, praying for sleep to end the pain.

"I know you want to sleep. And that is your choice, but if you do it will be your final rest." Tho-hoth was no longer on the cliff, but somehow beside him, one paw gently caressing his face. "Your Hyskos family is out there trying to rescue you, Windrusher, but unless you help them it will be too late. Too late for you and for them."

His family? It was coming back to him now, the awful shaking that left him cowering in the hole like a whimpering kitten. She was there. His young female had been calling his name, crying for him, reaching out for him. Then it happened—sudden darkness, the awful weight crushing him, burying him alive.

"Do you want to die in this dark hole?" Tho-hoth's question brought him back to the present. "Are you still that same cat, Pferusha-ulis, or is it time to put the legend aside and let you enjoy your long sleep?"

He squirmed, but was unable to move. "Help me, Tho-hoth. Don't leave me here." He wasn't sure if he spoke the words aloud or whether this was part of the dream.

"It is time for you to help yourself," Tho-hoth answered. "I'll be with you. I'll always be with you, but you must fight to save yourself, and save your Hyskos."

The words faded away along with the image of the god of wisdom. He was alone now and fully awake. Pain seeped into his consciousness along with the pressure that threatened to crush him. He attempted to move his head, and was surprised that it actually moved. The rocks and sand had apparently formed a small pocket around his upper torso, and he wiggled his head and neck hoping to make it larger. He struggled to move his front paws. The right one was tightly pinned against his body, but he was able to wrench the left one up toward his head.

With great effort, he forced his leg up, clawing at the dirt around his body. He scratched at the sand and rocks restraining his other leg, struggling to remain calm in the face of the paralyzing fear that had spread over and through him. Lungs aching, he breathed in with great care, swallowing grains of sand along with the tiny amount of stale air that remained in the pocket surrounding his head.

He panicked and pressed down with his back legs, trying to push his body forward with the sheer force of his will and diminishing strength. His leg muscles quivered with the effort until a spasm coursed through his back and he winced from the pain. But he couldn't stop. Time was running out, along with his air.

A sudden fury replaced the panic attack, and he clawed out at the injustice of his situation. With each scratch he tore at the hated Hyskos who was responsible for taking him from his home. He pictured the man's broad smile, heard the trusting voice, and despite the fact the high-legged being was now dead, he hated him even more. It wasn't fair that he end his days in this hole in the ground, and he clawed at the unknown force that had shaken the earth and buried him alive.

He continued clawing and pushing at the dirt above him until he felt his body edge upwards. He was moving, thanks be to Tho-hoth. With renewed energy, he scratched at the dirt on his right side, pushing aside small rocks and loose sand until finally he freed his other leg. Both paws were above him now, claws ripping into the soil, pushing it down beneath him. He used his back legs to propel himself forward, climbing the rocks and dirt that passed by him as if he was climbing a ladder.

The more he dug, the looser the earth seemed to be, and the more dirt he clawed aside. His heart fluttered wildly with hope. He was moving more rapidly now; and he let himself believe that he might actually dig his way out and see Rahhna's rays again. A vision of Rahhna shining in the heavens blossomed before him just as his left paw scraped violently against a large rock, tearing his pad and ripping out a nail. The pain furrowed through his paw and up his leg like a vicious parasite working its way into his heart.

His surge of frantic energy came to an abrupt stop, and he felt like he was collapsing into himself. He realized he had been holding his breath. Lungs strained to the breaking point, what little hope he had was now replaced by utter hopelessness. Why did he dare to think that he might dig his way out of this pit of death? He had been digging blindly, not knowing up from down. For all he knew, he had been digging himself a deeper grave.

A light went on in his brain, and he remembered the touch of Tho-hoth's paw on his face, and the look in those pale green eyes. No, I can't give up now, he told himself. Tho-hoth must have believed that there was a way out or he wouldn't have stayed with him, wouldn't have urged him on. Desperately, he scratched at the edges of the rock blocking his way. With bleeding and torn claws, he ripped at the soil until slowly the rock slipped to one side and he squeezed past it with a painful grunt.

Despite his small victory, he was forced to stop. A series of whimpers escaped as he fought the urge to open his mouth and breathe. He knew that only death awaited that last gasp, picturing sand filling his mouth and throat. Would it be painful he wondered, or like falling asleep? Sleep was what he needed. He had tried bravely, but he knew it was over for him. With this acceptance, a stillness settled over him and he retreated into that small, quiet place that welcomes all beings home in their final moments.

Her voice seeped into his waning consciousness. "Tony, we're coming, baby."

He fought the urge to return to the pain, but he heard scraping over his head and frantic cries. Even with his eyes shut, with the dirt packed around him, he sensed a dim light in the distance. Was this Irissa-u calling him to the home of the gods on Rahhna?

"Tony, oh, Tony," the voice sounded again. He felt something brush against him, and realized the light had grown brighter. It hurt his eyes and, with a supreme effort, he lifted a paw to shield his face.

Quint was digging furiously, casting away stones, using his hands as shovels. Amy and Kimmy were beside him. Together they scraped at the mound of soil that had fallen from the bluff and entombed Tony. Only a minute or two had passed, but how long could a cat survive beneath this, he wondered? Even if he was lucky enough to avoid being hit by one of the big rocks, he must be out of air by now.

He ignored the pain in his hands and kept scraping away the layers of brown dirt. They had already dug down several feet, but would they get there in time? He heard Kimmy sobbing behind him, felt the sweat gathering in his armpits and on his chest. It was ironic that this case ended with him on another dig. But this is your most important dig, he told himself. This one is to find the living, not traces of a long-dead past.

They broke through into a dark hollow, scraped at the soil and instead of the harsh gravel and dirt, he felt a soft form beneath his fingers. Kimmy's scream made him wince. "Tony, oh, Tony."

They were all on their knees staring into the hole. Amazingly, Tony was moving a paw. He was still alive. Gently, Quint lifted him out of the hole, brushing the sand from his face, cradling him as a mother would cradle her baby. He was aware of Kimmy and Amy's cries of delight as he carefully backed away, stumbling a little over the loose sand and rocks.

They had done it. Had brought him out alive. He was on the verge of tears, caught in a wave of strong emotion. If he felt this way, he wondered how overwhelmed Kimmy and Amy must be.

"Be careful," Amy said, putting a hand on his shoulder to steady him.

He stood still for a moment holding the limp cat to his chest, and then pivoted to pass Tony to Kimmy who was holding her arms out, tears streaming down her dirty face. He only caught a momentary glimpse of a quickly moving form behind him before the pain struck him in the right temple. He staggered, his legs losing their strength, blackness sweeping away the daylight, and he dropped back into the hole still cradling Tony in his arms.

40

THE SOUND OF THE COLT smacking against Mitchell's head was satisfying, but not as satisfying as seeing the big man drop as if he had stepped into the path of a Louisville Slugger. Von Rothmann noted that the cat hadn't moved. It lay in Mitchell's arms in the ditch like some ancient Egyptian Pharaoh buried with his favorite pet.

He had arrived at the southwestern end of the reserve next to the sandstone cliffs just as the earthquake hit, and had ridden out the primary wave and the aftershock in his car. He made his way to the edge of the cliff in time to see Mitchell and the others running toward the mound of dirt and start digging.

He had always known he was smarter than anyone else, but he also considered himself lucky. Other physicists had been working on the same line of nanotechnology as he was, but he had been the one to make the breakthrough first. And his luck had held for his entire career. From being lucky enough to find the right venture capitalists to his good fortune in finding a buyer when he was ready to get out.

Now, he was lucky again. He might have driven to a half-dozen spots to park and enter the San Elijo Lagoon, but he picked a spot off I-5 near Glencrest, and it was the right one.

He had made his way into the reserve using a trail that circled the bluff and brought him behind them. The way they were digging, their heads down, frantically scattering sand and stones everywhere, he doubted if they would have noticed him anyway. Then it was only a matter of getting rid of the big guy so he could take care of Amy and Tony without any heroics from the private detective.

His face was flushed and sweaty, and his eyes had a feverish glow as he waved the Colt at Amy and Kimmy with trembling hands. The excitement of the moment was enough to make him forget the hammering in his temples that had begun when he entered the reserve.

"Amy, Amy, Amy," he sang, pointing the gun at her chest. "You thought I would listen to your abuse and forget about it?" He shook his head as a kindergarten teacher might do when correcting a misbehaving child.

"Karl, I'm sorry, I didn't mean to hurt you. Please put that gun away before—"

He stepped closer to Amy, pushing the gun into her breastbone. Her exhalation of breath stopped her in mid-sentence. It was evident that she was frightened, and this fueled his excitement, knowing the power he held over her. He wasn't exactly sure what he would do to her when the time came, if his fury would carry him along to the point that he would do something he might later regret.

"Shut up, Amy. I've heard all I want to hear from you," he snapped. The little girl was sobbing, hanging on to her mother's arm. He stepped back from them so he had a good view of the unconscious detective still holding the cat. He smiled his death's-head smile, and pointed the Colt into the pit with trembling hands.

"This cat of yours has been more trouble than he's worth," he said, closing his left hand over his right wrist to stabilize it. "You shouldn't have gone to all that trouble to dig him out, now you'll only have to bury him again."

Even with the bright sun beating down, a cool sea breeze sent a shiver through him as he raised the Colt and sighted down the barrel. Behind him he heard their pitiful cries of protest.

Amy knew that von Rothmann was strange, but not that he was so unstable. Why did she go to his house and provoke him? "Karl, let's talk about this," she said, using her nurse's voice and taking a tentative step toward him. "I was wrong about you; please, let me make it right."

He didn't respond other than twist his mouth into a menacing sneer. His hands were shaking almost uncontrollably, and she worried that he was losing all control. There was clearly something wrong with him; the sweats, his trembling hands. Maybe he's on drugs. Maybe he's having a psychotic reaction.

"Say goodbye to your cat," he mumbled.

The loud scream surprised both of them and von Rothmann swung around, the pistol wavering in his unsteady hands. Kimmy had leaped into the pit and covered Tony's body with her own. She was crying furiously, yelling at von Rothmann between the sobs. "No…don't hurt him. You can't hurt Tony."

She couldn't believe her daughter had put herself between Tony and this maniac with the gun. She noticed Quint's eye lids flutter and open. He stared unsteadily at her, obviously still dazed. She rushed forward to pull Kimmy from the pit, but von Rothmann grabbed her arm and sent her tumbling back with a vicious shove.

His hand went to the side of his head and he left it there as though trying to divine the answer to some complex problem. He was staring wide-eyed at Amy, and she saw that the color had drained from his usually ruddy face, and his body jerked like he was walking across hot coals.

"This is what she wants, your little girl? She wants to die with her cat?" He turned away from Amy and back toward the pit where Quint was squirming, trying to find the strength to rise from beneath the pile of bodies. Von Rothmann stumbled forward, the gun shaking in his hands.

Amy grabbed the large rock at her feet and without hesitation crashed it down on the back of his head. He staggered, falling forward onto one knee, and then the other. Von Rothmann grabbed the back of his head and moaned loudly, but his other hand still held the pistol. On his knees, holding his head, and shaking as if he was caught in the throes of some sacramental rite, he let out a series of shrill whines.

"Get out, Kimmy," she yelled and swung the rock at him again. This time the clump of sandstone broke over the top of his head and crumbled into pieces. He fell forward as Kimmy scrambled out of the pit clutching Tony in her arms.

Quint pushed himself up with one arm, his eyes not totally focused.

She was afraid he might have suffered a concussion, but with some effort Quint rose to his knees and grabbed von Rothmann's gun hand.

Quint towered over the smaller man, but von Rothmann was surprisingly strong and pulled away from him. Still shaking and growling like a maddened beast, he stood up in the rocky pit swinging the Colt at Quint's head. This time Quint saw the blow coming and stepped out of the way, grabbing von Rothmann's arm and attempting to twist the gun away.

He flung himself at Quint, wrapping his arms and legs around him until they toppled together like roped steers. Sand flew from the pit and they rolled over and over, flailing at one another. Quint grasped von Rothmann's right wrist, pushing the Colt to one side, trying to roll on top of him so he could use his leverage to force the gun out of his hand.

Through it all, Kimmy stood to one side, as though oblivious to the fight that was taking place at her feet. Wiping the sand from Tony's eyes and mouth, she covered him with kisses until he responded with a low purr and licked her face like a dog. "Oh baby, you're all right," she cried.

Amy saw von Rothmann jam the heel of his hand under Quint's chin and shove his head back. At the same time, he twisted his body toward him, forcing Quint's arm down, the Colt in his hand slowly moving toward Quint's chest.

She had seen too many gun shot wounds during her years as a nurse, and knew how much damage those grams of lead did as they rocketed through muscles and organs. She pictured von Rothmann twisting around until he had the gun against Quint's chest and then pulling the trigger.

Amy didn't wait to find a rock this time, but threw herself onto the two men. Von Rothmann somehow shrugged her off his back and swiveled away, leaving her lying beside Quint.

With a rush of understanding, it all came flooding back to Windrusher. He had been buried in the pit and his young female and the others had saved him. Pulled him back from his final sleep. Now, here he was in her arms, still alive because of her.

The Hyskos men were fighting with one another, rolling on the ground like crazed Setlos. He would never understand the things they did, but this was totally incomprehensible. Perhaps they were playing as young cats do, testing their strength, wrestling to protect their territory. But when his older female Hyskos, Kimmy's mother, leaped onto the others, he knew that something was terribly wrong.

The squat man who had been at the house where he and the other cats had been taken was snarling at them like a wild creature. He was pointing a metal object at the other two and the female was crying. Then he remembered what Tho-hoth had told him: *"...unless you help them it will be too late. Too late for you and for them."*

This is what Tho-hoth had warned him about. It was up to him to save his Hyskos family. The man was babbling again, his voice rising, and he was pointing the object at the woman. He reacted with the instincts of his jungle ancestors. Claws extended, he sprang from the girl's arms and landed on the two-legged being's upper back. A low growl gurgled deep in his throat as he dug his nails into the man's shoulder's and pulled himself up as he would climb a tree.

The man screamed in pain and swiped at him with his free hand. He shut out the noise, ignored the hand brushing over him, and sunk his teeth deep into his neck. Like a cornered prey, the man whimpered and thrashed trying desperately to dislodge him. But Windrusher held on, burying his teeth deeper, tasting the man's blood on his tongue.

His growl grew louder, and he shook his head as though extinguishing the life from a trembling field mouse. Lost in the fury of the moment, he bit down even harder, trying to tear away the panic and fear he had felt while buried under the earth. He was only dimly aware of his young female's cries, of the other female scrambling out of the pit. Everything seemed to be bathed in a reddish cast, and the brown cliffs hovering over them had taken on a crimson hue, as though shrouded in blood. The other male, the one who had helped to dig him out, was now pressing the other man's face into the dirt. He had torn the metal object from his grip and suddenly it was all over.

The man stepped back, and his female was pulling him away, speaking reassuringly, lovingly to him. They formed a semi-circle around the man who was clasping his neck, whimpering like a kitten. Windrusher breathed heavily, aware that something extraordinary had happened. He looked at his young female and saw that she was smiling at him. Then her expression changed to one of horror, and he was afraid the man was about to attack them once again.

He was carried back, down the path, away from the open pit. He heard the scream and turned to see sand and stones sliding down the cliff face and entombing the screaming Hyskos.

41

"CALL 911," QUINT SCREAMED, throwing his cell to Amy. He was digging furiously at the mound of dirt covering von Rothmann, slinging rocks and dirt aside. She watched Quint's swiftly moving hands as she waited for the 911 operator, and saw them uncover von Rothmann's shoulder. Fortunately for him, the slide wasn't as massive as the first one that had covered Tony, and he was close to the surface.

When the operator came on, Amy quickly told her where they were, what had happened, and asked for both the police and an EMT. Quint uncovered von Rothmann's upper torso, and she hurried over to help pull him out. His limbs and head were twitching uncontrollably, and she moved quickly to help drag him away from the cliff.

"Turn him over on his side," she said, checking to make sure he was able to breathe. She didn't see a medical alert bracelet and unbuttoned the first few buttons of his shirt to see if it was around his neck. She wasn't sure if he was epileptic, but the symptoms he had displayed earlier, the sweating and shakes, his apparent confusion, and now the seizure, led her to believe he was diabetic and hypoglycemic.

Fingering the chain around his neck, she pulled it out and stared at the small silver cross in disbelief. Her grandmother's cross. It had disappeared from her apartment in Boston, and now her suspicions were confirmed. She remembered returning to the apartment from classes one day somehow knowing that Karl had been there. Oh, he was careful not to disturb anything, but the image of that day came vividly back to her, and she shuddered picturing him going through her personal belongings and stealing her grandmother's cross.

The sky was a remarkably clear shade of blue, and Amy admired it as she inhaled the fragrance of the ocean blowing across the estuary. A detective had already taken their statements and she and Kimmy sat in the back seat of a patrol car waiting for a ride to Brad's house where they had left their car. She watched the medical tech finish dressing the bite on von Rothmann's neck, and knew that along with his legal problems, Tony's bite could prove to be quite serious for a person in his condition. The emergency technician had confirmed that he was suffering from insulin shock, and had given him three glucose tablets.

Kimmy leaned against her, one hand resting on Tony, who lay quietly in her lap. "Mom," Kimmy said quietly.

"Uhmm."

"Do you realize that Tony saved our lives?"

She watched her daughter gently stroking Tony, who was still covered with layers of sand. He needed a good bath, she thought. But then, didn't they all? She planned to spend an hour soaking in the tub when they got back to the hotel. "You're right, baby. Tony is definitely the hero of this story."

"What about you?" Kimmy cut her eyes toward von Rothmann. "He's going to have a mean headache, don't you think?"

She laughed despite herself. "I'm not sure where that came from. I guess it's true that a mother will do whatever is necessary to protect her children."

"Tony must have read that same parenting book the way he protected his family."

She looked at her daughter with surprise, then reached over and gently stroked Tony's head. "You're right. I don't know what would have happened if he hadn't been here."

Kimmy giggled.

"What's so funny?"

"We wouldn't have been here if Tony wasn't here."

"I guess you're right. But it all worked out, didn't it?" She studied the silver cross in her hand, and Kimmy ran a small finger over the delicate crucifix as though it contained magical powers.

"Did this really belong to your grandmother?"

"And your great-grandmother. Yes, and I'm so happy to have it back." She knew that she owed Kimmy and Quint an explanation of how her grandmother's cross ended up around von Rothmann's neck, but that would come later. Maybe after the bath. Yes, definitely after the bath.

The detective gave them a lift to Brad's house and they went inside to find the surfer waiting for them. His eyes went wide as he saw the three of them covered with sand, and the bandage on Quint's head. "Oh, God, you must have been caught in the quake." Then he spotted Tony in Kimmy's arms. "You found him. Wow, I was so worried, man. When that thing hit and everything shook, I just got under my table and waited for it to pass. Then the phones were out, and I was about to go look for you…"

"That's all right, the quake was the least of our worries," Quint said, giving Amy an ironic smile. "In a way, I guess it actually helped us out." He patted his head gently as though reassuring himself that the bandage was still there and told Brad about their encounter with von Rothmann.

Back at the hotel, Kimmy had asked some pointed questions before stepping into the shower. Amy had fended her off, telling her she would explain everything after they had both scrubbed the grime from their bodies. First she showered; the water sharp like pin pricks, washing away the dust and dirt. Then she filled the tub with hot water, mixing it with half of the small bottle of hotel shampoo, and soaked. She leaned back and closed her eyes, imagining that she was floating in a tropical sea, the night sky ablaze with stars, the scent of jasmine wafting through the air. Slowly, the knots of tension loosened, and she felt her fears slide away with the soap bubbles.

Tony wasn't happy about it, but he got a bath, too. It took both of them to hold him until he seemed to realize that his struggling was only prolonging the situation. He stood nearly motionless and accepted the indignation of soap suds with only a few peevish meows. Later, with Tony napping on a towel on the bed, Kimmy listened with quiet attention as she told her how she had first met Karl von Rothmann. She told her of their brief friendship, and how she hadn't seen or even thought of him in twenty years.

"I'm so sorry that you had to go through this terrible ordeal, baby. And Tony, too," she added quickly before Kimmy could remind her of who had suffered the most.

"What's going to happen to Mr. von Rothmann?" asked Kimmy.

"I don't know. He's got some serious mental problems, along with his poor health. I imagine that he'll have to get therapy, but he should be put in jail for what he tried to do to us."

"For a long time, I hope."

She smiled at her daughter in agreement. "Kimmy, I hope you realize that I would never have put us in such a dangerous situation if I knew that he was behind Tony's disappearance. We should have stayed in Florida and let Quint bring Tony back to us."

Kimmy was shaking her head. "No, I don't think so."

"What do you mean?"

"Think about it. Less than two weeks ago, before Tony was stolen, you hardly got out of bed. I don't know what happened to you, but you just weren't the same and it…" She paused, looking at her mother with tears in her eyes. "It scared me, thinking that maybe we'd never get our old mom back."

"Old!"

"You know what I mean. But look at you now. You're a fighting machine like Storm or Mystique." Her eyes gleamed with pride.

"Storm and Mystique?"

Her expression changed to exasperation. "Oh, mom, the X-Men. Storm and Mystique are awesome. Of course, they're not Wolverine, but they hold their own with the guys. "

"Thank you, honey, that's high praise indeed." Her daughter was right about the change in her. An image came to mind that nearly made her wince. She was lying in bed, filled with self-pity and wracked with doubt and depression, not able to even get out of bed and make breakfast for her children. How had she let herself slide into that dark pit of anxiety and despair? She wasn't sure, but she was glad that it was behind her.

She left Kimmy and Tony napping together and took the elevator down to the first floor restaurant. Quint was already there waiting for her with a cup of coffee in front of him. He had showered and changed clothes, and, except for the bandage on his forehead, looked none the worse for wear.

"How's the head?" she asked.

"Like my father was fond of saying whenever I fell and bumped my head, 'It's a good thing that nothing important was hurt.'" He gingerly touched his head and smiled.

She ordered a cup of iced coffee, and when the waitress brought it to her she stirred in a little cream and sugar, focusing on the coffee instead of looking at Quint. He hadn't spoken since she asked about his head and the silence hanging between them was growing uncomfortable.

She looked up from her glass to meet his eyes. "I guess I owe you an explanation."

"I figured you would eventually tell me what was going on," he said.

She nodded slowly, her eyes drifting to the windows behind him where a sprinkler was splashing the panes, then back to him. "It was so long ago…" She told him everything. "Honestly, I had no idea he was involved in this. And I wouldn't have gone to his house if I knew that it would set him off." She paused and sipped her coffee.

"After I left his house, I was confused and afraid. But then you called to say that they had found Brad and he had Tony." She spread her hands out in front of her, palms up. "I felt like my prayers had been answered." She gave him a tight smile, hoping that he understood.

"Confused and afraid?" He had a bemused look on his face. "You didn't look confused and afraid when you cracked him over the head with that rock," he said.

"Guess I wasn't thinking."

"You're one tough cookie, Amy. I'm glad you're on my side. I appreciate how you feel about all of this, but it isn't your fault."

She started to protest.

"No, listen to me. Von Rothmann is one sick puppy, and he's the one to blame for stealing Tony and the other cats. In a way, he's also responsible for McWaters' death. I hope they throw everything at him and then some. Nothing would have changed if you had told me about him earlier. Who knew that he would show up with a gun?"

"You're very kind, Quint, and one heck of an investigator. You can use us as a reference anytime you want, but I hope we never need your professional services again," she said with only the hint of a smile.

"I'll be happy to get back to Florida. I'm sure you feel the same way."

"We're taking the first flight out in the morning. The police said they'd be in touch if they needed me to testify."

"These things can drag on for years, but I expect you'll eventually hear from the prosecutor's office sooner or later."

She had resigned herself to having to relive this experience until von Rothmann was convicted. "How about you," she asked, "are you flying back tomorrow?"

"I'm going to hang here for another day and take care of a couple of odds and ends."

Quint had insisted on taking Amy and Kimmy to the airport. They checked their bags with the curbside attendant and walked into the entrance rotunda. Taking the escalator to the upper level where Joan Irving's massive glass mosaic, *Sunlight Juxtaposed*, cast violet and aqua reflections on the floor, they joined the long line of people waiting to pass through security. Amy held her carry-on bag, and Kimmy held Tony in a soft carrier.

They hugged and said their goodbyes. "Keep in touch," Amy said as they stepped toward the security table.

"You might change your mind when you get my bill," he called back with a laugh.

After they disappeared down the long hall toward Terminal 2, he returned to his car and drove to the San Diego Police Department where he spent more than an hour with the detective in charge of von Rothmann' case. After leaving them all his contact numbers, he was back in his rental car again cruising north on I-5 at nearly seventy miles an hour.

Despite the traffic and the brief visit he made to a shopping center on Mira Mesa Boulevard, it took less than an hour to get to Encinitas in his rented Buick. He had called earlier to let them know he was coming, and when he entered the small lobby, Libby, the girl with the Reese Witherspoon smile, was there to greet him.

"You're back," she said, as though she hadn't expected to see him again.

"As promised."

"Good, are you ready?"

"Yep," he held up the collapsible pet carrier he had bought at the PETCO after he left the police station.

"That's cool. Okay, as they say, walk this way." She stepped around the counter and they walked next door into the small cattery with its stacks of cages. He noticed the name on the door of Cattery Eight had been changed from *Tennille* to *Dudley*. The small cat purred loudly as Libby slowly opened the stainless steel door and reached inside. She pulled the cat out with one hand, and quickly placed her other hand under its hindquarters to support it.

"Here you go," she said, handing him the cat.

He let the carrier fall to the floor and took the small cat in his hands. His eyebrows arched up a notch. "Is this all there is to it?"

"Not quite. We have some paperwork, and there's the fee, of course. But we'll have you and Dudley on your way in time for rush hour traffic." There was that sly grin again.

He held Darwin up at eye level, staring into the cat's huge blue eyes. "You're getting to do something not many of us ever have a chance to do—start over. I hope you'll like living in Jax Beach."

EPILOGUE

"THAT'S WONDERFUL, JEANNIE. I have it marked on the calendar and you can plan on us being there." Amy smiled broadly at Gerry who gave her his patented *What are you getting us into?* look and poured a second cup of coffee for them both. "Yes, yes, I love you too. My love to Tom and Stacy. Bye."

She hung up the telephone and joined Gerry in the sun room. "She's doing wonderfully," she said in answer to Gerry's unasked question. "The little guy is growing like crazy and sleeping most of the night."

"They have to be thrilled after what she went through with this pregnancy."

Amy sipped from her cup and admired the hummingbird hovering over the feeder outside their window. "You know they are," she finally replied with a faraway look in her eye. Then she turned to Gerry and grabbed his hand. "Isn't it great to be home together like this?"

Saturday mornings together had been rare occasions in the past months, and she wanted to make sure he knew that she appreciated it.

"It has been a tough couple of months with the construction, the golf tournament, and…" he patted her hand, searching for words before continuing, his voice suddenly husky. "And your medical problems."

Amy was touched, but tried to laugh it off. "*Problems* is a kind way of putting it. I would have put it differently, maybe catastrophe or meltdown." she said. Turning serious, she added, "I can't tell you how much I appreciate your strength through all of this, Gerry. I know what a burden I must have been and how much stress I added to your life, but you came through like a champ." She leaned over and kissed him on the cheek, which turned a rosy hue.

"Stop it," he said, dipping his head in mock humility. "You're making me blush."

"Hey, I'm being serious. Thank you for everything. For holding us together while I was coming apart, and for holding down the fort when Kimmy and I went charging off to California."

"The important thing is that you're back, and that we're all together again. I hope we can spend a lot more Saturday and Sunday mornings like this."

Amy had forced herself to wait two weeks before returning to the hospital. Gerry wanted her to wait a little longer, but she missed her work so much that they compromised and she began working part-time. Energized by the interaction with the patients and doctors, she returned to a full-time schedule after four weeks. Every other week she had weekend duty, so they both appreciated this opportunity to just hang around the house together as a couple of slugs, as Gerry so delicately put it.

This morning was especially quiet. G.T. was playing football with friends, and Kimmy was in her room surfing through the online catalogs for more clothes now that she was back in school. Stella, their black Lab, was lying on the couch in the other room.

"Before I forget, you need to put October 23rd on your calendar. Don't make any plans for that weekend, because we're all flying back to Bloomfield."

Gerry raised an eyebrow, and she saw the anxiety start to build. She knew he was already juggling manager schedules, trying to remember what major events might be planned for that weekend, possibly looking for excuses to get out of the trip.

"What's happening on October 23rd?"

Her eyes cut away from his face to the chaise lounge in the corner of the room. She had picked out the lounge furniture with its beige and green cushions and admired the rows of blue hydrangeas printed down the middle. Her gaze stopped at the foot of the cushion where an orange and gray cat lay sprawled.

She looked back at Gerry with a sly smile. "I told Jeannie we'd all be there. That's the day our new nephew, Tony, will be baptized."

Upon returning to Florida, Amy found that the horrendous experience with Karl von Rothmann had been liberating in a strange way. It had given her a sense of confidence and appreciation for her life and family. It had also strengthened her determination to get back to work.

She had thought about those three days in San Diego as a journey through a foreign land; facing unexpected discomforts and emergencies, hearing strange and alien voices, but finding a certain satisfaction in having endured and grown through the experience. Mercifully, those dueling voices in her head had vanished, and she knew that she had regained control of her life.

From what she could tell, Kimmy hadn't suffered from their encounter with von Rothmann either. In fact, Amy swore that her daughter was growing accustomed to these strange escapades with Tony, and she had come to believe that her cat was some kind of superhero. For weeks, she impressed all her friends with the amazing story of how Tony had saved their lives, and how she had saved Tony from being shot.

Naturally, Amy had told Gerry everything about von Rothmann. He was sympathetic, although he did ask if she had "any other psychopathic ex-boyfriends he should know about?" She assured him that she did not, but added with a wink, "You can't expect me to keep up with all my ex-boyfriends."

Three days after her conversation with her sister, Amy had a surprise visit from Quint Mitchell.

"Quint, what in the world are you doing here?" she asked after getting over the shock of seeing him at her front door. She gave him a hug then stepped aside to let him in. That's when she noticed the cat peeking out from under his arm. "You brought Darwin with you," she squealed excitedly.

He smiled and held the cat up for her to take. "Dudley. I decided I liked Dudley, and she didn't seem to mind, so Dudley it is."

They fussed over the cat while walking toward the sun room. "I thought that Tony might like to see the little gal again. They were roommates once, remember?"

"I'm not sure where Tony is hiding, but we'll find him. But this isn't why you drove three hours, is it?"

"Actually, I took a few days off to check out some archaeological sites that I might volunteer with this fall. Did you know that Crystal River has a state park built around six pre-Columbian mounds? They've found some tools and artifacts dating back to 200 B.C., so I thought I'd check it out." He put Dudley on the floor and the small cat sniffed excitedly and ran into the next room.

"Hey," he yelled after the cat.

"Don't worry, she'll be all right. Probably looking for Tony." Amy reached over and grabbed Quint's hand, giving it a friendly shake. "You won't believe this, but I've been thinking about calling you to see how you were doing."

"I've been so busy that I needed this break. It seems that somehow word leaked out about our California exploits and my phone has been ringing off the hook."

"Just leaked out?" She knew that she hadn't said anything to the media, since she wanted to avoid the circus atmosphere that had swept their household when Tony had been rescued from the tornado.

"It might have had something to do with the interview I did with Denise Waters before I left, and…"

"And?"

"And the press releases I sent out," he said rather sheepishly.

"Quint, I'm just beginning to realize what a huckster you really are," she said with a laugh.

"You're right. Anyway, I have more work than I can handle. Even hired another P.I. to help out."

"Good for you. And has Dudley adapted to living with a real life private investigator?"

"She's great. I take her to the office with me and Charla spoils her rotten. The little gal has put on a couple of pounds—Dudley, not Charla."

Finally, she asked him what was happening with the von Rothmann case.

"Not much as yet," he answered. "The guy nearly died from an infection he got after Tony bit him."

She knew that cat bites were serious, but this still shocked her. "Almost died, what happened?"

"I spoke with Officer Lawson a few days ago—you remember him, don't you? The one with all the muscles."

"Uh huh."

"Anyway, he told me that the bite became infected and von Rothmann developed a brain abscess. Maybe there is such a thing as karma. They ended up operating, drilling holes into his head to drain the abscess. He was in the hospital for weeks."

"I guess that's why I haven't heard from the prosecutor's office," she said.

"Didn't I tell you that this was going to be a long, drawn-out affair? Lawson said they obtained a search warrant and found clippings of Tony's run-in with the tornado. He even had a tape of your appearance on the *Today Show*."

"So, he's been obsessing about this for a while," she mused. "What about those other cats?"

He shrugged. "My guess is they were his first test experiments. Who knows, he's not talking. But the good news is they're charging him with attempted murder, felony theft—since Katmandu was insured for $50,000. And with conspiracy in the death of McWaters."

"Good." She had feared he would be treated differently because of his money, that his high-priced lawyers would get him off on some technicality. But it sounded like they were going after him on all charges. "Any other news?"

"I've got a new client," he said with a smile. "Ms. Corcoran has officially hired me to find Katmandu. I'll be flying back to San Diego next week and see if I can pick up her trail. She has to be somewhere close by. Maybe I can get Denise Waters to help."

"Why doesn't that surprise me? Seriously, I know that you'll find Katmandu. Hey, maybe you've opened up a whole new line of investigation." She gazed over his head and waved a hand as though unveiling a sign. "Quint Mitchell: Cat Detective."

They laughed. "I think that was a movie, wasn't it? Oh, that reminds me, you're going to love this. I called Murray's trainer, Iona Wager, the other day to see how they were getting along, and—"

"I saw on one of the entertainment news shows that Murray was back on *Larry's Life*," she interrupted.

"Yes, but here's the best part, she and her boyfriend, a writer, have a script based on the von Rothmann case and Disney is interested in the project."

"No way."

"You should have heard her… 'It's an unbelievable story filled with danger, intrigue, and a heroic cat. It's perfect for Murray.'" His voice had notched up an octave and she could picture the conversation with Iona Wager.

"So Murray is going to play the hero in this movie?"

"Iona informed me that they're called films, not movies. And yes, Murray will be the hero of the film."

"Good for him," she said. And she meant it. She didn't think that Tony would mind since he was too busy sleeping to star in any films.

Windrusher and Bright Claw had enjoyed their own reunion. The young cat had followed his scent to the upstairs bedroom where she found him asleep on a bed. She leaped onto the bed and pounced on her friend, growling playfully as he came awake with a start.

"By the gods, you frightened me…" He suddenly realized who it was and where they were. "Bright Claw! How…what…are you really here?"

"To think that you taught me to speak properly," she gently mocked him. "My Hyskos male carried me with him to visit you. It is good to see you again."

"I have thought of you often, little one, hoping that you had found a new home." They spent the short time they had together telling of their travels, and rekindling the flame of friendship that had been ignited during those stressful days.

When the high-legged being entered the room with his own female, he knew they would be parted again. With a lick and nuzzle, he said his goodbyes to Bright Claw, knowing that his young friend was safe and well cared for.

Later that same day, he awoke on the porch wondering where his Hyskos family might be. They had been here when he fell asleep and he searched the room anxiously, his eyes cutting from one corner to the next. He heard voices inside and lay back down.

This home, with its family of high-legged beings, was now the center of his world. He felt the walls wrap themselves around him like a protective cocoon, and knew that he and the two-legged ones were safe. His young female Hyskos provided him with all the love and affection he wanted.

He had noticed subtle changes in her since they had returned. Like leaves shifting colors, she was radiating a new confidence, reflecting an inner serenity that seemed to glow from within. He didn't fully understand it, but he had developed an even stronger bond with this young female and believed he could sense her feelings reaching out to him like circles of spiritual vibrations.

The experience with the ugly Hyskos and the terror of being buried alive had shaken him. Many day globes had come and gone before he ventured out of her room, spending his days sleeping on her bed and nights wedged tightly against her. His dreams had been fitful, filled with dark scenes that frightened him and jerked him back to consciousness, his heart beating wildly, his eyes searching for hidden dangers.

More than once, he had dreamed of a smiling Hyskos with a soothing voice. In the dream, he rolled over, exposing his belly to the high-legged being. He waited, his eyes closed, for the man to rub his belly, to run gentle fingers along his flank. Instead, he would open his eyes to see the man grinning hideously, reaching toward him with a sharp blade.

He would awaken in a panic.

Other dreams found him charging through the fields with Chaser and Bright Claw running madly beside him. He would urge them on, leading them along a path that rose toward a high bluff. He ran so fast that his paws barely touched the ground, and when he turned toward his two friends they were gone. He was alone on the edge of a high cliff, the Hyskos coming closer and closer.

Eventually, this dream faded away like the others.

Memories of those dreadful moments were still with him, but were becoming more shadowy with each passing day, like old photographs that had lost distinctive details over the years, dimmed to an obscure and gray version of the original.

Shortly after he returned home, he had related his experiences to Short Shank and the multitude of cats during a visit to the Akhen-et-u. Because he disliked the constant attention, he had stayed away until one recent night when his growing curiosity about Rahhna's Light finally drove him into the whirling vortex of Akhen-et-u.

He had made the connection and was one with Tho-hoth's greatest gift to cats, the Inner Ear. For a time, he was content to ride the currents, lurking on the edges of myriad conversations. When he sensed a break he introduced himself and heard the familiar rush of voices filled with awe and excitement.

"Windrusher, is it really you?"

"Windrusher, we have missed you."

"Have you been off on another adventure?"

"Please, tell us the story of the shaking earth."

He felt that he was in the middle of a twisting sand devil, noise all around him, being pulled one way then another. "My travels are all behind me, my friends. You have heard them too many times, and from what I hear, they are beginning to sound like the tales that kittens tell to frighten one another."

An explosion of voices erupted, pleading with him, questioning, some even daring to challenge the truth of his experiences. He felt like he was being torn into little pieces.

"Quiet!" It was the unmistakable voice of Short Shank berating the babble. "You forget the Code of Akhen-et-u. You forget your manners. This is no way to treat Windrusher, nor any cat. Your mothers would be disgusted to witness such behavior."

The Inner Ear fell quiet. "Thank you, Short Shank. I'm sorry that I have brought such confusion to Akhen-et-u. How have you been, my old friend?"

"Time drags on for me, and sleep is sweeter than ever. What about you? It has been some time since we last heard from you."

"I have enjoyed being home with my Hyskos family, and tried to forget how I nearly reached the end of my Path. Thanks be to Tho-hoth that I survived to enjoy what I hope will be a long life filled with nothing more exciting than deciding where to take my next nap."

"That's difficult for me to believe," said Short Shank.

"Actually, the reason I joined you today was to ask about a cat that was with me for a short time. I'm afraid that we didn't part under the best of circumstances, and I was hoping that one of you may know what happened to her."

"You have our attention, Windrusher." Short Shank said. "What is this cat's name?"

"She calls herself Rahhna's Light. She is a noble and proud cat and was one of those I was imprisoned with before we escaped. Rahhna's Light, unfortunately, decided to return to the house, and I have no idea—"

"I am safe, Windrusher. And I'm happy to hear that you are the same."

"Is that you, Rahhna's Light?" he asked excitedly.

"Have I changed that much?"

Windrusher was puzzled, but still amazed that he had actually connected with her. He pictured the haughty Persian, her cold, piercing eyes and sharp tongue contrasting with her noble beauty. "I'm happy to hear your voice again," he said. "Are you back home again?"

"Not exactly." She paused so long that Windrusher thought she had left the Inner Ear. "I have a new home now and a new Hyskos to care for me. But I am pleased that you are safely home."

Again, an image came to him of the Persian with her carefully groomed coat and arrogant ways. This didn't sound like the same cat he remembered. "There were many times when I never thought I'd see my

Hyskos family again, but it sounds like you made the wise decision not to follow us down the hill."

"My pride and anger made that decision, certainly not any wisdom I might have."

He remembered how she had bragged of the fancy home she was taken from, and how much her Hyskos cared for her. "I suppose you found another home like your last one."

"My life is different now, but I'm treated well, fed, and cared for. It's not the same." He heard a wistfulness in her voice. "But I've come to understand that the things that seemed so important to me before were not that important."

This was definitely not the Rahhna's Light that he remembered.

"I am living very close to where I left you and the others. My new Hyskos is a bit strange, and I do miss my fine home and pleasing my female Hyskos. I hope she is content. Maybe…" she paused for a long moment. "Maybe, I will see her again one day."

She seemed to have accepted her new circumstances, but he could tell that she wasn't totally happy. "I was hoping you were safe, and hearing from you is a blessing from the Holy Mother."

"Perhaps Irissa-u had something to do with it," she said, "but I have you to thank for setting me free. You were the one with the brave heart who led us out of that place. So, thank you, Windrusher. Thank you, and may you live long and happy."

Windrusher dropped to the floor and padded to his water bowl. The memory of Rahhna's Light was still with him, and he had difficulty believing the remarkable change in the bitter Queen. She had even thanked him for setting her free. Some things he would never understand.

He drank slowly from the bowl and then sat and groomed himself. He heard his Hyskos male and female in the next room and wandered inside to see if they were eating. Unfortunately, they were not eating, only communicating in their strange, un-catlike language. Watching them made him feel more comfortable and secure. In fact, he was secure enough to go outside.

Since his return, he had been outside a few times, but only for a few minutes. It wasn't that he was afraid. He knew that the Hyskos who had stolen him was dead, and didn't believe that anything similar would happen again. Still, each time he looked through the window and saw the circle of plants with the birdbath, he couldn't help but remember that day when his life had changed so drastically.

He vocalized loudly to get his female's attention, and then walked to the back door waiting for her to let him out. When she did, he hesitated while his eyes adjusted to Rahhna's bright light, and then stepped out onto the soft grass. He turned and watched the door close behind him, feeling a shiver course along his flank. It was time to put it all behind him, he knew, and walked slowly toward the garden.

He circled the small garden warily and continued on, scanning the fields beyond. Groups of Hyskos sat in their small vehicles while another hit the little white ball. He knew that soon they would move on, chasing the white ball like a cat chases its prey.

When he was satisfied that everything was as it should be, he returned to the garden. The impression in the sand was still there, and he stared at it for a moment before easing himself under the leggy plants. He lay down, tucking his front paws under him, and dropping his head. Shaded from Rahhna's rays, he enjoyed the breeze blowing across the golf course that riffled through the clumps of border grass near his head. His ears twitched several times in response to the high-pitched murmurings of insects calling to one another.

This was the life he wanted, and had missed all these day globes. He enjoyed staying inside his Hyskos home, but was there anything better than falling asleep on a soft patch of earth, with the warmth of Rahhna sinking deep into his bones and tantalizing smells tickling his nose? He didn't think so.

Squirming into a ball, his tail tucked snugly against his body, he closed his eyes and was soon asleep.

He felt a slight vibration. The first thing that flashed through his mind was that he was experiencing another frightening episode with the shaking earth. He opened his eyes, ready to dash away, prepared to do whatever he could to avoid being buried again. Only darkness greeted him, and he felt his heart plunge. Was he too late?

He scratched tentatively at the blackness in front of him expecting to find that he was unable to move. Instead his leg moved easily, but touched nothing. His racing heart slowly settled into a steady beat as he realized that he was safe, but he still didn't know where he was.

His nose provided the first clue. A strong, musty odor wafted toward him, as though an ancient book had been opened for the first time in centuries. Then he saw a reddish glow in the periphery of his sight. It was faint, like a distant star, but appeared to be moving closer at a rapid pace.

The light grew brighter until he recognized the vast stone chamber with its odd symbols adorning the walls. The crimson glow bathed the chamber in dark hues, and odd squeaks and squawks echoed all around him. He craned his neck and saw strange winged creatures gliding in and out of the shadows, bulging red eyes staring at him.

He remained perfectly still, waiting. He was back in the Cave of Tho-hoth and knew that it was only a matter of time until he would be face to face with the great god himself.

The radiance of the scarlet beam nearly blinded him, forcing him to close his eyes. When he opened them, Tho-hoth sat like a massive stone pillar studying him with his huge sad eyes. Windrusher struggled to understand how it was possible to fall asleep in his backyard and awaken in the presence of the legendary god of wisdom. He knew by now that this was more than a dream, that he had been summoned once again to Tho-hoth's Cave.

Finally breaking the silence, he spoke. "Tho-hoth, your warnings… the Hyskos…buried…saved them." He spoke, but knew he wasn't making any sense. Quaking like a frightened kitten, he felt flush with fever, his thoughts a bubbling cauldron of confusion.

"I know," Tho-hoth said kindly. He bent his great head and tenderly licked him on the side of his face.

A jolt of emotion coursed though Wind's body, leaving him so wobbly he thought he'd have to drop to his knees to keep from falling over. "Of course," he managed to say, "you know everything."

Tho-hoth straightened and Wind saw the pulsating Stone of Life hanging from the leather collar that looked like it had been fashioned in some prehistoric time. He stared at the rhythmic light waiting for Tho-hoth to speak again. To tell him why he was here. Was this another warning of impending danger? Another mission that would take him far away from home facing unknown threats?

His mind had been wandering as he gazed at the hypnotic gem, and he was stunned to see that they were no longer inside the stone chamber, but atop a high cliff, an arid desert below them. It was nearly dark, and Rahhna was slipping below the horizon, leaving a trail of gauzy orange and coralline clouds. Tho-hoth sat before him, his back arched, the white splash on his chest a vermillion blaze from the glow of the stone. A hot wind whipped clouds of sand across the desert floor before climbing the cliff and blowing over them. He felt it slip past him like a fiery spirit and saw Tho-hoth's coat flutter, the fine black hairs drifting up and settling back.

"Windrusher, you have met every challenge set before you. The dangers in the world of high-legged beings would surely have been too much for an ordinary cat, but your courage and tenacity saved you. And you saved your Hyskos family."

His pale green eyes softened and seemed to hold all the love the world could offer. He flicked his tail and it swept across Windrusher's chest sending a shudder through his body. Tho-hoth's eyes drifted past him toward the darkening horizon. In the distance, threatening black squall clouds gathered, and Windrusher heard deep rolling thunder rumbling toward them.

Tho-hoth turned his attention to him once again, but a far-away look had entered his eyes as though reflecting on sights he had seen that had touched him in ways Windrusher could not imagine. "My work on your world is finished, Pferusha-ulis."

"But the cave…" he stammered.

"There is no longer a need for my cave. The Akhen-et-u is a reality, and forever will bind cats together. You were one of the few cats privileged to enter my cave. I know that it was difficult for you, but you overcame your fears. As I knew you would. You have earned a special place in the hearts and minds of all cats."

Tho-hoth looked up as the first few drops of rain spattered at their feet, then on their backs. "I must go now, Windrusher."

He was breathing hard, trying to gather words that were noble enough to say what was in his heart. "Take me with you, please," he blurted out, his voice sounding strange, as though it belonged to a much younger cat.

"Ah, my Pferusha-ulis, if that were only possible. But you will always remain with me." He leaned over and licked him under the chin and up his face. "And I will always be with you. Closer than you will ever know."

The words were spoken so softly that Windrusher wasn't sure he had heard them at all.

The sky was almost completely dark and large drops pelted them. He ignored the rain, luxuriating in the sensation of Tho-hoth's tongue. He stood with his eyes closed, lost in the warm glow of tenderness that enveloped him like a soft blanket.

And then it was gone.

He opened his eyes and saw that he was alone on the high bluff. Night had settled in, and the storm clouds had eliminated all traces of light from the sky. He had arrived in the dark, and now it had ended in the dark. Closing his eyes again, he hoped that when he opened them Tho-hoth would be there, that he hadn't left him behind.

He was still alone, and he stared at the sky, dense and black. Confused, he lowered his head and for the first time became aware of a tiny twinkle at his feet. It was the faintest of glows, growing dimmer and flickering like an ember about to wink out. He dropped to the ground to inspect it, although he knew what he would find.

Tho-hoth had gone, but he had left behind the Stone of Life.

The chatter of a jay cut through the haze, and Windrusher

awakened with a massive yawn. He stretched all four legs out, his back arching, muscles flexing. It had been a long time since he had awakened so refreshed, and he wondered how long he had been asleep. A gurgling in his stomach sent him a message that perhaps it was time for a mid-day meal and he lazily rose to his feet.

He studied the bright Florida sky and suddenly remembered Tho-hoth and the dream. It was so real. Was there any doubt that he had been with the god of wisdom in the Cave of Tho-hoth? In the dreams, Tho-hoth had warned him of the dangers ahead, and they had all come true.

Still, there was that tiny seed of uncertainty, and he scratched behind his ear, as though trying to scratch out the truth. Closing his eyes, he recalled the cloak of love and contentment that had covered him when Tho-hoth had groomed him. Was it only a dream? He didn't think so.

The gurgling in his stomach returned, this time more insistently. Stepping out of the garden, he stretched once again. He heard a chattering noise behind him and turned to see a squirrel nibbling at a seed that had fallen from the bird feeder. If he wasn't about to go inside to eat, he might have enjoyed chasing the scrawny creature up a tree.

He turned toward the house, giving the small garden one final glance. A spot of color among the summer plants caught his eye. Alternating rows of pink and purple impatiens and red begonias ringed the birdbath. Day lilies and border grass completed the plantings.

He had seen the Hyskos working in this garden, pulling weeds, planting, and watering. All that care was reflected in the bright plants that had doubled in size in a short time. On the grassy field several high-legged beings were standing quietly while another swung his metal stick, then he heard the sharp *twack*. He tried to follow the flight of the ball, but lost it in the clear blue sky.

He returned his gaze to the garden, wondering what it was that had caught his interest. Something was nestled between the begonias and impatiens, half buried in the cedar mulch. He stepped toward the plants, sniffing the crisp aromas, the newly mowed grass, the sharp scent of cedar.

With his right paw, he scratched at the ground, expecting to see a leaf from one of the plants, but instead his paw struck a hard surface.

He knew something about digging, didn't he? What other cat has had to dig its way out of a pit covered with rocks and dirt? He scratched again, pushing aside the faded brown mulch, but a movement along the roof line of his Hyskos home caught his eye.

Windrusher turned away from the garden, craning his neck and squinting directly into the powerful beams of Rahhna. In the distance he saw an inverted *V* of large birds flying toward the bay. His eyes were drawn back to the roof again. It was impossible, but for a moment, he saw what looked like the tail of a shaggy black cat disappear over the roof line. Rahhna was surely playing tricks with his eyes. He blinked several times and looked again, but there was nothing on the roof.

Turning back to the garden, he scratched at the hard substance again, uncovering a smooth rock the size of his paw. Anyone gazing on that insignificant scrap of glass might think that it was a fragment from a broken vase or bottle, sharp edges worn away over the years. It was smeared with dirt, a dull red surface that showed no sign of life or light. He jumped back in surprise, as if he had uncovered a vicious snake, and searched the yard for anything that might explain how Tho-hoth's Stone of Life had found its way to his backyard.

Staring at the roof again, he knew that Tho-hoth had kept his word. He was closer than he would ever know.

Photo by Brian DiGenti

ABOUT THE AUTHOR

Victor DiGenti is the author of the *Windrusher* series. He has worked in broadcasting, produced a nationally acclaimed jazz festival, written for magazines and newspapers, and was executive director of an organization that worked for the welfare and protection of abandoned and feral cats. He lives in Florida with his wife, Evanne, where they are closely watched for aberrant behavior by their six cats.

Be sure to visit www.windrusher.com for more information.